D1570669

YELLOWSTONE STANDOFF

A National Park Mystery
by Scott Graham

TORREY HOUSE PRESS

SALT LAKE CITY • TORREY

This is a work of fiction set in a real place. All characters in this novel are fictitious. Any resemblance to actual events or persons, living or dead, is entirely coincidental.

First Torrey House Press Edition, June 2016
Copyright © 2016 by Scott Graham

Published by Torrey House Press
Salt Lake City, Utah
www.torreyhouse.com

International Standard Book Number: 978-1-937226-59-6
E-book ISBN: 978-1-937226-60-2
Library of Congress Control Number: 2015945496

Cover design by Rick Whipple, Sky Island Studio
Interior design by Russel Davis, Gray Dog Press
Distributed to the trade by Consortium Book Sales and Distribution

For Kirsten, Mark, and Anne,
my respected Torrey House teammates.

YELLOWSTONE STANDOFF

Prologue

She saw them only as a result of happenstance and thin air. *The most remote place in the lower forty-eight,* the three friends had crowed to one another via email. They would ride in on horses, enter the park from the south, head up Trident Peak from there. A dude-ranch vacation with a day climb tagged on.

They'd planned the trip for July, but busy schedules pushed it back to October. They hadn't understood that the park's grizzlies would be in the midst of their pre-hibernation feeding frenzy by then, on the lookout for anything—or anyone—capable of adding to their monstrous caloric intake. The horse packer pointed out four of the massive creatures during the ride in from the south, all, thankfully, in the distance.

The wrangler dropped them with their gear high above tree line on the Absaroka divide, south of the peak. He departed at the head of his string of horses with the promise to return in two days, muttering to himself about the hunting parties he needed to resupply.

As with the grizzlies, they hadn't realized how thick with elk hunters the area would be this time of year. They'd thought their camp would be in the national park, where hunting was illegal. That's where the peak was located, after all. Actually, they admitted to each other upon consulting their map following the wrangler's departure, the summit of the massif was located across the park boundary a mile north.

A rifle shot cracked beyond a sloping ridge. Two dozen big, blocky elk topped the ridge and galloped across the divide, a pair of antlered bulls in the lead, making for the safety of the park.

After a freeze-dried dinner, they hunkered in their tent atop the divide through the night, blasted by wind and rain and ice pellets. The morning dawned calm and clear. They packed up camp and climbed hard and fast, leaving the grizzlies and elk hunters below.

She took a break a hundred feet below the summit, preparing herself for the final push behind the others. She planted her ice axe in the snow and leaned on it, drawing deep breaths, her boots wedged in the snowfield blanketing the ridge.

Yellowstone Lake spread expansively to the north. The Absaroka Mountain Range rose from the lake's near shore and spilled out of the park to the east, an immensity of granite and tundra skirted by conifers.

Thorofare Creek snaked across a flat, upper basin at the foot of the massif's west face. A grizzly, little more than a brown speck, foraged in a meadow beside the creek a mile below.

A tight drainage climbed east away from the creek between two ridges to the base of the massif. At the head of the drainage, far below where she stood, something unusual caught her eye. Something extraordinary, in fact.

They—whatever *they* were—stood like soldiers in a straight line, dark spots against bright white, early season snow. From this distance, she could determine with her naked eye only that, based on the uniformity of the line and the consistent shape of the objects, the distant spots were not the product of natural processes.

Someone or something had placed them at the base of the peak, out here in the middle of nowhere, for a reason.

Part One

"All my life, I have placed great store in civility and good manners, practices I find scarce among the often hard-edged, badly socialized scientists with whom I associate."

—Edward O. Wilson,
Pulitzer Prize-Winning Evolutionary Biologist

1

"Grizzly bears are unpredictable creatures. When they're surprised in the wild, they're as likely to rip somebody to shreds as they are to run the other way."

Yellowstone Grizzly Initiative junior researcher Justin Pickford, recently of Princeton, didn't really understand what he was saying. But as a brand new member of the park's grizzly research program, he clearly was pleased with the opportunity to say it.

"In the case of the Territory Team," Justin went on, "it just so happened the bear wanted to rip somebody to shreds."

Chuck Bender, junior even to Justin as a Yellowstone National Park researcher, looked the young man up and down. Justin wore the requisite park researcher outfit—sturdy hiking boots, Carhartt work jeans, untucked flannel shirt, and bandana headband, with bear-spray canister and all-purpose folding knife sheathed to his belt at his waist. While Justin's clothes and gear looked like those of his fellow scientists in the Canyon Ranger Station meeting room, his scrawny, reed-thin physique did not. During the next weeks in the park's rugged backcountry, Justin would bulk up to match the broad shoulders, trunk-like legs, and concomitant stamina of the three dozen more experienced researchers in the room. If he couldn't cut it, however, he'd be gone, back to the computer-tapping, paper-pushing world of academia on the East Coast.

Justin leaned toward Chuck and asked in a conspiratorial whisper, "Have you seen the footage?"

Chuck glanced around the log-walled room. Folding chairs lined its scuffed, pine-plank floor. A platter of chocolate chip

cookies and a three-gallon dispenser of lemonade sat on a table in back. The researchers were half Chuck's age, in their mid- to late twenties, roughly two males for each female. They visited with one another in small groups, cookies and plastic cups in hand, waiting to take their seats upon the arrival of Yellowstone National Park Chief Science Ranger Lex Hancock.

Chuck turned to Justin. "From two years ago?"

"Yep. The fall before last."

The video had been yanked from the internet the instant it appeared.

"Can't say as I have," Chuck said.

Justin's blue eyes glowed. "Want to?"

Chuck hesitated long enough to convince himself viewing the infamous footage qualified as worthwhile research that would add to his store of knowledge as he pursued the questions awaiting him at the foot of Trident Peak. He nodded. Justin headed for a windowed door leading to the building's side porch.

Reflected in the glass door, Chuck's attire matched the other scientists—hiking boots, work jeans, flannel shirt—though his shirttail was tucked and he needed no bandana to keep his short, thinning hair in place. The reflection displayed his lean, weatherbeaten frame and the deep crow's feet cutting from the corners of his blue-gray eyes to his silver-tinged sideburns.

On the porch outside, the chilly air bit through Chuck's cotton shirt. It was eight in the evening, the second week of June, the days long and lingering here in the northern Rockies. The sun, a white disk behind a veil of stratus, hung above a tall stand of Engelmann spruce rising beyond the parking lot to the west. He drew in his shoulders, shivering. Back home, at the edge of the desert in the far southwest corner of Colorado, daytime highs were in the nineties by now, and the nights, while crisp, weren't anywhere near as frigid as here in Yellowstone, where the last vestiges of winter held sway even as the longest day of the year approached.

"Let's make this quick," Chuck told Justin, rubbing his palms together. "Hancock will be here any minute."

Justin fished his phone from his pocket. "The video-frame sequence is every three seconds, but the sound runs in real time. That's what makes it so brutal."

The young researcher swiped the phone's face with his finger. "Martha forwarded this to me." Martha Augustine served as logistical coordinator for the park's research teams. "Said I should see it before I decided for sure if I was in." He tapped at his phone. "It happened in upper Lamar Valley, at the foot of Pyramid Peak."

"A long way from where we're headed," Chuck said.

"Thirty miles at least," Justin said, nodding. "With the lake in between."

He held up his phone and stood shoulder to shoulder with Chuck. A paused video feed filled the phone's tiny screen. The trunk of a tree framed one side of the shot. A sweep of meadow, brown with autumn, filled the remainder of the frame. Green lodgepole pines blanketed a hillside on the far side of the grassy meadow.

Justin punched play. A rasping noise issued from the phone's small speaker. Chuck frowned.

"That's the griz," Justin said. "Snoring."

A sudden grunt broke in. The bear had awakened.

"The Territory Team showed up," said Justin. "They were just doing their job, comparing carnivore biomass consumption in various pack territories. Blacktail Pack had taken down an elk at the base of Pyramid a week before. The wolfies—" he used the informal term for the park's Wolf Initiative team members

"—hiked in and rigged the camera to film the pack's behavior around the carcass. The two of them were coming back to retrieve the camera and find out what they'd managed to record. Little did they know, the griz had chased off the wolves and was sleeping right on top of the kill."

Chuck flinched when a dark shadow covered the video feed. When the video advanced to its next frame three seconds later, the shadow drew away to become the back of a grizzly bear's broad, brown head.

The bear remained still through the video's next three-second frame, its unmoving head captured from behind by the camera, the fur on its neck standing straight up, its stubby ears erect. A distinctive, V-shaped notch cut to the base of its right earflap.

Over the sound of the bear's gravelly breaths came unintelligible human voices, those of a young man and woman. The tone of their conversation, relaxed and jovial, was of co-workers comfortable in one another's presence.

The young woman laughed, a high-pitched peal, and the bear's head dropped from view. The animal growled deep in its throat, the pitch so low it rattled the phone.

The woman's laughter cut off. "Bear," she cried out. "There! See it?"

The bear reappeared on the video feed. The grizzly's body, thick and muscular, stretched full out as it sprinted toward the voices.

Chuck's heart tattooed his chest at the sound of the bear's harsh breaths as it charged.

The young man hollered, "Whoa, bear!"

The next screen shot captured half the bear's body as it angled out of the picture, running flat out across the meadow toward the off-screen man and woman.

The grizzly woofed, a dog-like exhalation of warning.

"Stop!" the young man yelled. "I said *stop!*"

Chuck sucked a gulp of air, his throat stiff. The man's exclamation should have given the bear pause. Instead, the bear woofed again, the sound farther away, and the video feed returned to a serene shot of the meadow and forested hillside beyond.

A terrified screech from the young woman came over the speaker, after which her voice and the young man's united in a powerful, "No!"

"Stop!" the man cried out a millisecond later. Then, under his breath, "Get behind me, Rebecca. Back up."

A savage roar shook the phone's speaker.

2

M e," the man shouted in response to the grizzly's roar, his voice strong and forceful. "Hey, bear. It's me you want."

Justin raised his free hand. "Wait for it," he said, his eyes big and round and shining.

Chuck's jaw tightened.

The hiss of releasing aerosol came over the phone. From the reports he'd read, Chuck knew the two wolf researchers were spraying a protective screen of red pepper mist between themselves and the charging bear.

Chuck envisioned the team members' desperate effort at self-preservation, comparing it to the practice session he'd held with Janelle and the girls and Clarence before they'd left Durango a few days ago. Standing side by side in the front yard, bear-spray cans at arm's length, all five of them had pressed the buttons on the top of their flashlight-sized canisters at once. The pressurized cans hissed and a red fog formed in the air in front of them. They stepped forward and took a sample whiff of the spray as it dissipated. Even in its dispersed form, the aerosolized pepper burned their noses and set their eyes watering.

On Justin's phone, the video feed remained fixed on the meadow and pines while the terror-filled voice of Rebecca, the young woman, came over the speaker. "Joe!" she screamed. "Joe!"

Justin narrated. "She did what the guy wanted. She backed off. The Incident Team figured it out when they reconstructed the event."

Two sharp pops sounded.

"That's the griz," Justin said, "snapping at the spray."

Chuck pictured the brown bear's powerful jaws and jagged teeth, saliva flying. The pepper mist should have turned the animal away.

"Back!" Joe yelled.

The bear snarled. The warning nature of its initial woofs was gone now, replaced by long bursts of deep, bellowing roars.

The sounds of a struggle came over the phone—exhalations, scuffling feet.

Joe screamed in agony. "It's got me," he screeched. "Rebecca. It's eating me! It's eating me!"

"Joe," Rebecca moaned. "Joe."

"Run," Joe cried. "Rebecca. Run!"

Chuck shot a sidelong glance at Justin, who gazed at the screen, the phone steady in his grip.

Growls and indistinct noises came from the speaker. Chuck's gut twisted.

"She didn't know what to do," Justin said. "No protocol existed for her situation. The spray had always worked."

"Oh, my God," Rebecca cried. "Oh, dear God. Joe!"

"She wouldn't leave him," Justin said. "Gotta give her props for that."

"Bear!" Rebecca yelled. "Leave him. Leave him!"

"The griz went for the guy's abdominal cavity," Justin said. "She stayed. She should've run. I bet she'd have gotten away."

"Bear," Rebecca said. Her voice was little more than a whimper now. "Bear."

There came a long pause. Chuck clenched his hands at his sides, his fingernails digging into his palms.

Rebecca screamed, loud and shrill. Her cry died in her throat, followed by snarls and sounds of ripping and snapping.

"Stop," Rebecca managed. Then, two final words, half cry, half sigh: "Please. No."

Silence. The video feed remained steady on the field and forest.

"Keep watching," Justin said. "This is the creepy part."

Half the bear's body appeared on the screen. The animal stood in profile, looking across the meadow.

When the next frame appeared, the bear had turned to look straight at the camera.

Chuck stared back at the creature—its massive, furred head and short, dark snout glistening with blood; its stubby ears, the notch plainly visible in its right flap; its blond hump, lit by the midday sun, rising between its wide shoulder blades.

The hunter in Chuck focused on the precise spot between the eyes where an adult grizzly was sure to be brought down by a bullet.

But researchers weren't allowed to carry firearms in the park.

The bear continued to stare at the camera.

"It's almost as if it's posing," Justin said. "Is that bizarre or what?"

No further sounds came from the wolf researchers. Three seconds later, the bear was gone, the camera back to recording the sun-dappled meadow, the lodgepole pines covering the distant hillside.

"That's all," Justin said. "Those poor wolfies." He tapped his phone with his fingertip. Its face went dark and he shoved the phone back in his pocket. "By the time the posse showed up, the grizzly had split."

"They tried to track it, from what I read," Chuck said.

"Yeah. But it rained later that day and they ended up losing the trail."

"They haven't spotted it in all this time? Even with that notch in its ear?"

"They're still trying."

"It's been two years."

"Grizzlies cover a lot of ground—and there's lots of ground out there for them to cover. Lamar Valley alone is forty miles long, almost all of it roadless. It's not like civilization starts right up at the park boundary, either. At this point, everyone figures the griz is so deep in the Absaroka wilderness east of the park no one will ever see it again."

"That'd be fine with me."

Justin gave Chuck a calculating look. "I'll bet. I hear your wife and kids are coming with us tomorrow."

"And my research assistant, my wife's brother. My contract calls for a quick recon, a few days at the site. We were planning to backpack in on our own from the south, over Two Ocean Pass. Then Hancock told me about the research teams basing out of Turret Cabin this summer, everyone together."

"Grizzly people and the wolfies and geologists and meteorologists and the new canine-tracker guy and the Drone Team—and now you, too." Justin's mouth twisted. "Going to be a whole herd of us out there."

"The site I'll be working, at the foot of Trident Peak, is only five miles from the cabin. The timing turned out to be perfect. I was glad to join in, to be honest."

"Sounds like a peachy little family vacation for you." Justin lifted an eyebrow. "Assuming the killer griz is as long gone as everybody says it is."

3

"All of you will use Turret Patrol Cabin as your base of operations for the summer," Chief Science Ranger Lex Hancock announced to the three dozen scientists seated on folding chairs in the Canyon meeting room.

A collective groan rose from the researchers.

Chuck sat in the back row beside Clarence, who'd slipped into the room behind Lex, just after eight. Justin sat a few rows ahead and to the left, with the other Grizzly Initiative team members.

Clarence shoved a length of black hair behind his ear, revealing the thick silver stud set in his lobe. He cast a questioning glance at Chuck, who shrugged, waiting to see how the ranger would respond to his disgruntled audience.

Lex stood at a podium at the front of the room, flanked by American and Wyoming flags, his appearance as crisp as Chuck remembered from the years they'd worked together during Lex's climb up the ranger ranks at Grand Canyon National Park. Lex's gray hair was combed back from his high forehead, his mustache neatly trimmed. Despite the jowly cheeks framing the sides of his wrinkled face, he stood erect, shoulders straight, aging body fit beneath his pressed, green and gray park service uniform, brass badge shining on his chest. As chief science ranger, Lex oversaw Yellowstone's scientific research operations while his boss, Park Superintendent Cameron Samson, served as Yellowstone's public face.

Lex waved his hands for quiet. "Now, now. I know this comes as no surprise to any of you. And I don't necessarily blame you for your complaints—which I've been reading online." He furrowed his bushy eyebrows at his audience. "Rather than complaining, might I suggest you instead welcome the opportunity to work in the backcountry at all this summer?" The room grew still as the ranger went on. "As all of you are well aware, last year was a dark time for our research efforts here in the park. After the attack the previous fall, Superintendent Samson and I made the difficult but prudent decision to end all backcountry science operations and, instead, limit research to only roadside activities for the duration of the summer season."

Lex pointed at a young man and woman in the front row. The two wore black fleece jackets emblazoned with logo patches of various outdoor and high-tech gear manufacturers, including the bright red logo of a company called AeroDrone. The woman, petite with long, ebony hair, straightened in her chair. Even so, her head barely reached the shoulder of the man seated beside her. He was tall, broad-shouldered, and clean-shaven, his head enveloped in a fluffy cloud of red curls.

"The fact of the matter is, if it weren't for the work of our Drone Team, we'd have conducted no backcountry research at all last summer." Lex inclined his head toward the two. "Thank you, Kaifong, Randall."

The woman looked at the floor while the puffy-haired man lifted a hand and turned to face the others with a broad smile.

Lex addressed the room: "One of several new faces with us tonight I'd like to introduce is Keith Wilhelmsen."

A young man in jeans and a plaid shirt twisted in his second-row seat to acknowledge those around him. His thick, black beard was untrimmed, his wavy, shoulder-length hair corralled into a ponytail by a braided leather cord.

"Keith is a Ph.D. candidate out of Cornell. He constitutes the human half of the park's latest research addition, our Canine Team. He and the second member of his team—his tracking dog, Chance—will work out of Turret camp this summer. Like all of you in your specialties, Keith is a top dog in his field—pun intended." Lex's joke drew a handful of chuckles. "He'll be conducting leading-edge work in a new field of inquiry: the use of service canines to track other mammals. I know it's unusual to use a domesticated animal in the course of backcountry field work in the park. It's unprecedented, in fact. But the potential to expand upon our abilities to track and survey predators in the backcountry makes this new option one we have deemed worth exploring this summer. Keith and Chance will provide us with a new and, dare I say, revolutionary tool as we continue to pursue the grizzly involved in the attack on the Wolf Initiative's Territory Team."

A number of scientists seated ahead and to the right of Chuck—clearly the wolfies—shifted in their seats.

"Please understand," Lex said in response to the show of unease, "we have no indication the bear we've come to call Notch is anywhere in the vicinity of Turret Cabin. Keith will spend the coming weeks testing and refining Chance's ability to track other grizzlies whose territories include the Thorofare region. The goal is for Keith and Chance to be prepared to help in the pursuit of Notch when the bear is spotted—something we are convinced will eventually happen."

A woman two rows ahead of Chuck raised her hand. Her hair was shaved close on both sides of her skull. Half a dozen hoop earrings dangled from piercings in each of her ears. A blond mohawk rose from the top of her head and swooped down the back of her neck to the collar of a vibrant pink down vest over a skin-tight top. The nylon top hugged her wide shoulders and muscled arms. She spoke before Lex acknowledged her. "All this talk about Notch, and the humiliation you put the Grizzly Initiative through last year. I, for one, am getting pretty tired of it."

The researchers seated around the woman nodded their approval. After a second's hesitation, Justin followed suit.

Lex crossed his arms, his face immobile, giving the woman the floor.

She shifted in her seat. "I know you're trying to do what's best. But I lost an entire year on my whitebark pine nut ingestion study because of your decision to pull everyone out of the field last summer, and the twelve-month gap in my data set has forced me to recast my entire dissertation. At this point, I'm not even sure my thesis committee will accept the changes I've had to make. It's not only me, either. Everyone who was here last year, and that's just about all of us, is faced with the same kind of problems—research screwed up, theses delayed—because of what I would argue was an overreaction on your part."

Lex grasped the sides of the podium and leaned forward. "We pulled you and everyone else out of the field last year for good reason, Sarah. We lost two of our people the previous fall. A terrible, terrible tragedy. The entire Yellowstone research community was, and remains, devastated by what happened."

"Understood," Sarah said. "Much as I continue to disagree with it, my point is not to rehash last year's decision. Rather, I'm speaking up now because those of us on the Grizzly Initiative—" she looked to her right and left "—believe your forcing all the park's backcountry science teams to work together out of Turret Cabin this summer will severely limit our opportunities to conduct decent research again this year, just like your roadside-only decision hurt us so much last year."

Lex released the podium and folded his arms across his chest as Sarah continued.

"Forty people working out of the same base camp? With that kind of crowd around, all of us involved in mammalian studies will have a tough time collecting meaningful data.

The only team that's sure to get any decent work done is the Archaeological Team. It's not like anything they're here to study will be going anywhere."

Clarence dug his elbow into Chuck's side.

"As for the Grizzly Initiative," Sarah went on, "we're studying real, live grizzly bears. We have to go deep into the backcountry on our own in small teams to assure our presence doesn't alter the bears' behavior patterns. We're trying to study their natural movements and traits, free of human interference, not their response to the crowd you've got heading across the lake to the Thorofare region tomorrow."

Lex's steel-gray eyes glinted behind his glasses. He touched his upper lip with the tip of his tongue before he spoke. "I've acknowledged the difficulties inherent in last year's decision, Sarah. Moreover, while your concerns are duly noted, I stand by this year's determination that all backcountry teams will do the best they can while performing their summer research out of, and spending every night at, Turret Cabin base camp—which, I might add, park staffers have spent the last two weeks working long and hard to set up on your behalf."

"It was a grizzly bear," Sarah said. "A grizzly bear doing what grizzly bears do." She turned in her seat to face the Wolf Initiative team members on the opposite side of the room. "I feel for you guys. I really do. I can only imagine how hard it's been for you after what happened to your Territory Team. But you've got to understand. Our two teams are studying different creatures with different study protocols, different needs."

"Sarah," Lex warned.

She continued to face the wolf researchers. "I don't think you people can really comprehend the risks those of us with the Grizzly Initiative take every single day we're in the field. Remember, it was a grizzly that attacked your team, not a wolf.

Do you know the last time a wolf attacked a human? I'll tell you when: never. But grizzlies? They attack. It's what they do. They defend their young, their food, their turf. Learning what we can about their natural behavior by studying them in the backcountry is the best way we have of determining how best to keep people safe around them—and keep what happened to your team from ever happening again." She turned to Lex. "You already cost us a year of critical research, along with the knowledge advancement that would have come with it. Now, with this group-camp requirement of yours, you're about to cost us another year of legitimate, backcountry-based research."

"That's enough, Sarah," a male voice said from among the wolf researchers.

Sarah spun in her seat, her mohawk swinging with her. "What was that?"

Silence.

"Too chicken to show yourself?" she challenged.

"No," the voice came again.

A head turned, revealing the profile of a man with a long, sloping ski jump of a nose. A brown beard hid his chin, and a thick mustache, big as a cigar, ran around his face, almost connecting with his long sideburns.

"No, I'm not chicken," the researcher said. "In case you didn't hear me, what I said was, 'That's enough.'"

"I'll decide what's enough, Toby," Sarah replied, climbing atop her folding chair. Before Chuck realized what was happening, Sarah launched herself at the mustachioed man with her arms outstretched, her hands aimed at his throat.

4

"Those are some fiery scientists you've got working for you."
Chuck sat across from Lex at one of the long tables in the bustling staff cafeteria. The segment of sky visible through the front window was a glowing rectangle of pre-dawn magenta. Janelle and the girls were still in bed, but the cavernous room was filled with uniformed rangers getting ready for their shifts, and with many of the researchers who'd attended last night's meeting.

Lex held up his white paper napkin like a bullfighter's cape, fending off Chuck's comment. "Just one, really. And there are extenuating circumstances involved. Besides, the scientists don't work for me. If they work for anybody, they work for Martha—or, more specifically, for themselves. You saw as much last night. They're focused on their personal research projects, as they should be, and on how the park's decisions will affect their studies and dissertations. They're a pretty hard-charging bunch of kids. All of them have been studying their butts off since kindergarten, making perfect grades every semester, getting their papers published in the most prestigious journals, attending the best grad schools. They're top-notch young scientists, and, what you witnessed last night between Sarah and Toby notwithstanding, they get along well together. They support one another, go out of their way to help each other out."

"They definitely were unified in their dislike of sharing a camp this summer."

Lex wiped his mouth and set his napkin next to his plate of bacon and eggs. "Like I told them, they're lucky to be going into the backcountry at all this summer."

"It *has* been two years, though."

"One year and eight months, to be exact."

"A long time—" Chuck hesitated "—even as bad as it was."

Lex pushed his glasses up the bridge of his nose. "Do tell."

"I saw the video last night," Chuck admitted. "Martha forwarded it to one of the Grizzly Initiative rookies. He showed it to me on his phone."

"Then you know there's lots of room for debate about what happened."

"It looked fairly straightforward to me. The grizzly acted like a grizzly would be expected to act when the wolfies didn't announce their approach."

"What do you mean? The two of them were talking and laughing. They were making their presence known."

"They weren't yelling out to let anything and everything know of their presence, even though they knew they were approaching a kill site. Everything I read over the winter told me grizzlies have to be shown who's boss. The wolf researchers didn't do that. They were thinking gray wolves when they should have been thinking brown bears, and they paid the ultimate price for their mistake."

"You're really suggesting the attack was their fault?"

"We both know I wouldn't be headed into the backcountry with my wife and kids if I thought otherwise, nor would you be letting me take them. I've come to the same conclusion I suspect you and all your grizzly experts have. What happened to the Territory Team was avoidable, preventable. Seeing the video last night reinforced that conclusion in my mind."

"What that bear did was *not* normal behavior," Lex said, his voice flat. "It went out of its way to attack."

"It was sleeping," Chuck countered. "It woke up startled. It went with its first and most basic instinct."

Lex bent forward, dropping his chin so the fluorescent ceiling lights shadowed his face. "Surprise leading to attack is instinctive grizzly behavior, yes," he said. He lowered his voice. "But the attack of the Territory Team had elements that weren't so common. Quite uncommon, in fact."

Chuck leaned forward. "Such as?"

"There isn't anything that can be put in writing. But there is enough circumstantial evidence to raise doubts. The distance to the attack, for one thing. You watched the video; you saw how far the bear ran when it charged—all the way across the meadow. Generally, grizzly attacks involve bears that have been surprised in close quarters, in deep brush or dense forest. They lash out defensively, then retreat. In the case of the Territory Team, the logical assumption is that the grizzly was defending its food source—the carcass it had commandeered from the wolves. That much fits. But the distance it charged was entirely out of the ordinary."

Lex rested his forearms on the edge of the table. "Then there's the fact that the bear somehow overcame the team members' pepper spray. Was the grizzly immune to it? That's a scary thought. But without video evidence, all we have is conjecture."

He let a beat pass. "The attack resulted in multiple fatalities, lending even more weight to the theory that it was a predatory attack as opposed to defensive. That, again, is highly unusual, and raises any number of questions about the bear itself, as well as how park scientists should conduct themselves in the backcountry until those questions are answered." Lex's face hardened. "All of that explains why we kept the science teams out of the backcountry last year, and why this year, still with no answers, they're lucky to be going into the backcountry at all. The universities and foundations that fund research in the park have been all over me, wanting me to let their people head off into the woods on their own again. Even so, the decision to allow the teams to head to Turret Cabin as a group is a significant compromise."

Chuck gripped the edge of the table with both hands. Lex's response several months ago to his request to have Janelle and the girls join him at Turret Cabin had been unreservedly affirmative. "Yet you *are* sending a group of scientists into the backcountry this summer. And you okayed my family going in with me, too."

"The key word is 'group.' Essentially, we're forming a small city at Turret. Everyone will go out from there to conduct their research in teams of three or more, just as we recommend to anyone headed away from populated areas of the park. The idea is that they'll be just as safe as if they were based here at Canyon for the summer, or at Lake or Old Faithful."

"Just as safe," Chuck repeated warily.

"Look," Lex said, turning his palms up. "I know you've worked contracts over the years at lots of national parks across the West. But I also know this is the first time you've ever worked at Yellowstone. You have to understand, Yellowstone National Park is different from every other park in the country—in the world, for that matter—in the way it mixes huge numbers of people with predatory animals. That's something we deal with every single day. Yellowstone is like the Serengeti: predators prowl here. They hunt, they kill, they eat. It's the real deal."

Chuck inclined his head in agreement. "Sure. Along with the geysers, that's what draws the crowds."

"But unlike the Serengeti," Lex continued, "Yellowstone's predators do what they do in the midst of more than three million human visitors each summer, with those numbers steadily increasing year after year." He shrugged. "We can't exactly lock the people—the public—out of their national park. They own it, after all. But the fact is, we're seeing mounting evidence that some of Yellowstone's animals are changing their behavior based on the growing number of human visitors to the park. There's the steady rise of bison attacks from too many people posing next to them for selfies. Plus, there's the escalating habituation of elk, which are growing increasingly comfortable even in the busiest places in Yellowstone—wandering across parking lots at Old Faithful, giving birth outside the front door of the Mammoth Hot Springs Post Office, tearing up the flower beds in the Lake Yellowstone Hotel courtyard."

"Those are grazing animals you're talking about."

"Not entirely. There's the behavior of gray wolves to consider, too. Before their extermination in the early 1900s, the last wolves in the park had learned to be extremely secretive—to stay out of sight, deep in the wilderness—in order to survive. Since their reintroduction, though, the wolves have made themselves comfortable everywhere within the park boundaries. Yes, they're in the backcountry. But they're equally comfortable in the front country, too, denning within sight of Northeast Entrance Road in Lamar Valley, taking down prey right alongside Grand Loop Road, a mile from Old Faithful Geyser with its tens of thousands of daily visitors. The wolves are doing so well that there's even talk they might be challenging grizzlies for supremacy at the top of the park's food chain."

"And now," Chuck said, "you're telling me you think the grizzly attack two years ago represented some new level of habituation by grizzlies as well."

Lex looked to his right and left. Assured no one was listening, he lowered his voice even more. "I'm saying the attack *may* have represented that. The question we want to answer is whether this particular grizzly might have become so habituated, so accustomed to the massive human presence in the park, that it came to see the Territory Team as prey."

Chuck sat up straight. "What?"

Lex crooked a finger, beckoning Chuck closer to him. "What if the bear didn't attack because it was alarmed? What if it knew exactly where it was, and waited for the humans who would be coming to retrieve their camera? And what if, when those humans showed up, the grizzly went on the attack not because it was surprised, but just the opposite: because it recognized the members of the Territory Team as easy takings?"

5

Chuck gaped at Lex from across the cafeteria table. "That's one helluva leap—from increased habituation of animal species to the idea that the park's grizzlies are actually beginning to hunt humans."

"Grizzly, not grizzlies. We're talking about one bear here, whose extreme behavior presents lots of questions. That's why we're still working so hard to locate it—bringing in the Canine Team, doing everything we can to track it down."

"You've even given it a name."

"Notch," Lex confirmed. He made air quotes with his fingers. "The 'killer grizzly.'"

"Doesn't the park service frown upon that kind of anthropomorphism?"

"We've made an exception in this case. Naming it, particularly by its defining feature, helps keep it in the public's mind. Our hope is, if someone spots it, they'll be more likely to recognize it and let us know."

"But the attack was two summers ago. No one's seen the bear since."

"Grizzlies live for a quarter century or more."

One of the scientists Chuck recognized from last night approached carrying a tray of food. Lex waited until she was well past their table before he resumed speaking, again bending toward Chuck with his shoulders hunched.

"I can tell you this much: Turret Patrol Cabin wasn't chosen by chance. The entire Thorofare region around the cabin—the upper Yellowstone River valley and the Thorofare Creek drainage branching off to the southeast—is prime grizzly habitat."

"Everybody knows that."

"Yes, but everybody doesn't necessarily know the area has become increasingly prime over the last few years. I'm sure you've learned Yellowstone's grizzlies gorge on the nuts that fall from the whitebark pine trees each fall."

Chuck nodded.

"And that the pine beetle population has exploded in the park in recent years as temperatures have increased with climate change and global warming. The beetles have munched through thousands of acres of whitebark pines across the Central Yellowstone Plateau, killing millions of trees."

"So I understand."

"The Thorofare region is the highest and coldest forested part of the park. The pine beetles haven't arrived there yet. As the beetles have wiped out the whitebark pine groves across the lower parts of the plateau, more and more grizzlies have shown up in the Thorofare to feed on the pine nuts still produced by the healthy trees there each autumn."

"Are you actually telling me you sited the research camp in the heart of the Thorofare region specifically because of its high grizzly population?"

"Turret Cabin is not far, as the crow flies, from where the Territory Team was attacked in Lamar Valley, and of all the places hit by beetles so far, Lamar's one of the worst."

"You're thinking Notch might head for the Thorofare on account of the pine nuts?"

"It's as good a guess as any."

"But the nuts won't ripen and fall from the trees until late August."

"The camp will be operational for ten weeks, through mid-September. Besides, the Thorofare region is a big draw for grizzlies throughout the summer, too. The open divides over the Absarokas provide easy passage for the elk herds scattered across the central plateau inside the park, and for the herds in the headwater drainages of the Snake River south of the park. This time of year, with fresh, new grass sprouting everywhere in the high country, and with elk calf births by the thousands, grizzlies are on the move over the divides big time, grazing on the grass and munching any calves they can sink their teeth into."

Chuck scrunched his face in bewilderment. "So you think this grizzly, Notch, might be a manhunter, and you've situated your research camp in the most likely place for the bear to show up?"

"The best outcome of all would be a safe sighting of Notch through the presence of lots of folks in a part of the park generally uninhabited by humans but well trafficked by grizzlies, then tracking down the bear from there."

"Okay. Fine. I get it," Chuck said. "But I still can't figure out why you gave the all-clear for me to bring my wife and kids."

"Because of what I just said—the presence of lots of other people."

Chuck closed one eye, frowning. "There's more going on here, isn't there?"

"How's that?"

"Jessie," Chuck said, his voice gentle. "And your kids."

Lex sat back, his eyes suddenly hooded. "What are you—?"

Chuck lifted a hand. "I'm sorry for your loss. You know how much I cared for her. I can only imagine how tough the last few months have been for you."

Lex settled forward with a heavy sigh. "Sometimes, it's all I can do to pull on my uniform in the morning."

"Carson and Lucy, how are they doing?"

"Oh, you know. They loved their mother as much as she loved them. And now, they miss her as much as I miss her. But they'll get through it. We'll get through it."

"It'll be good for you, getting out of the office this week, won't it?"

"Just what the doctor ordered. Or, the psychiatrist." Lex smiled wearily. "I'm twelve months from retirement. I don't know what I'm going to do when they shove me out the door next year. Jessie had all these plans for us—Alaska, Europe, time with the kids. I couldn't wait." Tears welled in his eyes. "We had such a good life together."

Lex blinked. A single tear trickled partway down his cheek. He brushed it away with a brusque stroke of his hand. "When Carson and Lucy were your kids' ages, Jessie and I got them out camping and hiking and backpacking every spare minute we had." A wistful look stole across his face. "Those were the best years of my life."

Chuck spoke carefully. "Do you think part of why you okayed my bringing my family into the backcountry had anything to do with how much you miss those years?"

Lex slowly nodded his head. "Maybe," he admitted. "I can't say it didn't. But I stand by the fact that it'll be fine for them to be out there."

"You're sure?"

"Yes. No question." His eyes took on a faraway look. "There's no place on Earth more beautiful than the Thorofare region. Gene Rouse, one of the many seasonal rangers who have spent lots of time at Turret, brought his wife and kids in with him every summer, and I'm telling you, his kids loved every minute of it. There's no better place for a family to be together, Chuck. Years from now, when your girls are teenagers and they're busy hating your guts for not letting them stay out all night, they'll still be thanking you for taking them to the Thorofare."

Chuck pushed eggs around his plate with a fork, his appetite gone, his thoughts on the Territory Team video. As a loner with no close family connections, his life until two years ago had been free of complication. Ideas of risk vs. reward had played no role in the decisions he made to head into the backcountry.

The arrival of Janelle and the girls in his life had required him to change his thinking. All spring, as he and Janelle had hiked with Carmelita and Rosie to build their stamina in preparation for their Thorofare visit, he'd privately battled concerns about taking his new family to a place thick with grizzlies even as he'd openly shared his excitement for the upcoming trip.

"With the crowd we'll have at the cabin," said Lex, "there's nothing to worry about."

Chuck exhaled until he sat slumped in his seat. "Right," he said. "Nothing to worry about at all."

6

"She actually attacked him?" Janelle asked Chuck. "They had to pull her off the guy. He's the lead researcher on the Wolf Initiative's field team—Toby. Sarah's the Grizzly Initiative's backcountry team lead. She looks like she could be the lead singer in a punk rock band, though—mohawk, nose ring, the whole bit. Not exactly what I'd expect of a Yellowstone scientist, but quite a character, that much is obvious."

"Clarence is interested in her, anyway."

"That's Clarence. As for her and Toby, they obviously hate each other. Chairs were flying all over the place, people scrambling for cover."

"Science nerds—who'd've ever thought?"

"Hey. Watch who you're calling nerds."

"Not you, my science prince. Never you." She leaned from the passenger seat of the pickup and kissed him on the cheek. A smile played at the corners of her mouth as she stroked his leg and whispered in his ear, her breath warm on the side of his face, "*Nunca, nunca, nunca.*"

Chuck grinned as he piloted the crew cab south from Canyon Village, headed for Yellowstone Lake. "That's better."

The girls occupied the back of the six-passenger half-ton he'd purchased for family-hauling purposes after his and Janelle's quick courtship and city hall marriage two years ago. Skinny, reserved Carmelita, ten years old, sat at one end of the rear bench seat, while chunky, brash Rosie, eight, sat at the other end. They stared out their respective side windows at the passing trees, their eyes glassy and half-closed after their morning buffet in the staff cafeteria an hour after Chuck's breakfast with

Lex. The girls wore matching nylon hiking pants and bulky fleece jackets. Janelle sported a stylish, form-fitting fleece pullover and trim khaki slacks made of wind- and water-shedding nylon engineered to look like cotton. Waterproof gear duffles in a rainbow of colors filled the truck's bed. The day was sweater cool, the morning sun climbing in the pale blue sky.

"We're finally here," Janelle said, looking out the window. "I'm *so* looking forward to this—our big summer adventure."

Chuck took her hand. No surprise there. Janelle—just shy of thirty, thin as Carmelita, dark haired, heart faced, and olive skinned—had been rebelliously adventurous all her life. The rebellious part explained how she'd wound up a young, unwed mother of two daughters born to a drug dealer, now deceased, in Albuquerque's rough South Valley neighborhood in spite of a loving upbringing along with Clarence, three years her junior, by their Mexican immigrant parents.

"Your new life as an outdoorswoman," Chuck said, pushing thoughts of the Territory Team video and Lex's speculation about the grizzly attack to the back of his mind.

"*Reality TV: Alone in the Wilderness,*" Janelle intoned.

"Sorry to burst your bubble, but there'll be a crowd of us out there. We'll have our own tent platform, a mess tent for meals, the cabin to hang out in if we want. Best of all, we'll be a week or two ahead of mosquito season."

"No mosquitoes? You really are a prince."

"Timing is everything when it comes to Yellowstone. The window of opportunity is so small—six weeks of full-on summer is about it."

"Even with global warming?"

"Even with. The last of the winter snow will just be finished melting about now."

"Which means whatever they saw..."

"...should be in plain sight. I can't wait to see it."

"It's really that big a deal?"

"It's pretty much the only thing the North American archaeological world has talked about all winter. We'll hike up from camp, see what's what, take some pictures, plot everything out. Should be the easiest contract I've ever worked—no excavation, hardly any cataloguing—especially with Clarence's help."

When things had calmed after the melee last night, Lex had introduced Chuck and Clarence to the other science teams. Lex told the scientists how much he'd enjoyed working with Chuck in Arizona, where Chuck's firm, Bender Archaeological, Inc., had been awarded temporary contracts over a number of years to perform archaeological surveys and digs in advance of new construction projects in Grand Canyon National Park.

After the meeting, Clarence made his way through the chairs to Sarah's side, his compact pot belly leading the way. He struck up a conversation with her, laughing and resting his fingers on her forearm as they spoke. He flashed Chuck a devilish grin a few minutes later as he escorted Sarah across the room, his hand at the back of her hot pink vest. Sarah aimed a look of her own at Toby, her eyes narrowed. Toby turned away from her in response.

Sarah's dangling earrings twinkled in the gleam of an overhead light as she left the building with Clarence. Toby turned back after they were gone, his eyes on the door through which Sarah had exited.

Clarence didn't respond to Chuck's texts in the morning, nor did he answer Chuck's knock at his cabin door. When Chuck peered through the front window, he noted the bed inside was crisply made.

With the Grizzly Initiative team scheduled to head across the lake to Turret Cabin two hours ahead of the Archaeological Team, Chuck wasn't too worried about Clarence's arriving at

Bridge Bay in time for their scheduled mid-afternoon launch. He did wonder, though, how hungover Clarence would be when he showed up at the marina.

"The effects of global warming in the park are showing themselves more?" Janelle asked.

Chuck guided the truck along the winding road with one hand. "It's the only reason we're here."

Janelle clicked the heater fan up a notch. "But it's so cold, even in June."

"Not as cold as it used to be. In the last twenty years, Yellowstone's glaciers have melted away to a few lumps of remnant ice. The park's alpine regions have lost half their year-round snow coverage, and the speed of the loss is increasing. If present trends continue, year-round snow coverage will be a thing of the past in the park's high country in another few years."

"That won't take much away from its beauty."

She leaned forward to peer out the windshield. Pines swept past along the side of the road and sunlit meadows showed through breaks in the trees.

"You're really okay with this, aren't you?" Chuck asked.

"With what?"

He waved out the window. "All of this. I was raised with it. I never can get enough. But you're a city girl."

"I *was* a city girl." She glanced at Carmelita and Rosie in the rearview mirror. "*We* were. You brought us something different. Something better." She slid her hand from his and rested it on his shoulder. "Way better. It's like I've been handed this gift— you, the mountains. It's a chance to really live, not just survive, like the girls and I were doing before you came along."

"Survive? I guess that explains the courses you've been taking—EMT Basic, Backcountry Medicine, Wilderness First Responder."

"The girls are growing up. I'm about to turn thirty. You've got your archaeology, your thing. It's time for me to find my thing, too."

"And you've decided medicine is it."

"You have to admit, it goes well with this outdoorsy life you've got us living."

They approached a slow-moving recreational vehicle on the narrow road. The lumbering vehicle blocked the lane ahead, leaning as it negotiated the curves.

The dense forest through which they traveled was one of the three major features of the Central Yellowstone Plateau, along with Hayden Valley just ahead and Yellowstone Lake beyond. The sprawling grasslands of Hayden Valley served as home to vast herds of elk and the wolves and grizzlies that fed on them. Yellowstone Lake, the largest natural body of water above seven thousand feet in North America, occupied the plateau's southeast corner.

They'd left the canyon of the Yellowstone River and the river's famous, thundering waterfalls behind. To the east, the river meandered northward from Yellowstone Lake across the central plateau before plunging over the falls at the north edge of the plateau and on to its junction with the Missouri River outside the park.

The fifty-mile-wide Yellowstone caldera, the national park's seething heart, bounded the plateau. The first reports of European fur traders who witnessed the caldera's erupting geysers, steaming hot springs, and bubbling mud pots had been met with disbelief and derision in the East. Not until members of the Lewis and Clark Expedition explored and provided official reports on the region did Americans accept the truth about the land of fire and brimstone that had come into their possession as a result of the Louisiana Purchase.

The road broke from the forest into the open. Prairie-like Hayden Valley stretched to the south and west, its grasslands interspersed with stands of lodgepole pines. The valley's lush, early summer grasses glowed emerald green in the morning sun.

"Wow," Janelle said.

Chuck goosed the truck, preparing to pass the camper on the open straightaway. He fell back when he spotted cars and RVs lining both sides of the road half a mile ahead, at a bridge over Elk Antler Creek, a tributary of the Hayden River.

Chuck caught the girls' eyes in the rearview mirror. "Bear jam," he announced.

Carmelita sat up, her sleepiness disappearing. "Really?"

Rosie punched the air with her pudgy fist. "Yes!" she hollered.

Janelle studied the line of vehicles. "You really think it might be a bear this time?"

"They're parked at a stream," Chuck said. "Maybe it's a moose."

Janelle's mouth turned down. "Or more ducks."

They'd come upon three so-called bear jams—lines of cars and campers halted along the park's roads—during their drive north through the park to Canyon Village the day before. Each time, they'd parked and joined the tourists thronged outside their vehicles, some peering through spotting scopes attached to tripods set up on the shoulders of the roads. The first group of tourists was fixated on a mallard duck and chicks nibbling shoreline grasses along the edge of a roadside stream. The second group ogled an osprey nest in a treetop several hundred yards from the road, with no ospreys in sight. The third admired a bison herd in a meadow nearly a mile away, the grazing bison little more than brown specks in the distance.

The recreational vehicle pulled to the side of the road behind the last of the parked vehicles, a hundred feet shy of the bridge.

Chuck parked behind the RV and turned to the girls. "Might be another mama duck and her chicks. That'd still be okay, wouldn't it?"

"Sure," Carmelita said.

"You betcha," Rosie agreed.

They made their way along the edge of the road past the line of cars. The vehicles' occupants, more than two dozen in all, stood together where the bridge crossed the stream. They looked northward from the road's raised shoulder. Children held the hands of their parents. Elderly couples in matching jackets stood close beside each other. A pair of heavyset, middle-aged men were positioned at the front of the group, their eyes to head-high spotting scopes.

Chuck stopped at the edge of the gathered tourists. "What have we got?" he asked a woman in loose slacks and thick-soled walking shoes, her gray hair twisted into a bun.

"I'm not sure." She stood next to an elderly man in a navy overcoat. "We just got here."

One of the men in front turned from his scope and addressed the group. "Bear," he said, pointing past his tripod at a thick stand of willows sprouting at the side of the stream thirty yards from the road.

Carmelita pressed herself against Chuck's side. He put an arm around her shoulders.

"Are you sure?" the elderly man asked. He raised his hand to his brow, shielding the morning sun. "I don't see anything."

"We were the first ones here," the man at the spotting scope said. "It went into the willows when we pulled up."

The tall bushes filled a stream-side depression a hundred feet long and half again as wide.

The second spotter spoke without taking his eye from his scope. "It won't come back out," he said. "Not as long as all of us are here."

"Black or brown?" Chuck asked.

"Brown," the first spotter said. "We got a good look at it. It's a grizzly, all right."

"Black bears can be pretty light colored."

The man squinted at Chuck. "This is my nineteenth summer spotting in the park."

"Did you hear that, Daddy?" a boy's voice asked from among the onlookers. "A grizzly! There's a grizzly bear in the bushes!"

"Yes, Henry. I heard," replied a man in his late thirties, the nine- or ten-year-old boy jumping up and down in excitement at his side.

The man wore an urbanite's idea of a wilderness visitor's outfit: khaki slacks and an oiled-cotton jacket featuring shoulder epaulets and shiny brass snaps at the wrists. "My son wants to see the bear," the father said to the pair of men standing behind their spotting scopes.

"Too bad," the second spotter said, still without removing his eye from the scope.

"It's right there in the bushes?"

"It's waiting for everyone to leave."

"Well, then," the man declared, "I'll flush it out."

The father nudged the boy to the side of the woman standing next to him, then strode off the shoulder of the road and along the stream bank toward the willows.

The second spotter removed his eye from the scope for the first time, watching the father's progress. "Wouldn't do that if I was you."

7

I promised my boy we'd see a grizzly bear," the man called over his shoulder as he walked away from the road. "That's why we drove all this way."

Chuck gathered Carmelita and Rosie to him, his hands on their shoulders. "Idiot," he muttered in Janelle's ear.

"Shouldn't somebody stop him?" she asked.

The man was fifty feet from the road now, nearing the willows.

"Too late. Besides, it'll just run away, like he wants."

"You're sure?"

"I'm pretty sure."

Despite Justin's declaration last night that grizzlies were unpredictable creatures, Chuck knew Yellowstone's famed predators to be precisely the opposite. As Lex had noted over breakfast, when presented the opportunity to attack or flee, grizzlies almost always fled, even sows protecting their cubs. On the rare occasions they did go on the offensive, they were usually startled, and were prone to attack only those traveling alone or in pairs.

Given the absence of surprise and the two dozen onlookers at his back, the man faced virtually no risk from the hidden grizzly. Even so, Chuck held his breath as the man neared the thicket. He slowed, shortening his stride, then stopped before the wall of willows. The bushes stood fifteen feet high and grew so close together it was impossible to see more than a few feet into their depths.

"Hey!" the man hollered.

Seconds passed. Nothing.

"Hey," he repeated with less certainty.

The woman with the boy stepped forward. "Russell," she barked. "Get back here this instant."

Russell responded by straightening to full height and stepping forward, parting the pliant stalks in front of him with his hands. He disappeared into the willows, the tops of the spindly shoots waving as he wormed his way deeper into them. The willows stopped moving ten feet into the dense stand of brush. "Hey," he said again, his voice faltering.

In silent answer, a three-foot section of willows quivered with movement near the far end of the thicket.

A collective gasp rose from those gathered at the side of the road. The gray-haired woman next to Chuck stepped backward, her hand covering her mouth.

The heads of the displaced willows bent forward and returned to their upright position in a shimmering wave that advanced through the center of the willow patch, headed straight for the place where the man had come to a stop.

A snarl broke from the thicket, identical to the recorded growls of the grizzly that had come from Justin's phone the night before. Chuck tightened his grip on the girls' shoulders, his fingers digging into their fleece jackets.

"Aaahhh!" the man cried, his voice squeaky with terror.

Chuck clamped his lips together. Carmelita and Rosie slipped behind him, their heads poking around his sides. The tourists drew back as one.

The tops of the willows twitched as the father thrashed his way back the way he'd come, racing toward the front of the thicket. The wave from the rear of the patch rolled toward the man, marking the bear's continued advance. The bear surged through the willows, moving twice as fast as the man. The wave almost reached him before he stumbled into the open and sprinted for the roadside.

The wave came to a stop just shy of the front of the thicket. The bear, unseen, snarled once more, low and threatening. Then the motion of the willows reversed as the bear changed course, its movement back through the willow patch slow and leisurely.

The bear emerged from the far end of the patch and strode westward, away from the road, across the open ground beside the stream. It was a grizzly all right, medium-sized at about three hundred pounds, its broad shoulders tapering only slightly to its haunches, its fur the light brown color of coarse sand, the distinctive hump between its shoulders blond in the mid-morning sun.

Fifty feet from the thicket, the grizzly turned and rose on its hind legs, forelegs dangling in front of its chest. Standing taller than a human, it looked over the top of the willow patch at the tourists.

As cameras clicked around him, Chuck shivered at the memory of the grizzly staring at the Territory Team's remote camera after its attack. He leaned forward, squinting at the bear. Its ears swiveled one way, then the other, its right earflap smooth and undamaged.

The bear dropped to all fours and padded away through the knee-high grass until it disappeared into a stand of pines a quarter-mile downstream.

The man stood, quaking, at the side of the road, his hand on his son's shoulder as if for support, gawking at the place where the grizzly had vanished in the trees. The two spotters remained at their scopes. Tourists headed for their cars, chattering excitedly with one another about what they'd just seen. Chuck took the girls' hands and led them back along the roadside with Janelle.

"That was scary," Rosie announced.

"Will there be bears like that where we're going?" Carmelita asked, her eyes wide.

Chuck drew a quick breath. Last night, the video of the Territory Team attack. Earlier this morning, Lex's wild suppositions about the killer grizzly. And now, the idiot father.

In three hours, Janelle and the girls were scheduled to board a boat with him that would take them across Yellowstone Lake to the Thorofare region in Yellowstone National Park's isolated southeast corner, by many accounts the single most remote region in the lower forty-eight states, an area as populated with grizzlies as anyplace in North America, and where help was a long way off.

He pressed his hands to his stomach, containing a full-body shudder. No one had told him about the fears for Carmelita and Rosie he'd be subject to the instant he became a stepfather—worries of their being bullied at school, irrational concerns for their health, anxiety about the hits their self-esteem might take when they reached middle school.

What had possessed him to bring the girls here?

He lowered his hands, flexing his fingers. "Bears live everywhere in the park," he said, offering reassurance to himself as much as to the girls and Janelle. "This is their home. We're headed higher in the mountains on the south side of the central plateau where there'll be less for them to eat until later on in the summer and fall. They'll still be passing through, though, mostly going over the Absarokas from one side of the mountains to the other."

"Like on a road?" Rosie asked.

"Yep. Except there aren't any roads where we're going. Just trails up and over passes to the headwaters of the Snake River and on south to the Tetons."

They reached the truck. He took a map from the front seat, unfolded it, and pressed it against the side of the pickup with one hand.

"See?" he said to the girls, pointing at the small, green square with a peaked roof that marked the location of Turret Cabin at the foot of Turret Peak. "Here's where we'll be camped."

He slid his finger south, where two trails Y'ed, heading up matching, broad valleys above the junction of Thorofare Creek and the upper Yellowstone River. He tracked the Thorofare Creek drainage with his finger to where 10,971-foot Trident Peak climbed high above tree line near the head of the valley, the map thick with topo lines rising to the mountain's summit just inside the park's southern boundary. He tapped the map at the base of the peak, where three ridges fell away to the west in parallel lines. "This is where the mystery is."

"Oooo," Rosie murmured.

"You and Uncle Clarence are going to figure it out, aren't you?" Carmelita asked Chuck.

"That's what we've been hired to do."

He drew a circle with his finger around the area between the peak and cabin, taking in the Thorofare Creek and upper Yellowstone River drainages. "These are big valleys with lots of forests and meadows that climb all the way to high passes over the Absaroka Mountains. When the summer grasses get tall and thick there later on, big herds of elk will come to graze on them, and the bears will follow. Things won't really get crowded with bears until the end of the summer, though, when the whitebark pine nuts drop from the trees."

"I thought grizzly bears ate meat," Carmelita said.

"They like meat and plants both. They're omnivorous, the same as us. They eat almost anything."

"Including people?" Rosie asked, her eyes wide.

"Mostly they avoid people, like what happened back there. They just want to be left alone."

"They'll leave us alone where we're going?"

"Yes."

Rosie nodded. "If they don't, we'll spray them with our cans, won't we?"

"That's why we practiced. But we'll always be in a group, so they'll stay away from us."

Carmelita and Rosie climbed into the rear seat of the truck. Chuck closed the door and turned to Janelle. "I'm having second thoughts," he admitted.

Janelle looked at him, giving him time.

He cleared his throat. "You could drop me off at the dock and go back to Canyon Village with the girls. It's only five nights. Clarence and I can go on in and do the survey on our own. We might even be able to finish up and come out early. We'd be back in no time."

"You've been building up this discovery to the girls for the last six months."

"It *is* a big discovery."

"Which is what you've been telling them, over and over—that it's such a cool mystery, that they'll get to help solve it. You know how disappointed they'll be if you take that away from them."

"It's a site survey, Janelle. That's all the contract calls for. A simple, straightforward site survey. Stake it out, do the measurements, report back."

"Try telling the girls that, after what you've led them to believe. To them, it's the biggest thing ever."

Chuck's face flushed. "Yes, it's a site survey. But it's a survey of what might prove to be a truly significant discovery."

"Then stick to your guns. You just told Carm and Rosie we'll be fine out there as long as we stay in a group. That's exactly what we've planned to do all along."

"Yes, but..." Chuck looked at the patch of willows.

Janelle waited until he turned back to her before she spoke. "Were you telling them the truth?"

"Yes, I was." He took a deep breath. "But I have to tell you about something else, something I saw last night."

He described the video of the Territory Team attack, leaving nothing out. "Lex thinks the grizzly might actually have been hunting the team," he concluded.

"There were two team members?" Janelle asked.

"Yes."

"Grizzlies don't attack large groups, right? Just ones or twos. And we're going out there with forty or so people, *verdad*?"

"*Sí.*"

Janelle looked Chuck in the eye. "All of this might give me second thoughts if we were going camping on our own. But we're heading out there with an army." She stuck out her chin. "The girls and I are going with you. I want them to experience the world, your world, and I want to experience it, too."

Chuck hid the start of a smile. "Did I know you were this stubborn when I married you?"

"You didn't know the first thing about me when we got married."

"I thought the learning curve would be over by now."

"You thought wrong." She hesitated, searching his face. "We will be safe out there, won't we?"

He looked at the ground. The cold ache of responsibility gripped him with icy fingers. He'd promised his family the adventure of a lifetime. All this was his doing.

He'd been ecstatic two years ago when Janelle had agreed to marry him. Like Lex, he'd never been happier than the last twenty-four months, as a family man.

He settled himself on the soles of his feet. He was in Yellowstone with his family by choice, and he was heading into the backcountry with them today by the same choice. No need for mental histrionics.

He raised his eyes to Janelle. "Any bears in the vicinity of Turret Cabin will want nothing to do with our busy camp. That's why Lex is requiring everyone to base out of the same place this summer. As long as we're in camp or in a group, we'll have nothing to worry about."

"You're sure about that?"

He took her in his arms. "Absolutely."

His eyes strayed to the place where the grizzly had risen on its hind legs to observe the tourists gathered at the side of the road. Though only medium-sized, the grizzly had been tall and striking, and it had shown no hint of fear.

8

They ate their sack lunches at a picnic table on the north shore of Yellowstone Lake, down the hill from the porticoed front entrance to historic Lake Yellowstone Hotel with its vibrant, yellow-and-white paint scheme. Afterward, they drove on around the lake's western shoreline to Bridge Bay Marina.

Yellowstone Lake stretched fourteen miles from the mouth of Bridge Bay to the foot of the Absaroka Mountains, the swath of forests, tundra, talus fields, and barren peaks that continued eastward out of the park to form one of the largest roadless areas in North America. Beyond the mouth of the bay, a cold, hard breeze piled waves into whitecaps. The wind rushed across the harbor, up the concrete boat ramp, and through the marina's gravel lot, lifting dust in tight, spiraling dervishes.

Chuck put a protective hand to his nose and mouth as he crossed the lot while Janelle and the girls waited in the truck. A wooden dock, gray and weathered, extended a hundred feet into the water next to the ramp. Halfway down the dock, the two boats that made up the park's cross-lake transportation fleet bobbed in the water, snugged by their boxy sterns to the dock's rubber bumpers. The diesel-powered launches, thirty feet long by fifteen feet wide, squatted in the bay like miniature tugboats, their bows upswept to break the lake's notorious swells, their open sterns low in the water. Three-sided wheelhouses, each big enough to accommodate a single, standing pilot, stood near the bows of the matching boats' otherwise open decks.

A handful of scientists unloaded blue plastic storage containers in the shape of beer kegs, hinged plastic boxes the size of suitcases, and rubber-coated duffle bags from a pair of white cargo vans parked at the head of the ramp. The researchers carried the gear to a growing pile on the dock next to the secured boats. A woman stood beside the stack of gear, a clipboard in her hand and a nylon satchel draped from her shoulder.

"And you are...?" she asked Chuck upon his approach.

"Chuck Bender. You're Martha?"

She nodded, a crisp tic of her chin.

Yellowstone National Park Research Logistical Coordinator Martha Augustine was as legendary for her drill-sergeant-like officiousness as for the power she was said to wield over scientific work in the park. According to widely accepted rumor, proposed research projects in Yellowstone gained approval only with Martha's assent. It was whispered she could sabotage a project or researcher she didn't like—and was regularly accused of having done so—with a mere stroke of her pen.

Martha's fine silver hair poked from beneath her Smokey Bear hat. Wrinkles fanned out from her thin lips like the spokes of a wheel. A translucent plastic cover known among park personnel as a hat condom protected the hat's porous straw material from spray coming off the lake. Crisp creases ran the length of her forest green, park-service-issue slacks. The badge on the breast of her gray jacket gleamed. Above the reading glasses perched on the end of her nose, her brown eyes glinted with sharp intelligence.

"You're the Archaeology Team, correct?"

"I am. With one other."

"More than one, as I recall."

Chuck risked a smile. "I do have three members of my fan club with me."

Martha's face turned to marble. "Five total," she said. "You, team lead. Clarence Ortega, assistant. Janelle Ortega—" she paused before biting off the word "—*wife*. Carmelita and Rosalita Ortega, *daughters*."

She glowered at him over her glasses, her eyes flinty.

"Lex approved it," Chuck said.

"His decision, not mine." She checked her watch. "I've got you for 2:00. Place your things here with the rest and be ready to board at 1:30. That's thirty minutes from now."

"Got it."

"Two boats every ninety minutes. One for gear, the other for passengers. The Wolf Initiative made their two runs first thing this morning. Lex and Jorge, the cook, went in with the first boat. The Grizzly Initiative made their runs next. The 2:00 is for the rest of you—Meteorology, Geology, Drone, Canine."

"We get the afternoon wind and swell," Chuck noted.

"From what I understand, you brought your family along for the experience." She jabbed her pen at the white-capping waves beyond the narrow neck of the bay. "There's part of your experience right there."

She tucked her pen in her clipboard, reached into the satchel hanging at her side, and extracted a handful of plastic items. The bright red objects, three inches long by an inch wide, looked like fishing bobbers. Each one tapered to a recessed button and tiny LED light at one end and a metal clip at the other.

"Personal locator beacons to be attached to your packs," she explained as she counted five beacons into Chuck's cupped hands. "One for each member of your group. Required equipment as of this year, along with the camp satellite phone." Each beacon had a small sticker naming a member of Chuck's group. "Attach the beacon corresponding with the correct recipient to each of your packs—" she flattened her lips "—fan club members included. The beacons are to remain with you at all times. When the button is pressed and held for three seconds in the event of an emergency, a distress signal and locational coordinates will be sent via GPS, the Global Positioning System." She slitted her eyes at Chuck. "You'll make certain your daughters understand what 'in the event of an emergency' means, do I make myself clear?"

"Crystal."

Back at the truck, Chuck clipped the appropriate beacons to zipper pulls on his, Janelle's, and the girls' daypacks. He wrestled Rosie into her rain jacket, and they all walked across the parking lot to the dock, where they left their duffles with the growing gear pile. They returned to the emptied truck for their daypacks just as Clarence sped into the parking lot. He slid his dented hatchback to a stop, raising a cloud of dust, and hopped out.

"Can I help unload?" he asked.

"Just finished," Chuck told him.

"Yessss." He struck a pose, thumbs raised at his sides, pelvis pumping. Chuck handed him a beacon.

The five of them headed to the boats, their hiking boots echoing on the dock's thick planks. Clarence added his own armful of duffles from his hatchback to the stack on the dock. A pair of park staffers loaded the gear into the nearer of the two boats. The staffers lined the stern of the craft with the plastic storage containers, piled the duffles on top, and strapped the mound into place.

Kaifong, from the Drone Team, wandered up to Clarence. They struck up a conversation, her smooth face breaking open in a wide grin at his banter within seconds. She belly-laughed along with him a moment later.

Chuck rolled his eyes at Janelle. "Your brother," he said to her out the side of his mouth.

"You're the one who hired him. And let's remember: he's the reason you and I met."

"That's one thing in his favor. In fact, that may be the only thing."

The park staffer who'd loaded the boat took up his position in the windowed wheelhouse. The man turned a key in the ignition, and the boat's inboard engine coughed to life, then purred with a guttural murmur.

Martha unhooked the heavy ropes that secured the stern of the vessel to the dock and tossed them into the back of the boat. The pilot shifted the engine into gear. Diesel exhaust drifted across the water, acrid and pungent, as the boat chuffed toward the open water beyond the harbor mouth.

"Greetings," the other staffer said to those waiting on the dock.

The scientists turned their attention to the staffer, a woman in her mid-forties with collar-length brown hair, her bangs pressed to her forehead by a dark green baseball cap emblazoned with the arrowhead-shaped National Park Service logo.

The woman stood below the dock in the open stern of the second boat. "I'll be master and commander of your cruise to the southeast arm trailhead," she told them. "I understand this will be the first time most of you have crossed Yellowstone Lake." Her sparkling green eyes found Carmelita and Rosie. "Certainly for the two of you, am I right?"

Carmelita studied the laces of her hiking boots while Rosie clapped her hands and crowed to the woman, "I'm going on a boat ride!"

The pilot beamed. "That's right." Her brows drew together. "Most people think the biggest danger in Yellowstone National Park is the wildlife. But did you know Yellowstone Lake actually is the single most dangerous place in the whole park?"

9

Carmelita looked up from her shoes.

Rosie grabbed her sister's hand. "No," she said breathily to the pilot.

From behind Carmelita and Rosie, Chuck directed a look of warning at the woman. Who did she think she was, playing the part of drama queen in front of the girls?

"You'll be entirely safe today, of course," she told them, hurrying on. "Our boats are specially designed to take on the roughest weather Yellowstone has to offer." She licked her lips, avoiding Chuck's gaze. "But that wasn't always the case."

"It wasn't?" Rosie croaked.

"Anyone who tried to cross the lake before the invention of PFDs—personal flotation devices—took their lives into their hands," the pilot said. "At 7,775 feet above sea level this far north of the equator, Yellowstone Lake is one of the coldest navigable bodies of water on Earth, if not *the* coldest. The lake is covered with ice most of the year, and for the few summer weeks when the ice melts, the water temperature is barely above freezing." She lifted her eyebrows until they nearly reached the brim of her cap. "Yellowstone Lake is big, deep, and cold. In the old days, before PFDs, anyone who fell into the water was paralyzed within seconds and sank to the bottom of the lake like a stone, their bodies never to be recovered." The pilot's tone lightened. "But you can rest assured that Bessie here—" she tapped the rear deck of the boat with the toe of her black work boot "—couldn't flip in the worst Yellowstone storm if she wanted to. Even so, PFDs are mandatory."

She beckoned the scientists into the back of the boat.

Chuck rolled his shoulders, loosening the muscles at the back of his neck. It probably wasn't such a bad idea for the pilot to emphasize the danger of the lake to the girls.

Inward-facing bench seats lined both sides of the long, narrow stern. The pilot lifted each of the hinged seats in turn, pulling PFDs from the storage compartments beneath and passing them out before donning one herself.

The researchers slung their PFDs loosely over their shoulders and took their seats on either side of the stern, facing one another, their backs to the gunwales.

The Canine Team researcher, Keith, climbed into the boat and lowered his dog, Chance, to the rear deck. The dog, a shepherd with brown and black fur and a long, black snout, stood thigh-high next to Keith as he accepted his PFD.

Chuck sifted among the PFDs until he found a pair small enough to fit the girls. He fastened his own life jacket tight around his chest, then strapped the smaller flotation devices snug around Carmelita and Rosie.

"The temperature of the lake reminds me of the water in the Colorado River through the Grand Canyon," he remarked as he worked, squatting in front of them. "The river there is freezing cold, too."

"But that's in the desert," Carmelita said. "It should be warm."

"The water in the Colorado comes out of the bottom of Glen Canyon Dam, upstream from the canyon, so it's ice cold."

"Just like here," Rosie said, eyeing the bay water lapping against the boat. "Can I feel it?"

Without waiting for an answer, she set off for the center of the boat's stern, where a break in the railing allowed for easy loading and unloading of gear and passengers. Chuck chased her down before she could plunge her hand into the water that showed in the gap between the dock and the rear of the rocking boat.

"Maybe when we get to the other side," he told her. "There's sure to be some sort of a beach there."

He sat her beside him on one of the bench seats while the pilot entered the wheelhouse and started the engine. Janelle and Carmelita settled next to Rosie. Keith sat a few seats away, Chance tucked between his legs.

Chuck rested his elbows on the gunwale behind him as Clarence took a seat on the opposite side of the boat, still in an animated exchange with Kaifong. The second Drone Team member, Randall, sat with them. He joined their conversation, throwing his head back in a full-throated guffaw at something Clarence said.

Martha freed the ropes securing the boat to the dock and tossed them into the stern. The pilot engaged the throttle and the boat accelerated across the smooth water of the bay, the noisy cough of the engine forcing the researchers around Chuck to speak directly into one another's ears to continue their conversations.

Clarence rested a hand on Kaifong's knee and said something to her with an accompanying grin. Clarence's comment brought a smile to Kaifong's lips. She turned to Randall and, still smiling, spoke into his ear, obviously repeating what Clarence had said. Randall leaned around Kaifong and bumped Clarence's fist with his own.

The three settled back in their seats as the boat left the bay and headed out onto the open water of the lake. The boat pitched and rolled, rising and falling with the windswept swells. The pilot spun the spoked wheel, setting course across the broad body of water toward the lake's distant southeast shoreline.

The pilot leaned out of the open back of the vessel's tiny wheelhouse, her hand on the boat's wheel behind her, and faced her passengers. She pointed at a black spot making its way across the sky, trailing the boat. "Osprey," she called out, yelling to make herself heard above the engine noise and rhythmic slaps of spray arcing from the sides of the hull as the boat cut through the swells. "It's tracking us, waiting to see what we send its way."

The osprey tucked its wings and plummeted toward the water behind the boat. Just before the bird rocketed into the lake, it spread its wings, slowing itself. It skimmed along the boat's wake for an instant before plunging its clawed feet into the water. With powerful flaps of its wings, the bird rose from the surface grasping a shiny, silver fish in its talons. The fish struggled, flinging water from its tail, as the osprey flew back toward shore.

"Never fails," the pilot hollered to her passengers. "Bessie gets the fish moving, and the osprey take advantage. We're doing our part to help the park service get rid of the non-native lake trout so the native cutthroat can return." She smiled and turned back to the wheel.

As the marina receded into the distance, Chuck and Janelle wrapped their arms around the girls, who bent forward to avoid the brisk breeze curling past the wheelhouse.

Ahead, the Absarokas drew nearer. To the southeast, the snow-covered summit of Trident Peak reared highest above the lake's shoreline. After twenty minutes of plowing through the waves, the pilot again adjusted course, aiming the boat toward the opening into the lake's southeast arm, a two-mile-long, finger-shaped bay extending south from the lake's most remote reach. The upper Yellowstone River emptied into the head of the narrow bay, where the trail to Turret Cabin and on into the heart of the Thorofare region began.

Ahead, the gear boat exited the southeast arm on its return trip to Bridge Bay. The pilots exchanged waves as the boats passed one another. The stern of the gear boat was empty, the teams' duffles and cases waiting at the trailhead landing.

Opposite Chuck, Randall spun and knelt on his seat. Facing the open water of the lake, he trailed his fingers in the bursts of spray flying from the boat's hull. He lifted his hand from the water and shook it, then turned to Kaifong and Clarence and gritted his teeth. The pair twisted and knelt on their seats beside him, taking turns diving their hands into the spray.

Rosie turned to reach for the spray on her side of the boat. Chuck pressed her back into place. "Oh, no, you don't," he said in her ear.

"But they get to," she shouted over the roar of the engine.

"Sorry," Chuck told her. "They're bigger than you."

She crossed her arms over her PFD and thrust out her lower lip in an exaggerated pout.

Randall stood up. Grinning and beckoning Kaifong and Clarence to follow, he crossed the boat's white, fiberglass deck. "Come on," he encouraged them, his voice carrying above the engine noise. "We'll really be able to tell how cold the water is."

He hammed it up as he walked to the back railing, staggering like a drunk across the rising and falling deck. "Whoa!" he cried out, waving his arms for balance, as Kaifong and Clarence approached behind him.

He bent at the opening in the railing and stuck his hand into the lake water. He straightened as Kaifong and Clarence reached him at the back of the boat. "Ow, ow, ow," he cried, laughing and shaking his hand, his red halo of hair pressed back from his forehead by the wind. "That's what I call *freezin'!*"

He shook his hand once more and stepped aside, allowing Kaifong to take his place at the back of the boat. He gave a playful clap to her life jacket, slung over one of her shoulders, as she passed him. At the same instant his hand met her PFD, the bow of the boat climbed through a wave while the stern remained low in the wave's trough, causing the deck of the vessel to cant sharply upward. Randall's clap and the sudden upward pitch of the boat threw Kaifong off balance. She tripped over the coils of rope on the stern's floor and teetered, windmilling her arms.

Randall's eyes widened as he shot out his hand, reaching for her. Clarence grabbed for her, too. Their fingers closed on air. Kaifong's unfastened PFD swung free from her shoulder as she tumbled, screaming, into the lake.

10

Chuck scrambled to his feet and charged toward the stern of the boat between the stunned, seated researchers.

"Hey!" he yelled over his shoulder to the pilot.

"Overboard!" one of the scientists yelled.

Kaifong surfaced behind the boat. The wind blew her PFD, floating atop the water, away from her. She thrashed in the water while Clarence worked frantically to buckle the straps of his PFD. Randall stared at Kaifong, shock etched on his face, his own PFD hanging unfastened over one shoulder.

The wind would propel Kaifong's PFD away from her faster than she would be able to swim after it. There was no way she'd be able to tread water in her heavy clothing long enough for the boat to circle around and return to her; she would sink into the freezing lake well before the pilot completed the turn.

Chuck did not pause. He rushed past Clarence and Randall and dove from the stern into the lake. The cold poleaxed his head and chest as he entered the water. Pain exploded in his frontal lobes. The icy water slammed his chest, forcing his lungs to contract. He closed his mouth, fighting the panicked urge to inhale and take in a lungful of liquid.

His PFD, strapped tight around his torso, propelled him to the surface. He swam hard for Kaifong, fifty feet away from him, stroking his arms and kicking his booted feet. Behind him, the sound of the boat's engine deepened as the pilot cut the vessel into its turn.

Kaifong's pale face showed above the surface of the lake. She splashed toward her PFD, but her arms, weighed down by the water-absorbing fabric of her fleece jacket, barely broke through the waves. Meanwhile, the breeze propelled the PFD quickly away from her.

Within seconds, Kaifong's arm movements grew clumsy and robotic, and she sank in the water until only her mouth and nose showed above the surface. By the time Chuck drew within twenty feet of her, only the top of her head remained visible above the surface of the lake, her fingers floundering weakly at the waves.

The cold knotted Chuck's legs as he churned toward Kaifong. She sank from sight. He swam, his gaze fixed on the spot where she'd disappeared. A wave slapped the side of his head, filling his ear with freezing water. He drew air into his lungs, forcing them to expand.

He reached the place where he'd last seen her. She hung suspended in the clear water below him, four feet beneath the surface, her outstretched arms speckled by the sun, her black hair floating like seaweed around her head and shoulders. Even as he spotted her, she sank deeper, her body still, her fingers curled inward.

Chuck porpoised out of the water and dove. He stretched his arms down against the buoyancy of his PFD but missed Kaifong by inches before the life jacket shot him back to the surface.

He sucked a mouthful of air, the cold settling in his bones. The diesel engine roared as the boat, having completed its arc, raced back. Kaifong was deeper now, slipping away.

He cursed. The PFD trapped him at the surface. He unclipped the three buckles at the front of the life jacket, his fingers stiff and unwieldy, raised his arms, and sank out of the shoulders of the jacket and beneath the surface of the lake. Snagging one of the PFD's dangling straps with his left hand, he dove again, plunging his right hand downward, his eyes fixed on Kaifong below.

Twelve inches away. Six inches. Clinging with his other hand to the strap of his life jacket, he reached the extent of his dive when the PFD, acting as a cork atop the water, halted his descent.

Kaifong continued to sink below him.

He clawed at the water while holding his breath, his cheeks bulging. If he took the time to return to the surface for more air, he would lose Kaifong to the depths.

He stretched full out, scrabbling with his fingers, but Kaifong was too far away.

He couldn't release the PFD, lest he follow Kaifong into the depths.

One last, desperate idea occurred to him. He spun his body and shoved his feet toward the surface. Slipping one boot through the shoulder strap of his PFD and hooking the ankle of his other foot around the strap, he secured his feet in place. Battling the urge to breathe, his vision blurring, he strained toward Kaifong's suspended body with both hands.

His fingers swept past her. Missed. She was too deep.

But the motion of his hands created an underwater wave that pressed the floating tendrils of her hair against her head, then lifted them toward him in a rebound.

Chuck jabbed his hands into the depths, his feet locked to the PFD, his lungs screaming. He grasped a few strands of Kaifong's hair and tugged upward. The strands ripped free from her scalp, but not before the action lifted her body a few inches in the water.

He grabbed a handful of her hair, now within reach, and swam upward, the last of the air in his depleted lungs bubbling from his nostrils. He broke the surface of the lake and gasped, sucking oxygen into his seizing chest.

He looped his free arm through a strap of his life jacket and hoisted Kaifong to the surface beside him. Her head fell backward, her wan face to the sky, her lips blue and slack.

"Breathe," Chuck pleaded, clutching Kaifong. "Please. Breathe."

The whites of her eyes showed between her eyelids. Blood vessels, purple against her blanched skin, spiderwebbed her cheeks.

Chuck held her at the surface as his own strength waned. She hung limp in his arms.

11

The boat powered up to Chuck and Kaifong. Its engine chunked hard into reverse, then idled as the boat drifted alongside them. The pilot appeared at the gunwale, her face white. Randall and Clarence lifted Kaifong over the railing. Chuck clung to his PFD until they dragged him into the boat seconds later.

He lay on his back in the open stern of the vessel, vaguely aware of Janelle crouched over him. "I'm okay," he told her, his teeth chattering. He aimed a shaking finger at Kaifong, on her back beside him. "Her."

Janelle reached beneath Kaifong's neck and gently lifted, opening the airway, then locked her hands together and compressed Kaifong's chest in a steady rhythm. She counted out loud with each compression. "One, two, three..."

Randall knelt at the other side of Kaifong.

"Two breaths after every fifteen compressions," Janelle instructed him.

He hesitated.

"Now," she commanded. "Pinch her nose. Keep her chin lifted so her airway stays open."

Randall bent over Kaifong. All was quiet as he and Janelle worked, Kaifong's chest rising with each pair of forced breaths.

The other scientists stripped Chuck's wet clothes and wrapped him in fleece blankets pulled from beneath the bench seats by the pilot, who slid a PFD under his head as a pillow.

Enveloped in the blankets, Chuck rocked with the boat on the swells of the lake. Carmelita and Rosie knelt beside him.

"Are you okay?" Carmelita asked, her frightened voice little more than a whisper.

Chuck reached a hand to her. "Just...cold."

Seconds ticked by as Janelle and Randall continued their efforts. Kaifong lay still. Chuck willed her to live.

Suddenly, Kaifong's body stiffened. Her heels pounded the deck of the boat. She gagged and coughed. Her chest heaved and water streamed from the corner of her mouth and she drew an enormous lungful of air. She turned her head to the side and spat weakly, then took a second, trembling breath. Her eyes opened and she stared dully at Chuck.

She blinked once, twice, three times, more awareness returning to her walnut eyes with each blink. Her breathing grew steady.

The researchers stripped her clothes and wrapped her in blankets.

She turned her head, taking in Janelle and Randall kneeling over her, the researchers and pilot hovering above. "What happened?" she asked, her voice weak.

"I'll radio in and get us headed back," the pilot said.

"No," Janelle responded. "She'll freeze if we try to go all the way back across."

"Agreed," Chuck said, his own body shaking. "We need to get her warmed up, fast."

"The landing's only two miles away," the pilot said. "There's lots of driftwood." She darted to the wheelhouse and gunned the engine, aiming the boat across the last of the open water and into the southeast arm of the lake.

Kaifong lay on the deck, her eyes open but unfocused, her chest rising and falling.

"How is she?" Chuck asked Janelle.

"She was breathing and had a pulse the whole time, but I wanted to be certain. I wasn't sure what else to do."

The boat shot up the narrow bay. Forested ridges rose from both shorelines. The vessel slowed a few minutes later. The pilot worked the throttle, maneuvering the boat against an aluminum dock extending from shore.

Janelle and Randall lifted Kaifong, shivering and unsteady, to her feet. Clarence clambered from the boat and hustled off the dock past the pile of gear on shore. He and the other scientists collected driftwood from the rocky beach. Janelle and Randall helped Kaifong down the pier, supporting her between them, while the pilot secured the boat. Chuck made his way to shore. He clutched the blankets around him, glad to walk on his own.

By the time Clarence and the researchers assembled the driftwood in a tall pyre, the pilot arrived with a tin of gasoline from the boat. She doused the wood and put a lighter to it. The fuel ignited with an oxygen-sucking whoomp. Flames climbed into the air while smoke from the damp wood smudged the afternoon sky.

Janelle settled Kaifong on a patch of open sand close to the flames. Chuck slumped beside her. Welcoming heat emanated from the fire, warming his face.

Thirty minutes later, Kaifong sat before the roaring fire on a log next to Chuck, her palms held out to the flames. They wore fresh clothes from their personal duffles, their hiking boots drying on rocks beside them.

Kaifong's cheeks glowed. "Well, that sucked," she announced.

"I'm sorry, Kaifong," Randall said from where he stood on the far side of the fire, his voice cracking. "I'm so, so sorry, chickadee."

She waved him off. "I shouldn't have gotten so close to the back of the boat—and I should have buckled my life jacket."

"I never should've left my seat," Randall said, twisting his hands in front of him.

"At least it all ended okay," Chuck said. He glanced at the boat, where the pilot returned PFDs to the compartments beneath the bench seats. "About ready to head back across?" he asked Kaifong.

"I'm not sure I want to go back out to sea so soon." She pressed her hands between her knees and gazed at the roiling water of the open lake beyond the mouth of the arm before turning to Chuck. "What about you?"

"I'm staying. But it wasn't me who almost drowned."

Randall said to Kaifong, "Don't you think you should have a doctor check you out?"

"We've been waiting two years to get into the backcountry," she replied. "We're finally here."

She shifted on the log to face the upper Yellowstone River valley rising to the south, mile after mile of pristine forest broken by grassy meadows, every bit of it devoid of human development. Groves of whitebark pines climbed the sides of the broad valley, blanketing ridges that swept upward to alpine tundra studded by snowcapped peaks.

Janelle, standing behind Chuck, said, "There's still plenty of daylight. We can call in a med-evac if you have trouble on the hike to camp—in which case, you'll be choppered out instead of having to go back out on the lake."

"Once the boat's gone, there'll be no radio," Chuck warned. "Someone would have to make it to the cabin to use the satellite phone before any evacuation could happen. There's no cell phone service out here."

"Or," Janelle said, "she could press the button on her emergency beacon."

"True, I suppose," Chuck said. "As a last resort."

A horse whinnied from out of sight in the forest to the south, followed by a pair of whinnies in response.

65

Janelle cocked her head at the sound of the horses. "Maybe you could ride to camp," she told Kaifong.

"Me? Ride a horse?" Kaifong shook her head. "Never. Those things terrify me." She reached for her boots.

"It's four miles," Chuck warned her. He pulled the map from his pack, flipped it open, and showed her the trail winding upstream east of the river. "Not steep, but uphill all the way."

"I'll be fine. I'm sure of it."

A string of ten pack horses, their saddles empty, emerged from the woods. A mounted wrangler led the string, reins loose in his leather-gloved hand. A second wrangler brought up the rear. The two horsemen, square-jawed and middle-aged, wore Stetsons low over their eyes, their faces shadowed in the afternoon sunlight. The horses made their way along a well-trodden path toward the pier.

"Guess I'd better get to it, then," Randall said.

He left the fire and worked alongside the others, placing the duffles, storage kegs, and plastic cases from the gear boat in an orderly line, ready for loading on the pack animals.

Kaifong stood up after lacing her hiking boots. "Thank you," she said to Chuck as he tied his own boots, still damp from their dunking in the lake. "You saved my life."

He looked up at her from his seat on the log. "Glad I could be of service."

Beyond the pier, Clarence and the girls stood at the edge of the lake. They skipped rocks toward the Molly Islands, two rounded humps of sand and stone rising out of the southeast arm. White pelicans circled the barren islands in tight formations. The big, heavy birds skimmed the surface of the water like squadrons of World War II bombers. The islands served as the endangered pelicans' rookery, separating the birds from onshore predators. The upper Yellowstone emptied into the arm of the lake south of the islands. The river's surface was dark in the shadows of the lodgepole pines rising close on both banks.

Chuck turned to Janelle, who held her hands out to the crackling flames. "You did an amazing job out there."

"I felt good about it," she admitted. She tucked her hands in her jacket pockets. "Like that was what I was supposed to be doing."

"You've found your true calling: saving lives."

Her cheeks reddened.

"I'm not joking," he said.

"I know. That's why I'm blushing. I feel like, finally, I'm getting to grow up. You have no idea what having two little girls can do to you, especially if you're just a girl yourself when you have them."

He grinned. "You're right. I have no idea what it's like to be a girl, or to give birth."

Janelle shook her head. "Diapers and baby food and kiddie TV, that's been my life for as long as I can remember. I traded away my twenties—" She stopped, the color in her cheeks deepening. "Don't get me wrong. I wouldn't trade Carm and Rosie for anything."

"I know that."

"It's just, finally, they're getting bigger. I mean, look at them over there with Clarence." She waved at the shoreline. "They couldn't care less if I'm here, which is about the first time that's ever happened."

"They're great kids because you devoted yourself to them," Chuck said.

She tucked her hands in her jacket pockets. "I know what it has cost me—in a good way, that is. But now, thanks to you—thanks to us, together—there's a real future out there for the four of us, and just for me, too. And that last part feels good."

"I'm glad." He slipped his hand into her jacket pocket and wrapped his fingers around hers. "So tell me, are you still up for this?"

"Why wouldn't I be?"

"You've watched two people almost get killed today."

"The thing with Kaifong was an accident, the result of carelessness. And *el stupido* with the bear got exactly what he was asking for."

Chuck waited, wanting her to be sure.

"The girls have been looking forward to this trip as much as I have," she said. She aimed a finger from inside her jacket pocket at Kaifong, sorting the Drone Team's plastic storage cases.

"That's who I want the girls to be when they grow up. If she's not quitting after what she just went through, then the girls and I aren't quitting, either. Got it, *muchacho*?"

"*Sí, esposa mia*," Chuck said. He squeezed her hand. "*Claro que sí.*"

He turned away before she could see the worry in his eyes.

12

At Turret Cabin, Lex drew Chuck aside.
"I owe you some pretty big thanks, from what I hear," the ranger said. "Your wife, too."

"Right place, right time," Chuck replied.

"What happened, exactly?"

"They were messing around at the back of the boat when it hit a swell. Bad timing."

Kaifong had completed the hike to the cabin without difficulty.

"Not a good way to start the summer."

"Everyone will be more careful now."

Lex chortled darkly. "We'll see."

The two men observed the research camp springing to life before them.

A white, rectangular mess tent towered beside Turret Patrol Cabin. The historic log cabin, half the size of the tent, was one in a string of "snowshoe cabins" built in the Yellowstone backcountry in the late nineteenth and early twentieth centuries. The cabins sheltered rangers chasing poachers who slaughtered animals slowed by deep snow during the winter months. In recent decades, with winter poaching under control, Turret Cabin had served as a lonely summer outpost for seasonal rangers—though this summer, with the arrival of the research teams, the cabin site would be anything but lonely.

The one-room cabin and canvas mess tent faced north at the base of an open, grass-covered slope. A wooden picnic table, its planks as weathered and gray as those lining the dock at Bridge

Bay, sat in front of the cabin. The plastic storage drums containing the camp's supplies lined the outside walls between the tent and cabin. On the east side of the mess tent, the wranglers loosened straps and removed the last of the geology, meteorology, canine, drone, and archaeology teams' gear from the pack horses, lining the duffles and storage containers in the grass for retrieval by the team members. Fifty yards east of the horses, the beige cloth walls of the multi-seat camp latrine rose head-high at the foot of a stand of pines.

The scent of freshly cut lumber wafted from a dozen newly erected tent platforms, each fifteen feet wide by twenty feet deep. The platforms lined the hillside from east to west, a hundred feet above the cabin and mess tent. Team members swarmed their assigned platforms, putting up tents, setting out webbed camp chairs, and erecting mosquito-screened, nylon-roofed day rooms. Already, a number of fold-out solar panels lay face-up on the slope above the platforms. Wires from the panels fed juice into stacks of rechargeable batteries that would power the research teams' computers, LED lanterns, and walkie talkies over the course of the summer.

"What do you mean, 'We'll see'?" Chuck asked as he and Lex watched the activity.

"How many contracts did you win at the Grand Canyon during the years I was there?" Lex asked. "Six? Eight?"

"Plenty."

"So you know what it takes to score a research position in any national park, much less Yellowstone." The ranger eyed the scientists as they assembled tent poles and unfolded camp tables. "I already told you what a bunch of Type A personalities these kids are. They're good people, no question. Talented. Whip-smart. Capable. But they're high strung, too."

"Meaning...?"

"Meaning accidents are going to happen this summer; there'll be too many people here together for them not to—along with the sort of thing Sarah pulled last night, going for Toby's throat." Lex lowered his voice. "Speak of the devil."

Sarah approached with a large duffle over her shoulder, angling past the cabin from the trampled area where the wranglers unstrapped the last of the gear from the pack horses. She stopped before Lex and Chuck.

"Toby's making threats," she announced. She flopped the duffle to the ground at her feet.

Lex closed his eyes, then slowly opened them. "You tried to strangle him, Sarah."

"Do I look like the kind of person who goes around trying to choke people to death just for the fun of it?"

"Well..."

Sarah had traded her pink vest for a brown, camouflage-patterned jacket. A ball cap bearing the Grizzly Initiative logo of a bear's hulking outline hid her mohawk, and she'd removed all but the least showy of her earrings. She still sported plenty of attitude, however, with her hooped, gold nose ring; the rakish angle of her cap, its flat trucker bill set high and to one side so that it covered the top of one ear; the chipped black polish on her fingernails, banded with thin, orange stripes; and the multi-hued tattoo of a snake that wrapped around her wrist and across the back of her hand, the serpent's tongue extending past pointed fangs to flick between two knuckles.

"Well, I'm not that kind of person," Sarah declared. "What you saw last night was the finish. Toby started it before the meeting. I was just standing there, enjoying my punch and cookies, and he comes up to me and says, 'We'll see about that.' And I'm like, 'We'll see about what?' And he's like, 'If you can't take it, you shouldn't even be here this summer.' I'm like, 'Can't take what?'

And he's all, 'Being second fiddle.' Which is the last thing I am. We are."

"Wait, wait, wait," Lex said, waving his hands. "What in the world are you talking about?"

"Our studies. Our funding. You. Martha." Sarah raised her eyebrows. "It's been the same thing every year for the last three years. Every summer, a little more for the wolfies, a little less for the Grizzly Initiative. It's like the National Science Institute can't get enough of the poor, wittle endangered gray wolf. Year after year, a bigger percentage for them, a smaller one for us. And then, this year, the Center for Predator Studies shifted all their funding, every last dime, to the Wolf Initiative." She pointed up the slope at the row of tent platforms. "Look up there," she demanded, spittle flying from her lips. "There were tags with the platform assignments. The Wolf Initiative has four platforms. Four. We only have three. And Martha gave them the first boat over this morning. We had to sit around and wait."

Chuck looked from Sarah to Lex. It appeared the ranger was counting silently, working to control himself. "You said something about being threatened," he said finally.

She nodded vigorously, her remaining earrings bouncing. "By Toby. Yeah. He said if I complained about funding levels, he'd make sure the Grizzly Initiative got even less next year. He said he knew enough people to make it happen."

"That's it? That's the threat you're talking about?"

"It's pretty legit, I'd say."

Lex shot a glance at Chuck, then looked Sarah over. "I'm going to tell you this one time, Sarah, and one time only: your emails last summer, with your concerns about not getting to go out into the field, got old real fast. Martha didn't want you invited back this year, but I stood up for you. I know you were solid in the field two years ago, and I understand how frustrating last year was for you. I told her you deserved another season in the backcountry, that your thesis was riding on it." Lex lifted a finger. "But I'm telling you right now, I expect you to get along with everyone this summer, just as you've always done—Toby included. No more childishness like you pulled last night. One of the reasons I'm out here these first few days is to make sure everyone is going to play nice for the next ten weeks. If you can't manage that, then you can leave when I do."

"Sure, but—" Sarah began, but Lex interrupted her.

"This is a new situation, this group camp," he said. "It's something we've never tried. Everyone will be working together here, in close quarters. Sharing will be the name of the game, not worrying about who's getting more money than who." Lex's voice grew brittle. "I've looked at the list of your team members. You've only got one rookie, the kid from Princeton, which means there are plenty of experienced people on your team. I'll put one of them in charge out here for the summer if I have to."

Sarah started to speak, then snapped her mouth shut. The muscles at the sides of her face worked beneath her skin. "Okay," she said. "All right. Message received. And just wait till you see the body of data we're going to come out of here with by the end of the summer—" she flicked her fingers at the long row of tent platforms, swarmed by researchers "—frickin' Boy Scout camp and all."

She lifted the duffle with her sinewy arms, threw it back over her shoulder, and trudged off.

"Whew," Lex said, sagging.

"You're way more patient with her than I ever would be," Chuck said.

"You're probably right." His eyes followed Sarah as she cut behind the cabin and climbed toward the platforms. "She reminds me of Lucy. And Jessie."

"Your daughter *and* your wife?"

"You know full well how Jessie could be."

Chuck nodded. He remembered many evenings at the Grand Canyon, after dinner and plenty of red wine, when Jessie had stood up for herself in heated conversations with the ever-changing cast of park workers, many of them know-it-all males, who gathered around the Hancock table night after night.

"You never really knew Lucy," Lex went on. "She was in college by the time you and I met at the canyon. She got every bit of her mother's feistiness. She's a good bit older than Sarah, but she looks a lot like her—minus the mohawk and tattoos, that is. She's been a big help to me, since Jessie...since the cancer..." He choked up.

"How has she helped?" Chuck asked softly.

"Oh, you know, just being there. Calling. Letting me know she cares." He sniffled and waved a hand, taking in the camp and the valley around it. "But this is what really helps. God, it feels good to be out here."

"Even if you have to deal with the likes of Sarah."

"She's no problem. Not when you realize that what's going on with her has nothing to do with what she's talking about."

"Oh, yeah. You said something at breakfast about extenuating circumstances, didn't you?"

Lex raised an eyebrow and tightened the corner of his mouth, pulling his mustache down on one side. "Toby," he said.

Chuck recalled the look Sarah had directed at the lead wolf researcher as she'd left the meeting room with Clarence the night before. "Ahh," he said. "Sarah and Toby. They were an item at one point, is that it?"

"The last two summers," Lex confirmed. "Hot and torrid, from what I heard. And it's not like I was trying to hear anything."

"That explains a lot."

"Sarah is dedicated to her team, tireless, smart. A lot of people have a hard time getting past her earrings and tattoos. But you should've seen her two summers ago. Last year, too. No one works harder than she does. She's a natural-born leader, too. And she leads by example. Nobody's more willing to pitch in and help out, anywhere, anytime, than she is."

"What about her complaining that the wolfies are getting more money than the Grizzly Initiative?"

Lex flapped a hand dismissively. "That was all about Toby. Clearly, she's still in the process of getting over him. And just as clearly, she's not doing a very good job of it. That said, it's true that the research teams are pretty aware of who's getting what when it comes to grant money. But they tend to be very positive about it. They share information, give each other hints about what funding sources might be available, write letters of recommendation for one another."

"So her concerns aren't...?"

"There's some truth to what she's saying. But it's just the pendulum swinging—funding amounts going up and down a little bit. And I won't kid you. As supportive as the teams are of each other, there's competition between them as well, most of all between the wolf and grizzly teams. That's what made the relationship between Sarah and Toby, as team leads for the two programs, a bit dicey the last couple of years. And that's why the aftermath has the potential to be a bit more problematic than the breakup of normal inter-team relationships. The things Sarah has been carping about—all that's factual enough. But the way she's been carping is what's out of character for her."

"On account of her breakup with Toby."

"Yep. But she'll calm down. It'll sort itself out."

"Except that my assistant, Clarence, has just stepped right into the middle of it."

Lex nodded. "I saw him leave with Sarah last night. The truth is, he may be exactly what she needs to move on. Toby, too, for that matter. I wasn't kidding when I told Sarah how important it is for everyone to get along here in camp this summer. And I wasn't kidding, either, when I said she'll be out of here if she doesn't settle down and play nice."

"She clammed up pretty quick when you told her that."

"She did, didn't she? That's because she really is a good person. The best we've got. You'll see."

"I hope so." Chuck chuckled. "Silly me. I thought it was just the bears I had to be worried about out here."

13

Chuck caught up with Janelle and the girls on their assigned tent platform, fourth from the east end in the line of pine-plank decks bolted to wooden posts dug into the slope above the cabin. Janelle already had his wet clothes laid out on the grass behind their platform, drying in the last of the afternoon sun.

"We've got six days here," he told her as he climbed onto the deck. "Five nights. We'll spend our days going straight to and from the contract site or staying right here, in and around camp, and we'll stay close together the whole time, all of us, especially the girls."

Janelle looked down the hill at Lex. "What'd he say to you?"

"He reminded me again how many bears there are out here."

"We've known that all along, Chuck."

"It's more real now that we're here. A lot more real." He ran the tip of his tongue along his teeth. "Remember how I told you his wife, Jessie, died of cancer earlier this year? He's still at sea over it."

"That's to be expected."

"I know. But I'm getting the sense his okay for you and the girls to come out here is all wrapped up in her death, and how much he misses the time he spent outdoors with her and their kids in places like this."

"You're the one who asked if we could come. You have to remember that. You wanted us to see the site with you, to be a part of it all."

"I did, didn't I?"

Janelle patted Chuck's chest. "You're turning into a dad right in front of me. You're worrying about your kids, your family—which I like. The more worried you are, the safer we'll be." She rubbed his shoulder. "As for me, just so you know, I'm not worried, not one bit. We're going to have the time of our lives out here together, just like we've planned all along, all thanks to Lex—no matter why he decided to let us come."

On the far side of the platform, the girls squatted beside their unzipped duffles, giggling as they pawed through their clothes.

"Carm, Rosie," Janelle called to them. "*Ven aqui, por favor.* Time to help set up our tent."

Clarence arrived with the last of their duffles and the five of them set to work as the sun fell toward Two Ocean Plateau, a snow-covered promontory rising above the valley's forested west ridge. The girls helped Chuck and Janelle erect their family tent in one corner of the deck while Clarence put up his smaller tent in the opposite corner. They positioned a camp table and five fold-out chairs near the front of the platform between the tents, and arranged portable solar panels on the slope beside Chuck's drying clothes.

As he worked, Chuck kept an eye on the research teams setting up their tents and organizing their gear on the other platforms. The Grizzly Initiative team occupied the easternmost end of the row of platforms, while Martha had assigned the Wolf Initiative team to the far west end of the row. The smaller teams—meteorological, geological, drone, canine, and Chuck's archaeological crew—occupied the platforms in between. Chuck caught Clarence exchanging glances with Sarah as she set up her small tent in the corner of the nearest Grizzly Initiative platform, a few feet from Clarence's tent on the neighboring Archaeological Team deck.

As the evening shadows lengthened, the smell of broiling meat floated up the hill from the mess tent, mixing with the lumber-yard scent of the newly constructed platforms. At six, a cowbell rang. Up and down the row of platforms, team members abandoned their work and tramped down the hill, disappearing through the front flap into the steepled tent. The scientists emerged minutes later in ones and twos and headed back up the slope carrying plastic trays topped with lidded mugs and plates loaded with slabs of steak, fresh salad, slices of bread, and chocolate brownies.

Clarence and Sarah finished setting up their tents and walked down the slope to the mess tent together.

"When will it be our turn?" Rosie asked from where she sat with Carmelita at the front of the platform, her feet swinging.

Chuck tied a guy line from their tall family tent to the nearest of the deck's four corner posts. "Right now, if you're ready."

"I'm ready, ready, ready," Rosie said. She made chomping noises with her mouth and smacked her lips.

Chuck poked his head inside the tent, where Janelle tugged a sleeping bag from its stuff sack. "How about you?" he asked her.

Haloed by the yellow glow of the tent's interior, Janelle arranged the puffy red bag on one of the four pads she'd unrolled inside. "Just finished." She patted the bag into place and slipped past him. Chuck zipped the tent closed behind her as she climbed off the platform, helped the girls to the ground, and walked with them down the slope. Chuck paused at the edge of the deck above them to take in the view.

From where he stood, the meadows and forests of the upper Yellowstone River valley stretched north to the lake's southeast arm. Two ridge-walled miles farther on, the arm opened to the expanse of the lake itself. The rays of the descending sun shimmered on the lake's whitecaps, bright eyelashes sweeping across the distant body of water. On the far horizon, a low spot between dark ridges marked the place where the Yellowstone

River left the lake and made its languid way north across the plateau. Between the cabin and lake, dozens of meadows, some large, some small, tear-dropped the valley floor. New grass in the clearings glowed vibrant green in the last of the sunlight. The trail up the valley from the boat landing wound in a thin, brown line across several of the clearings on its way to the cabin.

Chuck swept the valley floor with his gaze, moving from one meadow to the next in methodical, hunter fashion. Now was the time, as afternoon gave way to evening, that the earliest arrivals of the Thorofare region's famous summer elk herds would filter from the trees into the open to graze on the fresh summer grasses.

As if on cue, a single cow elk, little more than a smudge of light brown topped by a darker brown neck and head, stepped from the forest into the open at the edge of the meadow nearest camp, just over half a mile to the north. More cows and smaller brown smudges denoting calves followed the lead cow into the open. The herd's huge bulls stepped from the trees last. The bulls appeared as large brown rectangles in the evening light, topped by forked sticks—their heavy, back-swept antlers.

More elk came into the open, cows as well as bulls. The herd moved away from the cover of the trees, several dozen animals in all, grazing toward the middle of the meadow, their heads to the ground. Suddenly, the animals stopped moving. The angled sun lit their still forms. Then, the elk turned and sprinted back the way they'd come, disappearing into the trees.

Chuck kept his eyes on the clearing. A rectangular shape the same tawny brown color as the elk emerged into the open on the opposite side of the meadow. The figure moved across the grass low to the ground, like a steamroller.

A stiff breeze cut across the platform and sliced through Chuck's fleece jacket, causing him to shiver. He squinted, convincing himself he saw a pale hump atop the brown profile in the clearing. Before he could retrieve his binoculars from his duffle bag for a good look, the figure crossed the opening and melted into the trees behind the elk.

14

Chuck woke early the next morning fired up for the day ahead. This was what he'd waited for all these months, what he'd built up in the girls' minds as, perhaps, the best archaeological discovery they might ever see. Today, finally, they would all find out.

The dawn sky shone lavender above camp as he followed the smell of fresh coffee down the hill to the mess tent. Frost clung to stems of grass on the slope, and the cold morning air fogged his breath. He ducked through the front flaps to find a squat, middle-aged Hispanic man working at a pair of gas stoves set at the back of the tent. On one of the waist-high stoves, the man poured and flipped pancakes on two griddles at once, stacking the cooked, golden pancakes in a covered pan on a side table. He paused at the second stove long enough to pour boiling water from a kettle through coffee grounds in a cloth filter fastened to the top of a large metal urn with a low flame burning beneath.

Chuck made his way between the tables, lined with folding chairs, that filled the front half of the tent. The air inside, toasty warm, smelled strongly of the fresh coffee. Upon spotting Chuck, the cook grabbed a plastic mug from a stack on a side table, filled it from a tap at the base of the urn, and presented it with both hands.

"You figure I'm a coffee drinker, do you?" Chuck asked him.

"If you aren't now, you're about to be," the cook said with a slight Latino accent.

"You're Jorge?"

"That would be me." The cook wiped his hands on a rag tucked through the strings of the white apron he wore over blue jeans and a long-sleeved dress shirt, with snaps instead of buttons, rolled to his elbows.

Chuck took a sip. The coffee was strong and crisp, with the perfect amount of bitterness. "You're right. I'm hooked."

"Martha thinks we're drinking Folgers out here," Jorge said. "Ha." He patted the urn. "Single source. One-hundred-percent Guatemalan, land of my forefathers. I'd never make it through the summer without it."

"You've done this before?"

"Out here in the middle of nowhere? Never. My lady, she works at Lake, in the hotel. I'm usually stationed in the staff kitchen at Canyon. We work winters at Big Sky, the ski resort over by Bozeman. They said they needed someone to come out here this summer. Seven days a week, twelve hours a day, ten weeks straight. I said okay, I'd give it a try: the mountains, the fresh air, the sunshine—and all the overtime pay. We got two in college. *Aiyee*, the tuition payments. But it's going to be a long summer. The two of us have never been apart this long."

Chuck raised his cup. "I agree with you: this'll help."

"That's what I'm hoping." Jorge turned back to his pancakes.

When Chuck walked up the hill from the mess tent with two lidded mugs of Jorge's brew, he found Janelle bundled up and seated in a camp chair at the front of the platform, overlooking the mist-shrouded valley.

"Today's the day," he said, setting the mugs on the edge of the platform and climbing up to join her. "I'm stoked."

"Me, too."

He handed her a mug. "It's five miles farther up the valley. Ten miles roundtrip. Think the girls are up for it?"

"They did the four miles from the lake without breaking a sweat. All the practice hikes this spring are paying off."

"Today's the real payoff."

"You really think they'll be there?"

"No one could have gotten to them over the winter."

"It just seems so odd, out here in the middle of nowhere."

"There's good reason, though. The passes provided easy summer access from the south—a thoroughfare—to the central plateau, with all its food and game."

Janelle hugged the mug to her chest and looked north, down the valley and across the lake. "It's beautiful, I'll grant you that. But cold."

"That's why the old ones spent their winters down low along the Snake, and only came up and over the passes to the plateau in the summer. When they got here, though, they were in the land of plenty."

Janelle's gaze took in the forested ridges and snow-covered peaks lining the sides of the valley, the whitebark pines waving in the chilly morning breeze. She drew her arms to her sides. "Doesn't look like the Garden of Eden to me."

"You'd be surprised." Chuck popped the lid off his mug and took a sip, savoring the tanginess of the coffee on the back of his tongue. "The early Sioux controlled the plains, and the Navajo and Apache and Utes were in charge farther south. That left the Yellowstone uplift to the predecessors of the Shoshone. They used atlatls—spear-throwers—to take down game. Plus, they collected the nuts and berries that grew in huge quantities up here, with all the moisture and long, summer hours of daylight."

"Which is what brings you here, among other things."

"Which is what brings *us* here—me and Clarence, and you and the girls, too—for the initial field survey of what may well be one of the top archaeological discoveries in North America in decades, all thanks to global warming."

"ExxonMobil should be proud."

"Spoken like a true greenie," Chuck said with a grin. "Wait. What 'other things'?"

She looked him in the eye. "You're a man of convictions. That's one of the things I love about you. You're an honest guy, living your life in an honest, hard-working way, unlike all the gang-bangers I grew up with in Albuquerque. What I saw of you when we met is what I got, and it's what I want to keep getting, even while you figure out what it means to be a parent—which is, basically, loving your kids while worrying about them all the time, too."

Chuck blinked. "I think I understand you."

"I know you understand me," she said. "All your worries about bringing the girls out here with you? Welcome to your new life. It's not the grizzlies, Chuck. It's parenthood." She smiled. "You may think you're here to find whatever there is to find up there at the base of Trident Peak. But the way I see it, you're actually here to find something else: balance. As long as you offset your fatherly worries with the person of conviction I know you are, this week will be the greatest ever. Got it?"

Chuck leaned from his seat and kissed her cheek. "Got it."

It was mid-morning by the time Chuck and Janelle rousted Carmelita and Rosie, and the four of them worked their way through Jorge's pancakes, assembled to-go lunches from fixings set out on the tables in the mess tent, and topped off their water bottles from the filtered supply outside.

"What's the rule?" Chuck asked the girls as he bent to cinch the laces on their hiking boots.

"Tight shoes rule!" they recited in unison. "Blister-free is blissful!"

"Any hot spots on those feet of yours, let me or your mom know right away." He straightened. "You did great yesterday, but it's a lot farther today."

"Piece of steak," Rosie declared.

Chuck grinned as she ran in place, her elbows flapping.

Carmelita beamed. "*No hay problema*," she said in a rare outward display of confidence.

Lex climbed the slope to the platforms from the cabin. His straw Smokey Bear hat cut straight across his forehead. The back of the hat's circular brim nearly touched the U-shaped aluminum frame of his decades-old, full-size backpack. The pack's cavernous storage compartment, faded from red to pink by years in the sun and empty of all but the day's worth of supplies he carried, swung loosely from the metal frame. A leather pocket-knife scabbard, inscribed with his initials, rode his belt at his waist next to a walkie-talkie and canister of bear spray.

"I'll lead since I know the trail," he said while he walked with Chuck, Janelle, and the girls to the east end of tent row, where the trail from the lake climbed past the platforms and on over the hill to the south. The trail split a mile farther up the valley at the base of Hawks Rest, a craggy peak at the junction of Thorofare Creek and the upper Yellowstone River. The east spur of the trail climbed around the base of Hawks Rest, past Trident Peak, and along Thorofare Creek to a high pass over the Absaroka divide favored by elk and grizzlies alike. The west spur of the trail climbed out of the headwaters of the Yellowstone and up along Atlantic Creek to the Continental Divide at Two Ocean Pass. Water in a bog atop of the broad, flat pass separated and ran down both sides of the divide, resulting in the only place in America where a water source split in half to feed both the Pacific Ocean, via Pacific Creek and the Snake River, and the Atlantic Ocean, via Atlantic Creek and the Yellowstone River.

Waiting at the end of the row were Clarence, Kaifong and Randall of the Drone Team, Keith and Chance of the Canine Team, and, to Chuck's surprise, Sarah.

"Why'd you invite her?" he said in Lex's ear as they approached the group.

"I told you, she's great," Lex answered, his voice also low. "She asked if she could come along. There are no wolf packs in the vicinity right now, so the wolfies are organizing their gear in camp today. But uncollared grizzlies could be anywhere around here. She said she'd like to be along for any sightings."

"I've never been too fond of hotheads," Chuck told Lex, "other than the one I'm married to." He glanced from Sarah to Clarence. The two stood well apart, each acting as if the other did not exist.

"All the better for you and me to keep an eye on her—make sure she's minding her P's and Q's."

All the better for Sarah to spend the day with Clarence, too, Chuck thought. "What about the others?"

"I invited them for a test run. This is the first time the drone and canine teams have been in the backcountry. It'll be good for me to spend some time with them away from camp. I want to make sure they're set for the summer before I head back to civilization."

Lex halted in front of the group. He toed a clod of dirt that had been kicked up from the damp, heavily chewed trail. Chuck had listened from his sleeping bag before dawn as the wranglers and their pack string headed south up the trail, the horses' hooves digging into the soft dirt of the path as they made their way past the row of tents.

"They were in a hurry to get back to civilization," Lex commented.

Over the preceding week, he explained, the wranglers and their pack horses had hauled from the boat landing to Turret Cabin the lumber for the tent platforms along with the kitchen equipment, mess tent and poles, latrines, and additional supplies needed at the camp for the summer.

"The wranglers built the platforms for you, too," Lex said.

The horsemen were headed over Two Ocean Pass and on south out of the park, down Pacific Creek to their waiting trucks and trailers at the end of the nearest Forest Service road more than thirty miles away.

"As early as they left," he concluded, "it'll still take them most of the day to get over the pass and all the way down to the road."

Chuck scanned the group. He stopped at Randall, who stood a full head taller than anyone else. In contrast to Lex's ancient backpack, the gear-hauling system on Randall's back was futuristically high-tech. Fiberglass stanchions rose from a web of shoulder and waist straps to form a cradle for the Drone Team's quad copter. Lashed to the frame and rising higher than Randall's head, the copter consisted of a square black aluminum frame two feet across topped by engines and rotors at each corner. Wires ran from a gray metal box at the center of the frame to each of the four engines. A small video camera hung from a bracket below the metal box at the base of the drone. A black plastic control console with a pair of thumb toggles and numerous buttons and switches on its face dangled in a holster of nylon webbing at Randall's waist.

Chuck pointed at the console. "That's a lot of controls."

Randall turned sideways, displaying the drone riding high on his back. "The flight capability of this thing is out of this world, man." He tapped the console at his waist. "But it takes a lot of operational capacity to take full advantage of it."

Next to Randall, the Canine Team's canine, Chance, panted at Keith's side, flank pressed against his master's leg. Keith held a retractable tether attached to the dog's collar.

Chuck glanced at the sun, already high in the sky. "Ready when you are," he said to Lex.

Walking single file behind the ranger, the hikers topped the hill above tent row and entered a thick grove of whitebark pines. Piles of moist horse dung littered the trail.

"Yuck," Rosie said, leaping a particularly voluminous mound in front of Chuck.

"Double yuck," Carmelita agreed from her place in line ahead of her sister. She held her nose against the stench.

"Poopy, poopy, poopy-head," Rosie chanted.

"*Rosie*," Janelle admonished from behind Chuck.

The trail soon cleared of the horses' start-of-the-day evacuations and the air filled with the piney scent of the forest. The path wound through the trees along the east side of the valley. To the west, bordered by shoreline ranks of brilliant purple lupine, the river swung back and forth, glittering in the sunlight as it meandered across the flat, marshy valley floor before straightening and picking up speed where the drainage steepened below camp.

After the first mile, the trail angled southeast to follow Thorofare Creek beneath Hawks Rest. Thorofare Creek flashed through openings in the trees, the creek bottom as wide and flat as the continuation of the upper Yellowstone River valley stretching away to the southwest. The only sounds were the morning breeze sighing through the treetops and the occasional caws of magpies flitting through the branches overhead.

"I'm surprised we haven't passed anyone on the trail," Chuck said to Lex.

"It's still early in the season. And we're inside the park, which requires permits with set user day limits."

"As it oughtta be, brah," Randall said from his place near the back of the line.

"It's a different story six miles farther up the creek," Lex continued, "where the park ends and the Teton Wilderness begins. Cross the boundary into the national forest in the middle of the summer and it's like you've stepped into downtown New York City. They'll start pouring in from the south on horseback in another week or two, when the snow on the divide fully clears. By the end of June, there'll be camps every few feet, people cheek by jowl, thick as the mosquitoes that'll be eating them alive, not to mention illegal campfires, and all the pack animals eating the grass down to the roots, leaving nothing for the elk." Lex shook his head wearily.

"I've heard the real yahoos show up in the fall," Chuck said. "The outfitters with their pay-to-play elk hunters. Rumor has it some of them have even set salt licks just outside the park in the past, to draw trophy bulls across the boundary for their clients to gun down. And I've heard, because the state of Wyoming won't limit the number of outfitters, some of them take matters into their own hands, sabotaging each others' camps, shooting over each other's heads to scare game away from one another. And God help you if you're a private hunter up here on your own, competing with the outfitters. They say you're liable to have your stock run off or your water supply fouled—anything to keep you away from the bulls the outfitters see as their divine right."

"The truth is, there actually are quite a few good, dedicated outfitters," Lex said. "The majority, I'd say. They understand the limited nature of the resource and are willing to work with each other and the game-and-fish folks to ensure its sustainability. As for the few bad apples, we keep waiting for natural selection to do something about them, but it hasn't happened yet."

"They can just get away with it?"

"We don't have any say. They operate outside the park. There are those who claim the outfitters own the Wyoming Fish and Game Department lock, stock, and barrel. I can't speak to that. But I do know this much: when you watch them from this side of the boundary, you get the pretty clear sense they'll do any-thing—*anything*—to score a trophy kill for their big-spending clients, and that goes for the good outfitters as well as the bad."

"Including killing wolves, I suppose."

The broad brim of Lex's hat tilted back and forth as he nodded. "Whenever they can, wherever they can, as many as they can. It's funny; the success rate for guided elk hunters in the Teton Wilderness went way up—from thirty or forty percent all the way to ninety percent—after the 1988 forest fires in and around Yellowstone. The fires were so destructive that there basi-cally was no cover left for the elk to hide in. These days, though, the new trees are tall enough to provide cover for the herds again, and the hunting success rate has fallen back to historic levels. But will the outfitters admit that's what's going on? Of course not. When the success rate was high, they started offering their cli-ents guarantees—kill a bull or get your money back. Now that things have returned to normal, where hunters actually have to go out and hunt if they're to get a shot, the outfitters are fit to be tied. And what do you think they blame their troubles on?"

"Wolves."

"Of course."

"Which explains the push by the states around here to get the feds to remove the gray wolf from the Endangered Species List."

"That's right. Gray wolves already are under what amounts to extermination orders outside the park. De-list them entirely, and who knows what'll happen."

"They're doing well inside the park, though, right?"

"That they are, thanks to the East Coast politicians who set aside the lands of Yellowstone National Park a century ago for the American people."

"*And* for the animals," Randall added.

"And for the animals," Lex agreed. "Can you imagine that happening in Congress today?"

They hiked on. After another mile, the smell of sulfur overrode the scent of the pines.

"What's that?" Rosie asked, sniffing.

"I know what it is," Carmelita said. She turned and walked backward up the trail, looking past Rosie at Chuck. "It's what you told us about, isn't it?"

Chuck nodded. "It's what Yellowstone is known for, along with all the critters."

"Oh, oh, oh," Rosie said, thrusting her hand skyward. "It's the Thermos stuff!"

"Thermal," Carmelita corrected, turning forward and hurrying to catch up with Lex.

Curving, the trail left the forest and cut across a grass-tufted hillside. A mile away, on the far side of the broad Thorofare valley, the creek flowed between stands of pines. Between the creek and trail stretched the Thorofare thermal basin, a pan-flat expanse of hissing steam columns, cauldrons of boiling water, and bubbling mud pots.

Lex stopped. Everyone piled up at his back, ogling the otherworldly scene before them. Pools of water in irregular shapes, some a few feet across, others as large as tennis courts, pocked the black crust of the barren basin. Scalded white rims bounded the pools of water, while the pools' underwater walls gleamed blaze orange in the sunlight. Mud filled a handful of the pools, churning and gurgling and spitting clods of viscous, lava-like muck into the air. Steam columns marked the location of fumaroles—openings in the earth's crust from which superheated water, sulfur, and carbon dioxide shot from the ground. The fumaroles spewed upward, forming bright white pillars that dissipated in the morning breeze.

"Never gets old," Lex said.

"Incredible," Sarah agreed from the back of the line, her voice filled with wonder.

A yelp sounded from the middle of the line. Chuck turned in time to see Chance shoot from Keith's side. The retractable leash swung from the dog's collar. Keith grabbed for the leash but missed. The animal raced down the grassy hillside, straight for the thermal basin.

"Chance!" Keith yelled as he charged down the slope after his dog. "Heel, boy!"

"Keith!" Lex hollered after him. "Stop! The crust is only a few inches thick. It'll never hold your weight!"

Chance reached the base of the slope a hundred feet below the trail and galloped onto the basin. The dog's claws dug into the black surface as it cut between bubbling pools of water and mud, the leash trailing between its front legs.

Keith sprinted down the hill, steps from the thin crust of the superheated basin.

15

For God's sake, stop!" Lex yelled at Keith.

When Keith kept running, Chuck plunged off the trail and down the slope. Clarence followed.

"Keith! Stop!" Kaifong's high-pitched cry sounded from the trail. Then she admonished, "Hold still, Randall."

Chuck glanced back to see her wrestling with the straps that secured the drone in its frame on Randall's back.

Keith slid to a stop at the foot of the hill and cupped his hands around his mouth. "Chance," he bellowed. "Chance. Here, boy. Come!"

"Doggie!" Rosie screeched from above. "You come back here right now!"

The dog, sprinting across the thermal crust, paid no heed. Chuck and Clarence slid to a halt on either side of Keith.

"Chance!" Keith cried again. The dog kept running. Keith leaned forward.

"Oh, no, you don't," Chuck told him between heavy breaths. "You can't go out there. You'll kill yourself."

Keith's gaze remained fixed on his dog. He stepped from the solid earth of the hillside onto the crust. Chuck and Clarence grabbed him from either side and the three fell forward together to their knees, fracturing the crust beneath them. Ooze, mucky and lukewarm at the edge of the basin, rose around their legs.

Chuck and Clarence struggled to their feet and dragged Keith back to the base of the hill. Chance had made it halfway across the thermal area. Keith stood at the edge of the basin, arms locked at his sides, gaze fixed on his racing dog. Chuck slumped down on a hummock of grass, his hands on his mud-coated knees.

"What were you thinking, letting go of the leash like that?" Clarence demanded of Keith.

"He caught me by surprise, yanked it right out of my hand," Keith responded. "I've worked with him every day for the last three years. He does what he's told, *only* what he's told."

"Looks like you've got more work to do."

Keith watched as Chance galloped across a narrow isthmus between two large pools of water. "Chance!" he cried. "Chance!"

The dog didn't slow.

Chuck used one of Keith's mud-caked pant legs to pull himself to a standing position. A loud whirring noise, like a room fan at maximum speed, came from behind him. Kaifong stood in the middle of the trail holding the drone out from her body, the copter's spinning rotors a blur in front of her.

Randall pulled the plastic, batwing-shaped control console from his waist holster. He thumbed one of the console's toggle sticks forward. The whir became a high-pitched whine as the speed of the drone's rotors increased.

Randall nodded at Kaifong. She opened her fingers. The drone lifted off her palms and climbed into the air. Randall cradled the console in both hands, working its controls with his thumbs and forefingers. The drone flew down the hill, tracking the angle of the slope. It zoomed past Chuck, Clarence, and Keith, and shot across the thermal basin, ten feet above the crust.

Far out on the basin, Chance stopped and turned to face the noisy, oncoming drone. The racing copter neared Chance in seconds. The dog crouched with its belly to the crust. The miniature helicopter flew straight over Chance and stopped beyond the animal, hovering in midair.

The whine of the machine's rotors increased as the drone shot straight at Chance, angling toward the ground. The dog leapt away and ran ahead of the trailing copter with its tail tucked between its legs. Randall flew the drone a few feet above and behind the animal, using the aircraft to herd the dog back across the basin.

"Here, Chance," Keith called as the dog neared the base of the hill. "Here, boy."

Chance ran to Keith and pressed, quivering, against his muddy legs while the drone flew up the hill and returned to a gentle landing on Kaifong's outstretched hands.

Keith grabbed the leash reel from where it dangled between Chance's legs and, holding tight to the lead, climbed with the dog back up the hillside.

Lex awaited him on the trail. "What were you thinking, letting go like that?" he growled.

"He's never done that in all the time we've been together," Keith said. Chance panted at his side.

Lex aimed a finger at the tether. "From now on, hold tight."

Keith gave the nylon line a tug. "Got it."

Chuck and Clarence arrived back at the trail. Lex eyed the sulfurous ooze dripping from their legs. "You guys stink," he said, wrinkling his nose.

"Pumpkin Hot Spring is somewhere around here, isn't it?" Chuck asked.

"You know about that?"

"I had all winter to research this area."

"It's not in the guidebooks."

"But it's all over the internet."

"Is nothing sacred anymore?" Lex sighed. "By the way, good job keeping Keith from killing himself."

Chuck pointed at the Drone Team members—Kaifong, reattaching the copter to the frame on Randall's back while Randall strapped the control console back into the webbed holster at his waist. "They're the ones to thank."

With the console secured, Randall flicked a switch on its face. A green diode light in one corner died out as the console turned off.

"Thank you," Keith said to Randall and Kaifong, "from both me and my doofus dog here." He scratched Chance's ears. "That was some pretty sick flying."

Randall shrugged. "It's what we do, man."

Lex returned to the front of the line and led the hikers past the thermal basin and into a stand of pines. The sulfurous odor of the basin died away as they continued up the creek drainage. The cool breeze flowing down the valley from the divide pressed Chuck's muddy pants against his legs. The smell of sulfur picked up again half a mile farther on, riding the breeze where the forest grew sparse near tree line.

The hiking group climbed out of the last of the low, bent trees toward a grassy bench. To the south, the divide cut the skyline below hulking Trident massif and its high point, Trident Peak. The three parallel finger ridges that gave the massif its name dropped east to west from near the top of the snow-covered summit into the upper Thorofare Creek drainage. Snowfields fronted the north faces of the three finger ridges, and shadows filled the two deep canyons between them.

As the hikers topped the grass-covered bench, they saw steam rising from the surface of Pumpkin Hot Spring, fifty feet off the trail. In the 1950s, horsemen frequenting the trail had channeled hot water flowing from a steaming vent in a nearby hillside to a galvanized steel stock tank pieced together on site and dug into the ground. A chalky, orange-tinged coating of travertine around the rim of the ten-foot-diameter tank gave the manmade soaking pool its name. Freshly trampled grass surrounded the sunken pool.

"Somebody beat us to it," Chuck noted.

"The wranglers," Lex said. "Can't blame them. They hit it pretty hard the last two weeks." He turned to the group. "Everyone but Chuck, Clarence, and Keith, keep moving. We'll wait ahead while they get cleaned up."

Janelle walked with the girls and the others up the trail and out of sight over a rocky lip.

Lex stood at the edge of the pool. "We keep threatening to shut this thing down," he said, "but people really like it."

"Especially the rangers assigned to Turret Cabin each summer, I'll bet," Chuck said.

"Especially them," Lex agreed. "Can't beat the view, that's for sure." He turned a slow circle, taking in the surrounding ridges and peaks, the broad Thorofare Creek drainage, the even broader river valley below Turret Cabin, and the southeast arm and rippled, open lake in the distance.

Chuck shucked his daypack, stepped out of his nylon hiking pants, and dunked the pants' dirty lower legs in the narrow stream of warm water flowing out of the pool. Next to him, Clarence and Keith pulled off their muddy pants, too.

"Be careful if you decide to get in. Wouldn't want you to scald yourself," Lex said. "Thermal temps across the park have been fluctuating quite a bit lately."

Chuck looked up from where he knelt at the edge of the pool. "I hadn't heard about that."

"We've kept it quiet so far—and offline, too, I guess, if you haven't caught wind of it. We're still trying to get a handle on what's going on." Lex squatted and dipped his hand into the pool. "Still perfect here." He rose and turned to the trail. "Join us when you're done."

Chuck, Clarence, and Keith finished rinsing their pants and laid them on the grass. Chuck stripped and slid into the spring.

"Can't resist," he said. "Just for a minute while our pants dry a bit."

He rested his head against the pool's travertine rim, up to his neck in the warm water.

"Ahh." He closed his eyes, his arms floating at his sides. "I wish the lake had been this temperature yesterday."

Keith set his pack on the ground and secured Chance's leash to it. He and Clarence disrobed and slipped into the pool with Chuck.

"I'm not sure I deserve this," Keith said, sinking to his chin, "but it sure feels—"

A yell came from out of sight beyond the rock rib. "Bear!" Sarah's voice cried out. "Grizzly!"

16

Chuck scrambled out of the water and yanked his wet pants up his legs. Were Janelle and the girls safe? No more shouts came from above as he hurried up the trail, boots untied, pack in hand, Clarence and Keith close behind. He topped the rocky rise and found the others peering across the rolling terrain of the upper Thorofare Creek basin. Janelle stood among the hikers, the girls holding hands at her side.

Chuck slowed, catching his breath. "What's going on?"

"Bear sighting," Janelle said evenly. She pointed at a tiny, brown dot crossing an open stretch of tundra more than half a mile away, on the far side of Thorofare Creek.

Clarence bent beside the girls, his hands on his knees, breathing hard. "*Que bonita*," he said to them.

The girls nodded, their eyes on the grizzly.

Chance trembled at Keith's side, ears forward, eyes on the brown, moving spot.

Lex faced the hikers, his back to the distant grizzly. "It's doing exactly what it's supposed to be doing. It's going about its business, just like us."

"You mean," Randall said, "in spite of us."

"You don't think we should be here?" Lex asked him.

"This is the grizzly's pad, not ours. We should be chill with it, man. Instead, we show up here, see the bear, and start screaming and yelling."

"I was letting it know we're here," Sarah said. "It's what Grizzly Initiative team members are trained to do."

"You're cool," Randall assured her. "It's just that what you're trained to do is not a part of this environment. *You're* not a part of this environment. None of us are. It's foreign to us, so we end up screaming and yelling instead of hanging and chilling. Dogs run off for no reason. We build huge camps in the middle of nowhere. We make a mess of things, when, really, we don't even have to be out here to do research anymore in the first place."

Sarah raised her head, her neck stiff. "What's that supposed to mean?"

Uh-oh, Chuck thought.

Randall aimed a thumb at the drone riding in its fiberglass frame high on his shoulders behind him. "We've got these things now, lady-cakes."

Sarah's face flushed. "The very idea that—"

Lex raised a hand, cutting her off before Chuck could tell if she was responding to Randall's boastfulness about the drone or his calling her lady-cakes.

"Who knows?" Lex said to Randall. "Maybe someday your contraption will take all of us humans out of the backcountry. We'll be like those drone operators in the Air Force who blow up people in the Middle East from air-conditioned offices in Las Vegas. At this point, though, your contraption has a total possible flying time of what? Ten minutes?"

Randall avoided Lex's gaze. "Fifteen," he admitted grudgingly.

"You're not going to make it too far into the backcountry in seven and a half minutes."

"It won't be long before—"

"I know, I know," Lex broke in. "Someday you'll be able to fly that thing for hours on end. But that's in the future, maybe way in the future. For now, today, the only way we can conduct research is to get up close and personal with the creatures we're studying." He glanced at the bear. "Just not too close."

He addressed all of the hikers. "Roughly two hundred brown bears call Yellowstone National Park home at any given time, and each of them covers a lot of territory. It makes sense that you'll see grizzlies like this one as they move around. It's important to understand you'll be surrounded by them all summer."

"Surrounded?" Rosie yelped.

"We're supposed to be surrounded by them," Lex told her. "That's the whole idea. We're out here where they live—in their pad—" he raised an eyebrow at Randall "—so we can study them. But as long as we give the bears plenty of warning, they won't bother us. In fact, they're probably used to having us around. A recent tracking study in Montana found that grizzlies actually trail elk hunters on national forest lands in the fall. They wait until the hunters make a kill. After the hunters quarter their elk and leave, the bears swoop in to feast on the rest of the carcass." Lex directed a sharp look at Randall. "In that case, at least, the grizzlies appreciate having humans around."

"Opportunism, pure and simple, dude," Randall responded. "Can't blame the grizzlies. But it certainly doesn't make it cool."

Sarah bent toward Rosie. "The key is letting them know we're here."

"Sarah did what she should have done," Lex said, "in crying out when she spotted our friend over there. That's a good thing to do upon first sighting a grizzly." He gazed around the group. "For those of you new to the Yellowstone backcountry, it's worth repeating: none of us wants to surprise a grizzly out here. Surprise triggers a brown bear's attack response. We made plenty of noise talking with one another as we hiked through the forest this morning. Any bears in the vicinity would have heard us and moved away without our even knowing they were there. Up here above tree line, as we continue to make noise, the odds of our seeing bears as they move away from us—like the one across the valley—will logically be higher."

The grizzly topped a rise and passed from sight.

Lex turned to Chuck. "Do you need to go back to the spring?"

Chuck glanced at Clarence and Keith. "We rinsed off the muck. The sun will dry our pants quickly enough."

"Onward, then?"

"Can't wait."

Trident Peak loomed ahead, its three prong-like ridges falling away to the west. Fifty years ago, a pair of matching glaciers, Trident One and Trident Two, had spilled from the two shadowed canyons between the three ridges all the way to Thorofare Creek. In the years since, the glaciers had retreated to the heads of the matching side canyons. Today, Trident One and Trident Two were classified as snowfields rather than glaciers. Though the two snowfields grew and shrank between winter and summer, they contained little, if any, of the expanding and contracting glacial ice that had led to their original classification as glaciers when the park first was mapped in the 1800s.

The pack trail skirted the base of the northernmost ridge. From the base of the first ridge, the trail cut across the green tundra of the upper valley away from the next two ridges and along Thorofare Creek toward the top of the divide.

Where the trail turned away from the three ridges, Lex forged a cross-country route up an open slope. The mossy tundra depressed like a wet sponge beneath Chuck's boots as he trailed the girls and Lex past the toe of the first ridge and on to the second.

He stopped to gaze up the canyon. Snow spilled down the north-facing wall, while the south face glowed green with newly sprouted tundra grass. The deep cleft between the first two ridges doglegged half a mile up. The dogleg hid the canyon's terminus, where the remnants of Trident Two Glacier awaited exploration. But Chuck was here to see what last summer's melt-off had revealed to the climbers who had looked down from the summit of Trident Peak at the remnants of Trident One, where the higher of the two canyons ended at the base of the mountain.

Lex set a slow, steady pace up the slope. They were over nine thousand feet in elevation here, the air thin. Finally, after six months of anticipation, the climbers' discovery waited just ahead.

The hikers passed the toe of the center ridge and turned into the second canyon. As in the lower canyon, tundra blanketed the upper canyon's south-facing wall, and snow covered the opposite slope.

Chuck's heart thudded as he headed up the narrow defile. He'd looked forward to this moment since the offer had come his way from the Greater Yellowstone Anthropological Foundation to be the initial on-site archaeologist to investigate what first had been spotted by the climbers last fall, before winter snows entombed the park's high country.

Ahead, the canyon canted sharply upward. Before its recent retreat, Trident One Glacier had worn the pitched granite floor of the canyon to a smooth sheen over thousands of years. The hikers helped one another up the steep, glistening rock, their boots slipping on the canyon floor's burnished surface.

The canyon leveled and turned south, matching the dogleg in the lower canyon. The hikers continued the steady climb up the drainage. The air in the bottom of the canyon was cool and wet. Chuck's nostrils filled with the mossy scent of fungal spores launching from the surrounding tundra with the onset of summer.

The walls of the canyon closed in from both sides and the last of the winter's snow filled the shaded canyon bottom. Carmelita and Rosie scurried atop the crust while the adults sank to their knees, post-holing through the snow. Behind Chuck, Clarence plunged to his waist at regular intervals. Each time, Chuck pulled him back to the surface.

"Snow snakes," Chuck said upon offering his hand a third time. "They'll get you every time."

"Not snakes." Clarence patted his belly. "Burgers and fries."

The walls fell back near the canyon's head, allowing the sun's rays to reach the canyon floor. The snow gave way to rock and mud. They rounded a sweeping turn and came to the end of the defile. They spread out, gaping at the scene before them.

Where the mountainside fell almost vertically from the summit to the head of the canyon, the white blanket of mountaintop snow was broken by a wall of aquamarine ice rising twenty feet from the canyon floor—the last remnant of what once had been Trident One Glacier. The wall of ice glittered like a long-lost jewel in the midday sun, but the real treasure waited at the foot of the ice, newly exposed to the elements by the glacier's retreat.

"Remarkable," Lex whispered.

"Unbelievable," Sarah said, staring.

"*Jesucristo*," Clarence murmured from where he stood at Chuck's shoulder.

Chuck's breaths came fast and shallow. At the foot of the wall of ice stood what he'd waited all these months to see.

17

Twenty reed baskets sat in two uneven lines at the base of the shimmering ice wall. Each basket was three feet high by two feet wide and half encased in mud. The baskets rested next to one another, some upright, others on their sides, with dank, loamy sludge spilling from their mouths. Geometric designs showed through the crust of dirt that covered each of the storage vessels. The designs, simple zigzags and squares, consisted of thicker strips of reeds woven through the thinner reeds that made up the main bodies of the vessels.

Rosie lifted her shoulders to her ears in an exaggerated shrug. "It's just a bunch of muddy baskets."

"Yeah," Carmelita said. "I don't get it."

"Actually," Chuck told them, his voice trembling, "this is as good as archaeology gets. Somebody left these here in the ice a long time ago. What were they doing here with so many baskets? Why didn't they ever come back?"

"They must've forgotten where they put them," Rosie reasoned.

"Maybe they got chased away by grizzly bears," Carmelita said.

"Or wooly mammoths," Kaifong added with a smile.

"Grizzlies, maybe," Chuck said. "Not mammoths. Or saber-toothed tigers, either, for that matter. That would date these baskets to the time of the Ice Age, twenty thousand years ago."

"They're not that old?" Kaifong asked.

"A group of climbers spotted the baskets from high on Trident Peak last October. The baskets were just emerging from the melting ice. One of the climbers dropped down here and tore off a piece of one of the baskets—not the correct thing to do, but that's what she did. At least the climbers were smart enough to keep their pictures of the baskets off the internet so thieves wouldn't come prowling. The climbers turned over the basket piece and their photos to the Greater Yellowstone Anthropological Foundation. The foundation carbon-dated the specimen over the winter."

"And?"

"The baskets date to between four and six thousand years old."

Randall whistled.

"Yeah," Chuck said. "Not the Ice Age, but pretty old none-theless. Archaeologists have known for a long time that Native Americans came over the Absarokas from the south to the Central Yellowstone Plateau during the summer months. They've found obsidian hunting points on the banks of Yellowstone Lake smeared with blood of bison, elk, deer, bear, rabbit, you name it. Carbon dating of the blood shows that most of the hunting and gathering by natives on the uplift was concentrated in the last fifteen hundred years, with the vast majority in the last five hundred years."

"But you just said the baskets are thousands of years old," said Kaifong.

"That's what makes this find so incredible. The age of these baskets, their large size, and their significant number indicate that substantial visitation to the Yellowstone uplift by Native Americans appears to stretch back thousands of years further than previously thought. The carbon dating of the basket piece has chucked a wrench in everything Yellowstone's anthropolo-gists thought until now about the park's human timeline. This discovery is the sort of thing archaeologists live for."

"Wait, I'm confused. Archaeology or anthropology?" Kaifong asked.

"Both. Anthropology is the study of people. Archaeology is the study of people's old stuff and what that stuff tells us about ancient peoples."

"And these baskets...?"

"May have a lot to tell us about the correct human-history timeline on the Central Yellowstone Plateau," Chuck said. "Clarence and I have been hired to initiate the process of finding that out. The GYAF's members are all retired anthropologists and archaeologists from around the country. They're too old to make the trip to the site. They contracted with my company to complete a preliminary survey of the baskets on behalf of the foundation and the park service."

"Is there anything we can do to help? We don't have anything specific on our agenda today."

"Except saving dogs," Randall said.

"Which," Keith said, "I totally appreciate."

"No worries, dude."

"Well," Chuck said to Kaifong, "now that you mention it, maybe there is something you can do. Clarence and I are scheduled for several days of survey work here. Today, we'll take pictures and do our initial measuring and plotting. I'd love to provide the foundation with some aerial footage of the site, if you're up for it."

She nodded, studying the baskets and glittering wall of ice. "Anything in particular you're looking for?"

Chuck pointed at the snow covering the slope above the wall of ice. "I'd appreciate your scanning the snowfield up there to see if there's any sign of anything else melting out. We'll climb up and have a look, too, of course, but your eye-in-the-sky might spot something we can't see from ground level."

"Anything else we can try to capture for you?" Kaifong asked.

"Yeah, man," Randall added. "Our camera is ultra high def. In good light like today, whatever we shoot is crisp as bacon."

Chuck crossed his arms, studying the reed storage containers. "Maybe," he said. "People are pretty fired up about the in-situ placement of the baskets."

"The what?" Kaifong asked.

"The way they're lined up in such orderly fashion. It's obvious they were placed here for a reason. Care to guess the experts' opinion so far?"

"The baskets are filled with dirt. Was it for constructing insulated earthen homes of some sort?" Kaifong ventured.

"Not a bad idea," Chuck said. "But check out the color of the contents—dark brown, almost black—significantly darker than normal soil."

"It's not dirt."

"It's not dirt *yet*. Based on the climbers' pictures, the thinking is the stuff in the baskets is in the process of *becoming* soil."

"So it used to be something else."

"As of a few thousand years ago."

"Hunters and gatherers," Kaifong noted. "That's what you said the Indians were. It stands to reason, then, that these baskets contain the remains of something they hunted or gathered."

"You got it. Which takes us to the next question. Why did they leave such a huge store of what they hunted or gathered buried way up here in the ice?"

Kaifong frowned. Then her brown eyes brightened. "Got it," she said. "They were using the glacier as a deep freeze."

"Precisely," Chuck said. "At least, that's the general consensus. It's one of the things the foundation wants to find out for sure."

"You're saying there's something else we can do to help with that?"

"The working theory, so far, is that the baskets were filled with berries or nuts or smoked and dried meat at the end of the summer. They were then stored in holes gouged in the ice before the natives headed for lower ground with the coming of winter. When the Indians returned over the divide the next spring, the food stored in the glacier served as an early-season supply depot for them on their way to the lower parts of the plateau like Hayden and Lamar valleys."

"Seems like pretty sophisticated planning for such ancient people," Kaifong said.

"The first thing is to find out if it's true."

"How do you go about proving something like that?"

"We'll gather samples of the baskets' contents along with more reed samples from the baskets themselves. A full dig later on, by a full archaeological team, will provide lots more evidence."

"Could there be more baskets than just these?"

"I don't think there's enough ice left for that. But you and Randall can help us be sure."

"You got it." Kaifong turned to Randall. "Shall we?"

"Yes, dear." Randall looked at Chuck. "This is our third summer together. She has no idea how to chill. I've even met her parents." He chuckled. "Talk about the perfectly predictable guerrilla-girl result of a Tiger Mom upbringing."

"Impressive," Kaifong shot back. "A sexist *and* racist comment, all in one breath."

Randall grinned. "My abilities are straight-up awesome, babe," he told her. "But, of course, you already knew that, didn't you?"

They bumped fists.

Lex rolled his eyes and turned to Chuck. "What about the rest of us? We're at your service, too, if you'd like."

"It'd be great to have everyone's help with an outlying survey." Chuck faced the group. "Clarence and I will assess the baskets and the area immediately surrounding them. The rest of you can search outward in all directions. The idea is to use an informal, expanding-circles approach. Your movements can be pretty relaxed; everything we're doing at this point is preliminary, to get a sense of how to proceed."

"What are we looking for?" Lex asked.

"Anything manmade. Scarring on any remaining glacial ice. Hunting points, of course. Any further signs of baskets or reed material. No one should touch whatever they come across. I'll warn you, though: the most likely scenario is that nobody will find anything. That's the nature of archaeology—lots of looking, little finding."

Janelle said, "Hear that, girls? Let's help look."

Lex said to Carmelita and Rosie, "I'll bet you're going to be famous archaeologists someday, just like your dad."

"Maybe," Carmelita said.

"Not me," Rosie announced. "I'm going to be an astronaut." She swung her hips back and forth. "Or a supermodel."

After a quick group lunch, Chuck took pictures, made notations in his tablet computer, and drew rough diagrams on his sketch pad while Clarence pounded a length of rebar into the ground, fixing the central datum point for the basket site. He measured and recorded in his tablet computer various site and artifact dimensions and distances from the datum point—the size of individual baskets, the lengths of the two lines of baskets, the range of the baskets in relation to each other, and the projected depth of the baskets in the muddy soil at the base of the ice wall.

Kaifong and Randall launched their overview flight with the drone from the far side of the canyon. A few minutes later, Randall flew the drone back to a smooth touchdown on Kaifong's outstretched hands.

Kaifong called across the canyon to Chuck, "With the earlier flight at the thermal area, the batteries are about dead. But we'll still have plenty of footage to review with you."

"Did you see anything out of the ordinary?" Chuck asked her.

"We won't really know until we see what we've got back at camp." She hesitated. "But…"

"Yeah?"

"It's probably nothing. From over here, though, it looks like there's something stuck in the ice." She pointed at the glacier. "It's white, or whitish."

Chuck looked where she pointed. He saw only the blue of the ice and, in several places, the gray of the rock, behind the ice, where the glacier met the mountain. He made his way across the canyon to Kaifong's side.

"There," she said, pointing again. "See?"

He put his hands to the sides of his cap brim, shading his eyes from the glaring sun. In the middle of the wall of ice, eight feet above the canyon floor, visible only from Kaifong's oblique viewpoint because of undulations in the face of the melting glacier, a small, light-colored object shone in the sunlight.

"Good work," he told Kaifong.

He edged behind the baskets, his boots sinking into the mud at the foot of the ice, until he stood before the object, looking straight up at it.

He knew immediately what it was—a sliver of bone, two inches long and an inch wide. The sliver was off-white, almost tan. It sat out from the glacial wall on a thin ice tendril shaded from the sun by the piece of bone itself. The tendril of ice appeared ready to give way at any second, sending the bone fragment tumbling into the mud.

He took pictures of the bone fragment from several angles, then noted the distance from the hanging sliver to the datum point set by Clarence. Finally, he pulled from his pack a clear, plastic Ziploc bag and plucked the sliver from the wall of ice. The sliver of bone was soft to his touch; it would not have lasted long had it fallen unnoticed into the mud, there to rot away to nothing.

He held the sliver of bone beneath his nose and sniffed. It exuded a slightly rotten smell that mixed with the clammy odor of the wet earth at his feet.

He sealed the sliver in the plastic bag and held it up before him. The shard was uniformly beige except at one end. He brought the bag close to his eyes. Four indentations, spaced a quarter-inch apart, marked the end of the piece of bone.

A blast of adrenalin coursed through him. The indentations clearly were cut marks. Sometime in the distant past, a human had butchered meat from the bone and discarded the sliver here, in the ice.

This sort of discovery—this direct connection with the past—was what Chuck loved about archaeology. Even as he marveled at the butchered sliver of bone, his blood running hot in his veins, he knew most others wouldn't understand why he found this kind of thing so enthralling. He didn't blame them for their lack of understanding; in fact, he barely understood it himself.

He gave a thumbs up to Kaifong. "Excellent!" he called to her.

"Glad I could be of service," she said.

The group's outlying survey revealed no additional signs of human activity at the head of the canyon. No matter, though.

In Chuck's view, the day was an unrivaled success. The baskets had been waiting, recently melted out of the winter snow, as he'd hoped. And they'd discovered an accessory find in addition to the baskets themselves.

Chuck rubbed the sliver of bone, through the baggie, with his thumb. Before the sliver's discovery, he'd have bet the loamy substance in the baskets would turn out to be rotted nuts and berries. But the piece of bone sent his thoughts in a new direction. Until now, butchered bones on the Central Yellowstone Plateau had been discovered only on the shores of Yellowstone Lake. The finding of this butchered piece of bone so high in the Absarokas would engender all sorts of fresh thinking about how extensively the park's ancient human visitors had hunted on the plateau—and, thanks to Kaifong's keen eye, Chuck would get to report the new discovery to the archaeological world.

He tucked the baggie containing the sliver in the outside pocket of his pack, where it wouldn't be crushed, and returned to the survey work with Clarence.

At Chuck's request, Lex broke from the return route to camp and led the hikers up the side canyon between Trident Peak's middle and lowest ridges. They found Trident Two Glacier melted away to nothing, leaving no manmade objects—baskets, bone slivers, or otherwise—on the muddy ground at the head of the canyon.

They stopped for an afternoon snack on the hillside overlooking Thorofare thermal basin. The smell of sulfur rolled up the slope from the bubbling pools. Keith kept Chance leashed tight. Chuck shook dried cranberries into the cupped hands of Carmelita and Rosie. Randall stretched out full length in the middle of the trail, his face to the sky and his hands clasped over his chest.

"Check this out," he called to the girls.

Carmelita and Rosie stuffed their cranberries into their mouths and ran to him. Rosie flopped to her back on the grassy hillside next to Randall and imitated him, knitting her fingers over her plump stomach and looking up at the sky. "What?" she demanded.

"The clouds, baby-cakes." Overhead, puffs of white cumulus floated against the azure backdrop. "They're sky pillows. Can't you feel them behind your head?"

Rosie giggled. "I don't feel anything."

Carmelita lay down beside her sister. They snuggled close together on the slope next to Randall. "I feel them," Carmelita declared. "They're soft."

Rosie giggled some more. "You're so crazy, Carm," she said.

Chuck traded smiles with Janelle. He leaned back on his elbows and closed his eyes. His forearms, resting on the ground, tingled. The sensation increased, becoming a subtle vibration wherever his body touched the earth.

Everyone stopped talking. Randall and the girls sat up. The vibration vanished, and Chuck tensed. The trembling returned, stronger this time, coming from somewhere deep underground.

18

Steam erupted from a fissure on the near side of the thermal area, less than fifty feet from the foot of the slope below the trail. A thick, white cloud wafted away from the jet of super-heated water spewing from the black crust.

The rumbling faded away, and the jet of steam subsided. A third vibration did not come. Chuck pressed a palm to the hillside. Nothing.

"Kowabunga," Randall said from where he sat in the middle of the trail. "Dude!"

"What the hell was that?" Rosie asked.

"Rosie!" Janelle exclaimed.

"Chuck says it all the time."

Carmelita shook a finger at her sister. "'Heck. You're supposed to say heck."

Rosie wrapped her arms around her torso, her hands gripping her sides. "I will if Chuck will."

Chuck felt Janelle's eyes on him. "Heck it is," he said.

Rosie asked Lex, "What the heck was that? Was it an earthquake?"

"That's exactly what it was," Lex said.

"Like in the movies? Holy shlamolies."

"They're to be expected, of course. Yellowstone is one of the most active seismic zones on the planet."

Janelle said, "You don't sound too worried."

"Big quakes are rare here—that is, in human time. But small quakes of the sort we just felt have been occurring in the park more and more frequently the last couple of years. The Geology Team is looking into what's causing them."

"And their hypothesis at this point?" Chuck asked, anticipating the answer.

"Hydraulic fracturing around the park perimeter."

Chuck told the girls, "That's where companies pump water and chemicals into the ground to release oil trapped in layers of rock. There was a bunch of that kind of drilling during the last natural-gas boom. Now, the drilled wells are producing—that is, sucking the gas out of the ground." He asked Lex, "Could the tremors be causing temperature fluctuations in the thermal basins?"

"At this point," Lex replied, "I'd say it's logical to assume the mini-quakes and temperature fluctuations and hydraulic fracturing are related. But, like I said, that's what the Geology Team is studying."

"I read that plain old, everyday earthquakes—with no hydraulic fracturing involved—tilted Yellowstone Lake back and forth over and over in the past, so it drained down one side of the Continental Divide, then the other."

"Millions of years ago, yes. But there's no way fracking could set off an earthquake that big today."

"I thought that's what the Geology Team is trying to determine."

Lex averted his eyes. "Since the oil companies started working around here," he admitted, "they've written lots of checks to the park—for research, infrastructure upgrades, you name it. It's hard to point a finger at them with no proof."

"Spoken like a true bureaucrat."

Lex grunted. "Which is exactly what I am."

Clarence's stud earrings sparkled in the sunlight as he shook his head. "*Hombre.* Here we are in one of the most remote places in North America, and we've got manmade global warming melting the glaciers and manmade earthquakes messing with the geysers. It's like the start of the apocalypse or something."

"I wouldn't go that far," Lex said. "But humans certainly can alter things far from where their activities take place, Yellowstone included. More and more, the questions researchers are studying in the park revolve around what can be done to control, or at least minimize, the effects of those activities." He pushed himself to his feet. "Two miles to camp," he said to the hikers. "Shall we?"

They strode along the open hillside and into the trees, leaving the thermal area and smell of sulfur behind.

Rosie looked up at Chuck as they walked through the forest. "Is an earthquake going to come and swallow us up?"

"It'll take a lot more than a teeny, tiny tremor like that one to get us."

She nodded to herself. "So the grizzly bears will get us first."

"Rosie!" Janelle said.

"I think your mom's going to get you before an earthquake or a grizzly has the chance," said Chuck.

The trail wound in and out of the pines as it descended the east side of the valley. It was late afternoon by the time everyone left the last stand of trees and topped the hill overlooking camp. Above the hikers' cheerful chatter, the walkie-talkie clipped to Lex's belt beeped, signaling an incoming call. A cry rose from the foot of the slope. Chuck looked down toward the cabin, where a figure was heading up the trail toward them, waving and shouting.

Part Two

"Of all the national parks, I prefer Yellowstone because I like working in a park that has at least two man-eaters in it."

— Doug Peacock,
world-renowned authority on grizzly bears

19

Justin, the rookie Grizzly Initiative researcher, sprinted up the trail and stopped, out of breath, in front of Lex. "Double whammy," he declared, hands on hips, sucking air. "Wolf and grizzly, right outside camp."

Lex turned to Sarah, who held her walkie-talkie to her ear like a phone, its volume low. She nodded in confirmation, her eyes bright.

Justin spoke quickly. "Everyone's saying they've never seen anything like it. The bear and wolf went back into the woods together. Toby wants to go after them, but he says we need to check with you first."

"I have to know what happened," Lex said. "Everything." He stepped around Justin, heading down the hill at a fast clip. "Walk with me."

Justin fell in with Lex. Everyone hurried down the trail behind them. Carmelita gripped Janelle's hand and Rosie pressed herself to Chuck's side. He put his arm around her. A grizzly in camp? This shouldn't be happening.

Lichen on the shake-shingle roof of Turret Cabin shimmered in the late afternoon sunlight like a gray-green mirror. The meadow beyond the cabin sloped gently downward to a wall of lodgepole pines two hundred yards from the cabin and mess tent.

"Everyone's been sorting supplies," Justin explained to Lex, still breathless, as they passed the row of tent platforms and descended the trail toward the cabin. "Someone yelled. People were pointing. Sure enough, there at the edge of the meadow...I mean...right there in full view..." He stuttered to a stop.

"He's right," Sarah called out, walkie-talkie still to her ear. "A grizzly and a wolf, that's what I'm hearing."

"I saw them with my own eyes," Justin said. "But only for a few seconds. They turned—I swear to God, they did it together, like they were dancing—and disappeared in the trees."

Lex lifted his cap and scratched his head. "A grizzly and a wolf?"

"It was like they were checking up on us or something."

"In broad daylight? You're sure it was a wolf, not a coyote?"

"I'm not totally sure, but the wolfies are. I know my bears, though," Justin said with pride in his voice. "It was a grizzly, all right. Big."

"How far away were they?"

"The far edge of the meadow."

"My God." Lex resettled his hat on his head and gave the front of its brim a firm pull.

"Everybody saw them," Justin said.

"Only one wolf?"

"Just the one."

"So," Lex said, "no sign of any other members of its pack."

"Not at this point."

"Who got footage? Photos?"

"It happened so fast. Nobody had their phones handy since there's no signal out here. People were scrambling for cameras, phones, anything. Maybe somebody got something, but I don't think so. I spotted you up on the hill and took off."

"This just happened?"

"Less than five minutes ago."

Lex picked up his pace, jogging down the trail. "Toby's right," he said. "We'll go after them."

"I'm coming along," Sarah called ahead to Lex from the middle of the line, hustling with everyone else to keep up.

"I want Toby to come as well," Lex said. "Chuck," he called over his shoulder. "You're coming, too. Between the two of us, we should be able to keep Sarah and Toby from killing each other."

Chuck blanched at the thought of leaving Janelle and the girls to go after the predators.

"Can I join you?" Keith asked, his dog leashed at his side. "Chance can track both species at once. We'll be able to determine how long the griz and wolf stayed together."

Lex slowed. "Together," he muttered, shaking his head.

"You should include Randall and me, too," Kaifong chimed in from the back of the line, "in case you need some aerial recon."

Lex commented to Chuck, "That's a lot of people."

"With a lot of capabilities," Chuck replied.

Lex expelled a puff of air out his nose. He called back to Kaifong, "Okay. You're in."

"We'll get fresh batteries and meet you at the cabin." She left the trail and angled across the hillside toward the Drone Team platform.

"Wait up, babe," Randall called after her. She didn't respond. He groaned. "You never quit, do you?" he said to her receding back as he left the trail to follow.

Chuck took Rosie's hand in his and squeezed it. She and Carmelita would be safe in camp with Janelle and the rest of the scientists, he told himself. Meanwhile, by going after the bear and wolf with the others, he might well learn something that would provide assurance to him regarding the continued presence in the backcountry of Janelle and the girls—or convince him they needed to return to civilization immediately.

Moreover, he admitted to himself, the sighting of the wolf and grizzly together was fascinating—not ancient-baskets-and-butchered-bone-slivers fascinating, but intriguing enough.

Sarah lowered her walkie-talkie and ran alongside the trail until she drew even with Lex. "A single wolf," she reported to him. "Overriding color: gray. No collar, and no specific features to identify it or its pack. The griz was big. Over five hundred pounds. Presumably a male. Distinctive, light-colored hump."

"Two grizzlies in one day," Lex said.

"We haven't seen the second one yet."

Lex broke back into a jog. "Maybe there's still time."

20

Chuck turned to Janelle when they reached the cabin. "Why don't you and the girls grab a snack in the mess tent? I'm sure Jorge will have something set out. We should be back by dinner." He shrugged, working to display nonchalance. "Lex asked me to go along," he said. "What am I supposed to do?"

"You're supposed to go with him, that's what."

Chuck straightened. "Really?"

"It's part of what you're here for. This is a science expedition. You're a scientist. Lex says he needs you to go with him. So, go."

Chuck warmed at Janelle's words. "I don't mind helping him out," he replied, no longer hiding his excitement. "Odds are we won't see either the wolf or the bear again—though it does sound like Chance will be able to give us a sense of which way they headed and where they split up. We might even get an idea of what brought them together. My bet is one of them made a kill somewhere near here, and the other one was attracted to the carcass." He remembered the rectangular form, almost certainly a grizzly, he'd seen chasing the elk in the meadow yesterday at dusk.

"I wanna go, too," Rosie pleaded from Chuck's side.

"As *if*," Carmelita said.

"Your sister's right," Janelle told Rosie. Then she gripped Chuck's arm. "I know you'll be fine out there with everyone. But, still—" she arched her eyebrows "—no need to dive into any more lakes."

"Only if I have to."

She punched his arm, pecked him on the cheek, and herded the girls into the mess tent.

Kaifong and Randall joined Lex, Toby, Sarah, Chuck, and Keith, with Chance at his side, in front of the cabin. The drone rode in its frame on Randall's back.

"All batteried up," Kaifong reported.

Lex held out his hands. "As all of you know, observational analysis is the key to studying animal behavior. If we can catch up with the wolf and grizzly and capture them together on video, we'll document something never seen before. That's why I'm in agreement with Toby that we should head out right away. I want all of you to keep your eyes peeled. Toby will take us to the sighting location. Keith and Chance will lead from there." He glanced at the sun, just above the western ridge on the far side of the river. "It's later than I thought," he said. "Let's get moving."

With the rest of the scientists looking on from camp, the group set out behind Toby. He strode across the grass, Sarah close behind. Keith followed, with Chance on a short lead in front of him. Chance came to an abrupt halt after only two dozen yards. Everyone stopped as the dog snuffled at the grass.

"What are you onto?" Keith asked Chance, squatting. He parted the stalks with his free hand. "What the...?" He picked up a hunk of steak from last night's dinner. Chance's snout followed, sniffing. Keith held out the piece of meat.

Lex's face grew red. "This is ridiculous," he stormed. "I could not have made myself more clear about the need to dispose of all food scraps in the sealed refuse kegs in the mess tent."

"Looks to me," Chuck said, "like someone got more than they bargained for."

"You think someone did this on purpose?" asked Lex.

"Like you said, you've been adamant with everyone that all food scraps are to be thrown away in the kegs."

"But why...?" Lex asked, his face screwing up in consternation.

"I bet somebody left this out here on purpose, looking for a photo op. They probably thought a coyote would come by, or maybe a fox. Instead, they lured in a couple of examples of the park's megafauna."

"No one would do such a thing," Lex declared. "Everyone's a pro out here."

Chuck tilted his head to one side. "You're right," he said. "What's your idea, then?"

"The cook, maybe? He's new to the backcountry."

"Martha would have cleared him. She probably made him take a ten-page test before he came out here."

Lex shook his head. "I just don't know." His eyes went around the group, stopping at Sarah.

"What are you looking at me for?" she asked. She pointed at Toby. "He's the one who probably did it."

Toby stepped toward her. "If you think—"

"That's enough," Lex cut in. "Sarah," he continued, "take the scrap back to the mess tent and dispose of it properly."

"I didn't—"

"I don't care what you did or did not do. We're wasting time."

Keith gave Sarah the hunk of meat. Holding it away from her body with her thumb and forefinger, she set off toward the mess tent. Toby headed the other way, resuming his place at the head of the line. He stopped at the bottom of the meadow in front of the trees. Sarah, out of breath, rejoined the scientists as they formed a semi-circle around him.

"They were standing right here," he reported, "looking at camp."

"How far apart from each other?" Lex asked.

"Ten feet."

"That close?"

"Maybe closer."

"Unbelievable."

Kaifong asked, "Did you observe any acknowledgment between them of one another's presence?"

"Not that I could tell."

Chuck cleared his throat. "Any sign of a cut in the bear's right ear?"

"You mean a *notch*?" Toby glanced at Lex. "No. But it all happened pretty fast."

Lex clapped his hands. "Okay. Let's keep moving." He turned to Keith. "Ready?"

"Chance didn't get here by sitting around munching chew toys all day—" Keith rubbed his dog's ears "—did you, fella?" He pointed at the ground, then at Chance beside him, then back at the ground. "Search," he said to the dog. "*Search.*"

Chance sprang from Keith's side, sniffing at the earth. Keith released the spring-loaded reel on the leash as the dog nosed back and forth through the grass. Within seconds, Chance froze, snout to the ground, tail in the air.

"That's where the bear was," Keith announced.

Chance spun from the spot, padded across the grass, and halted once more with a foreleg raised.

Keith said, "That's the wolf."

Chuck asked, "How in the world do you know which is which?"

"He's predator-trained. We've developed a pecking order. Bears first, wolves second, mountain lions third, any other predators—coyotes, badgers, wolverines—fourth."

Sarah grunted in approval. "Bears first," she repeated. "Wolves second."

Toby shot back, "The opposite of all the funding lately."

Sarah whirled on him. Before she could respond, however, Lex stepped between them. "What did I tell you two?"

They turned away from each other, their jaws set.

"Good job," Keith commended his dog. "You're right, boy. There are two of them. Now, find. Find them both."

Chance entered the trees. Keith slowed the dog, the leash reel locked, allowing Chance to tug him forward. The others came behind as the sun winked out over the west ridge and the forest filled with shadow. They moved through the woods at a brisk pace until they came to a blowdown—trees felled by high winds, the downed trunks stacked haphazardly before them like giant, toppled matchsticks. The blowdown created a formidable barricade. Chance leapt atop the nearest trunk and jumped from it to the next, straining at the leash. Keith hoisted himself onto the first toppled tree and balanced there before stepping to the next. Chance leapt from trunk to trunk across the fallen timber, winding through upthrust branches while sniffing noisily and whining with excitement. Everyone stepped with care behind Keith and Chance, making slow progress as the evening shadows deepened.

Chance plunged belly-deep into a swampy pool of brackish water on the other side of the blowdown. Keith balanced on the trunk of a fallen tree above the pool. "They went in," he reported to Lex, who teetered atop a trunk behind him.

"Any sign of tracks?"

"Not that I can see."

"We'll go around. Can Chance pick up the scent on the other side?"

"No question."

Keith hauled Chance through the water as he made his way along the tree trunk. He hopped off the toppled tree and jogged with the dog around the edge of the standing pool. Upon reaching the far side, Chance nosed the pine-needle-covered ground and pressed on through the forest.

The western sky glowed crimson by the time the dog broke from the trees into a small meadow. A cold evening breeze blew down the shadowed valley from the high peaks to the south.

Chuck slipped his hands under his jacket and pressed them to his belly, warming them. Not much daylight left. The wolf and grizzly likely were far ahead by now and moving farther with each passing minute. If the two were still together this evening—a big if—they almost certainly would split up before tomorrow, which meant tonight was key. But Chance and Keith were moving slowly, and darkness was coming fast. There had to be some way to speed up the search.

Lex checked his watch. "We should turn back, start again at first light."

"There may be a better idea," Chuck said.

21

Chuck turned to Kaifong and Randall and pointed at the drone, riding high on Randall's back. "What do you guys think?"

Randall looked at Kaifong. "It's almost dark, chickadee," he said.

"I think we still have time, if we move fast."

Randall studied the sky, his hand resting on the control console at his waist. "Okay," he said. "I'm with you, babe."

Kaifong removed the drone from its frame and stood at the center of the meadow with the copter held out before her. The tiny video camera hung between her hands, attached to the bracket at the bottom of the drone.

Randall faced Kaifong at the edge of the trees, working the control console. The drone's four rotors spun to life, a low-pitched whir climbing to an ear-splitting whine as they sped up. The drone lifted from Kaifong's hands and hovered ten feet in the air. She pulled a tablet computer from a nylon pouch affixed below the frame on Randall's back. After tapping at the tablet, she held it in front of Randall. He glanced from the drone to the glowing computer screen as he adjusted the console's controls. The drone climbed straight up until it was a dark blob against the evening sky, then darted northward above the treetops and out of sight, the scream of its rotor blades diminishing as it departed.

"I didn't notice how loud your drone was when you herded the dog with it," Lex said.

Kaifong propped the computer screen with both hands, acting as a stand for the tablet. "Hovercrafts require lots of force to stay airborne," she said.

Randall bent toward the screen, fingers working the console.

"A lot of times," Kaifong continued, "the noise works in our favor. Like with Chance. The sound is new to animals. They're not sure what to make of it. Often, they'll stop to check it out."

"It's wild," Randall added, his eyes on the screen. "They'll even come out of the trees into the open sometimes, just to see what's making all the racket."

The members of the search team gathered behind him, looking over his shoulder as he controlled the drone. A live-streaming view from the drone's video camera showed treetops sweeping by beneath the speeding aircraft.

"Right toggle—throttle," he explained to his onlookers.

He thumbed the toggle to the side. On the tablet screen, the view of the trees beneath the drone shifted as the copter rose higher into the air. He moved the toggle the other direction. The treetops neared as the craft descended.

"Left toggle—direction," he said.

He pressed the lefthand toggle to the side with his thumb. The view of the forest canopy on the computer tablet spun as the drone turned 360 degrees.

As he watched, Chuck felt his stomach spin, too. "Whoa," he said. He tilted sideways, nearly stumbling.

Randall chuckled. "Happens all the time. Especially to gray-hairs."

"Thanks," Chuck said.

"There," Randall said, his eyes on the screen. "See? Next meadow. Bigger."

On the video feed, grass replaced the treetops.

Kaifong shifted the tablet to hold it in her left hand. The fingers of her right hand hovered over a row of glowing buttons at the bottom of the screen. "I'm in charge of the camera," she explained. "It's attached to a motorized swivel." She asked Randall, "Okay if I do some panning?"

Randall nodded. He said to Chuck out of the side of his mouth, "Get out your barf bag."

Chuck watched through squinted eyes as Kaifong tapped the buttons lined below the video feed. The scene through the drone's camera turned to one side, then the other, taking in the pine trees lining the meadow but revealing no sign of wolves or grizzlies or any other creatures lurking in the deepening shadows.

"I'm going to lift the view a little," Kaifong said to Randall, "so we can look ahead."

"Just make sure I've got the bottom axis at all times."

Kaifong tapped at the buttons along the base of the tablet screen. The scene shifted as the camera angle rose and the drone climbed above the meadow. A small, red light appeared in the upper corner of the computer screen.

Kaifong's voice grew tense. "We've got movement."

The red light went dark.

"Think it was legit?" Randall asked.

"It's not in this meadow, that's for sure." She pointed at the top of the screen. "We could have picked up something in the next one."

"Okay," Randall said through compressed lips. "Let's go there."

The drone sped above the treetops.

"That's something we just added," Kaifong explained. "Randall programmed the camera to pick up animal movement, like a motion detector in an alarm system."

The red light reappeared on the tablet.

"One," Kaifong said. "No. Correct that. *Two*."

Toby gasped. "They're still together?"

"They're heading for the trees," Kaifong told Randall. "Go, go, go."

"Speed's maxed," he replied. "Still at least half a mile. I don't think we'll make it."

"I'm getting a sense of size," Kaifong said. Her fingers tapped at the base of the computer screen. The camera zoomed in, focusing on a clearing in the forest still well ahead of the speeding drone. Two specks appeared on the screen against the lighter color of the grass in the opening. The specks moved toward a dark wall of trees.

"That's them," Kaifong declared. "It's gotta be."

She tapped the lit buttons on the screen below the video feed. The camera zoomed in and the moving objects disappeared.

"Too much," Randall hissed. "We're flat-out, remember? I've lost gyro. Zoom out! What's our elevation?"

"One-twenty," Kaifong reported, her eyes on a changing set of numbers in the lower left corner of the screen. "No. One-ten." Her voice shook. "You're dropping. Bring us up. *Bring us up.*"

"I'm trying!" Randall cried. "Zoom out, zoom out! I can't see anything. I told you, I've lost my bottom axis!"

His thumbs moved the toggles as Kaifong tapped at the buttons. The camera pulled back, showing the approaching edge of the meadow and a particularly tall tree, its top rising several feet above the rest of the forest canopy, directly ahead of the speeding drone.

Randall cursed as the drone flew straight into the top of the towering tree. The copter spun crazily. Chuck's stomach spun along with the drone as sky, trees, light, and shadow flashed across the computer screen.

Then the video feed went dark.

22

And...we're...down," Randall said. He lifted his thumbs from the toggles.

"I was trying to see ahead," Kaifong said. "I thought we were elevationally stable."

"We were," Randall told her. "Until we weren't." He turned to the others. "Usually, Kaifong can zoom in all she wants. But things can get janky pretty fast at top speed."

"That tree came out of nowhere," Kaifong said.

"Tell me about it," Randall agreed.

Chuck said, "You guys don't sound too upset."

"Drone plunge," said Randall.

"That's what it's called," Kaifong explained. "It's a fairly common occurrence, unfortunately. Which is why all drones are designed to withstand hard landings, and why we brought lots of spare parts with us this summer. You know when Randall asked me about the bottom axis? That's what we lost when I zoomed in so much."

"Always have to be ready to abort," Randall added.

"We had them, though," Kaifong said. "*We had them*."

Lex asked her, "Think the footage will show us anything?"

"Nothing too specific. We were still too far away."

Randall returned the control console to the webbed sling at his waist. "Guess we'd better go pick up the pieces."

Lex looked to the west, where a thin streak of purple lined the horizon. "I still can't believe the wolf and grizzly stayed together all the way here. We have to figure out what's brought them together, what's going on between them. But it's too dark to do anything more now. Let's come back tomorrow. We'll retrieve the drone then."

"No can do," Kaifong said. "Ground squirrels love gnawing on the plastic parts. Something to do with the chemical smell. There won't be much left to retrieve if we wait till morning."

"You just said you have lots of extra parts."

"Not a complete warehouse. If something gets munched that we can't replace, we're finished."

"We'd have Chance as a backup," Keith said. At his side, Chance's head rose.

Lex asked, "Think your dog can track the smell of plastic?"

Kaifong lifted her arm and pointed at an oversized watch that dwarfed her delicate wrist. "The drone has a GPS tag. My watch is GPS-enabled. It'll get us within a hundred yards."

"Okay if we keep tracking?" Keith asked Lex. "It'll be good practice for Chance."

At Lex's nod, Keith allowed the dog, ranging at the end of its leash, to lead everyone across the opening and back into the trees. No blowdowns or pools of water slowed their passage through the next stretch of forest. They broke into the next meadow. The clearing glowed a dim rose color, tranquil in the waning light.

Chance strained at the leash, nose to the fresh grass sprouting in the opening. "We're still on a dual trail—both animals," Keith told the group.

Chance and Keith crossed the meadow. Lex fell in behind, with the others. Chuck brought up the rear. They entered the deepening gloom of the forest, moving in silence through a section of old-growth lodgepole pines. The trees grew tall and thick, the north sides of their trunks covered in moss. Pools of water stood in low points on the forest floor, forcing everyone to wend their way around them.

"There!" Keith shouted when he and Chance reached the far side of one of the pools. He pointed at a pair of indentations in bare mud at the edge of the water.

Lex studied the indentations. He turned to Toby. "I'll be honest. I didn't fully believe what you said you'd seen until now."

The others crowded forward. Sarah pulled a headlamp from her pocket and aimed its beam at the ground. Over her shoulder, Chuck could see imprinted in the black mud the unmistakable paw print of a wolf, and beside it the track of a bear, big as an omelet pan and so fresh the wrinkles in the sole of the bear's paw cobwebbed the wet soil.

"*Dude*," Randall breathed.

Lex set his hands on the shoulders of Toby and Sarah. "Looks like your two teams are going to need to work together—and the two of you, as well."

Toby rested his fingers on Sarah's arm. "What do you think?"

Sarah shook off his touch. "You've gotta be kidding me."

Toby rolled his eyes. "Can we get this over with?" he asked Lex.

Chance and Keith headed deeper into the shadowed forest, Toby close behind.

"You need to get your act together," Lex said to Sarah.

"He just harassed me."

"He offered you an olive branch."

"He touched me. I could file suit if I wanted."

"I've about had it with you, Sarah," Lex said. "Whatever's going on between you and Toby, it's time for it to end. Right now."

She looked at the ground.

"You have to understand," he continued, his voice softening, "the success of the Wolf Initiative helps the Grizzly Initiative, too."

"True that, man," Randall said. "The grizzlies and wolves together in Yellowstone are showing the importance of the predator-prey relationship in, like, a balanced ecosystem."

Lex nodded, one of his bushy eyebrows cocked in response to Randall's bro-speak. "If grizzlies and wolves really are, like, starting to team up in the park," he told Sarah, "you and Toby are going to have to learn to team up again, too."

Sarah's body quivered. "This thing with the grizzly and wolf is a one-time deal," she said. "It has to be. One of them made a kill, the other was drawn to it. Then, while both of them were in the same area, they were attracted by the smell of the meat lying in the grass in front of the cabin, and they just happened to step out of the woods to check things out at the same time."

"Then why are they still traveling together this far from camp?" Chuck asked.

Sarah turned to him. "They're on their way back to the kill. That has to be it. Anything else would...would..."

"Anything else," Lex said, "would go against everything Yellowstone researchers have come to know and understand about the park's top two predators. If what we have here is more than just a grizzly and wolf posturing over a kill, it could change everything—*everything*. And you and Toby would be the lead scientists on the case."

Sarah looked after Toby as he departed through the trees. "Okay," she said. "All right. I'll be a team player." Her eyes narrowed. "But if he tries to shoot another move on me, I'll kick his balls into his throat."

"I'll be sure to warn him."

A low fog sifted along the forest floor with the coming of full dark. Chuck stuck his hands in his jacket pockets against the deepening chill and followed the others through the trees until he caught up with Keith and Chance. They doubled back time after time, skirting low areas of swamp and mud.

On several occasions, Chuck stumbled and almost fell, failing to spot depressions and downed branches in the gloom. Like Lex, just ahead, Chuck walked with his shoulders bowed and his eyes down, focused on the stretch of forest floor directly in front of him, while the other scientists strode through the forest with their heads up, looking forward, their bare hands swinging at their sides.

He worked his lower lip between his teeth. The benefits of youth. Not so long ago, he, too, would not have noticed the growing chill, and his youthful eyes would have registered all manner of definition on the shadowed forest floor at his feet.

He stopped and swung his daypack around to his chest. The others snaked away from him through the trees, leaving him on his own as he dug his headlamp from his pack, settled it on his forehead, and clicked it on. Its beam bathed the patch of ground in front of him with a welcome cone of blue-white LED light even as the rest of the forest around him plunged into contrastingly deeper shadow.

He resettled his pack on his shoulders. The others were out of sight in the forest ahead. He turned his head, the lamp sending shadows flitting through the trees.

A growl rumbled directly behind him. He stood in place, not daring to breathe.

The growl had the same low pitch as the grizzly in the willows in Hayden Valley yesterday morning, and the audio of Notch on Justin's phone the evening before that.

Another snarl froze him. Without moving his head, he glanced sideways, scanning the shapeless darkness. The second snarl, also behind him, was higher pitched and canine-like—wolf-like.

He spun and directed his headlamp the way he'd come. The beam lit tree trunks and skittered across the black surface of a pool of standing water. Two spots glowed yellow on the other side of the pool. No—four spots.

23

Chuck turned his back on the glowing spots and strode after the others as fast as he dared. He fought the urge to run, knowing if he did, he might well trigger the attack response in whatever was behind him—assuming, that is, anything actually was behind him.

He lengthened his strides, moving steadily through the trees. Only the sound of his footfalls broke the silence of the forest. He slowed when he caught up with the group, still weaving through the trees.

Had he truly just been threatened by a grizzly and wolf—*the* grizzly and wolf that had shown up at camp? No, he told himself. Impossible. This had to have been the product of his overwrought imagination. No other explanation fit.

Chance and Keith entered the next opening, this one broad and undulating. Behind, the others broke from the trees and formed a loose circle in the last of the evening light. They pulled headlamps from their packs and jacket pockets and centered them on their foreheads. Kaifong and Randall scurried off, returning after a moment with the drone. Chuck stood at the edge of the circle, his heart pounding.

"Lucked out," Kaifong reported, the drone in her hands. "Its momentum carried it into the open after it hit the tree, and it's all in one piece. Just a couple of snapped rotors."

"Good," Chuck said. His words came in a rush. "Then we can head back."

Lex eyed him. "You sound spooked."

Chuck looked back at the trees. No growls. No eyes glowing

from the shadows. "I'd just like to get back to camp. Janelle's waiting."

"Of course. Your husbandly duties." Lex turned to Keith. "Think the scent will still be strong enough for Chance to follow in the morning?"

"If we start out first thing."

"Sunup, then." Lex indicated the direction to the cabin with an open hand. "Shall we?"

Kaifong strapped the drone into its frame on Randall's back and everyone set off, retracing their route through the forest.

Chuck took a place in the middle of the line and directed his headlamp at the ground as he walked.

If the grizzly and wolf had circled back to stalk the group from behind, Chance surely would have sniffed them out.

Maybe, just maybe, Keith and his dog were overrated. Much more likely, though, was that the growls Chuck thought he'd heard had simply been trees rubbing together as the evening breeze swept through the forest. And the yellow spots that had looked like glowing eyes actually had been the play of light from his headlamp refracting off the pool and mixing with particles of mist hanging above the water.

He popped his tongue off the roof of his mouth in frustration. What a fool he was.

But at least he was headed back to Janelle and the girls. And today had been incredible, he reminded himself—his first glimpse, with his family at his side, of the reed baskets melting out of the remnant ice of Trident One Glacier, and the added discovery of the butchered sliver of bone, too.

After a late dinner, Chuck sat with Kaifong and Randall before a laptop computer at one of the long tables in the mess tent, viewing the few minutes of aerial footage captured by the drone during its short flight over the head of the canyon.

Rosie stood at Chuck's shoulder. "I saw a whole lot of neat rocks when I was searching," she said as she watched the streaming video. "But *Mamá* wouldn't let me pick them up."

Kaifong turned to Rosie from her seat in front of the computer. "It doesn't look like we found much more with our camera than you did."

Chuck watched as the footage streamed on the computer screen. Despite the bright midday sunlight, the definition on the surface of the snowfield above the ice wall was clearly discernible. When the drone passed over the lines of baskets, the baskets' loamy contents were dark as pitch.

"Ewww!" Rosie exclaimed. "They used to eat that stuff?"

"A long time ago," Carmelita, standing next to Rosie, explained, "when it was real food."

Chuck said to the girls, "We'll gather samples of it later this week, to find out for sure what it was. The butchered bone we found is making me think, more and more, that it might have been meat—which would really be something."

"How come?" Rosie asked.

He pointed at the contents of the baskets on the computer screen as the drone tracked slowly above. "See how everything in the baskets is the same color? That indicates the baskets were filled with the same thing. If they were filled with meat for winter storage, that would indicate a significant level of hunting on the Absaroka divide—far higher, even, than any of the more recent hunting by the predecessors to the Shoshone who came here over the last few hundred years. Yet these baskets are from thousands of years ago. If they were filled with hunted meat, then the people who filled them were incredibly talented hunters for such a long time ago, maybe the best hunters in ancient human history."

"Neat-o," Rosie said. Then she shrugged. "I guess."

Eight hours later, Chuck huddled with Janelle in their camp chairs in the early morning chill, the girls still asleep in the tent behind them. They sipped Jorge's strong coffee, carried up the hill from the mess tent, while awaiting the appearance of the sun over Turret Peak.

Janelle unscrewed the lid from her mug and blew across the steaming liquid, her hands wrapped around the cup. Her smooth face glowed in the morning light, her high cheekbones accentuated by spots of red from the cold.

She leaned toward Chuck, her voice low. "You're going out with Lex again this morning?"

Chuck kept his voice low, too. "He wants me to keep helping him out, as long as I'm here."

"I'm sure he can manage on his own."

"I'm sure he can, too."

"What about the baskets?"

"The follow-up search this morning shouldn't take long. Besides, as excited as I am to get back to the Trident site, I will say this whole thing with the bear and wolf is pretty incredible. The sighting of them together, not to mention their traveling with each other so far from camp, has never been observed before. It's even more fascinating when you take into account what Lex told me at breakfast the other day—that some of the park's scientists are wondering if wolves might be challenging brown bears at the top of the Yellowstone food chain."

"What's that mean, exactly?"

"If I understand it correctly, it means things may finally be getting back to normal in the park. In the past, grizzlies and wolves shared the spot at the top of the food chain on

the Yellowstone plateau. Then, after government extermina-
tors wiped out the wolves, grizzlies took over the top spot by
themselves. That was fine for the bears, but it turned out to be
terrible for the park, resulting in what's called a trophic cascade.
With wolves gone, the elk population exploded. All the hungry
elk wiped out the beavers' primary source of food, riverside
willows. The beaver population plummeted, their dams disinte-
grated, and severe erosion followed. Basically, the park's natural
ecosystem went into a death spiral, all because of the elimina-
tion of a single species, the gray wolf."

"So they brought the wolf back."

"Yes, finally, in 1995, and the results for the park ecosystem have been nothing short of miraculous. The reintroduced
wolves controlled the elk population, putting an end to over-
grazing. Plant life came back, the beavers rebounded, and
erosion slowed, all thanks to the hundred-plus gray wolves now
roaming the park."

"But a wolf and a grizzly bear hanging around together...that
would seem to be taking the idea of balance between the two
species to a whole new level."

"Which is what makes this so fascinating."

"But not as fascinating as your baskets." She lowered her
voice to a whisper, her back to Sarah's tent on the next platform
over. "Based on what Sarah pulled the other night in the meeting room, I take it balance isn't a big thing with the scientists."

Chuck leaned close to Janelle. "Lex says the researchers
actually get along great with each other. It's just that, in Sarah's
case, there's other stuff going on." Keeping his voice low, he told
her about Sarah's broken relationship with Toby.

"So Clarence is her rebound." Janelle nodded to herself.
"That makes sense. I've been wondering about them."

"Hope Clarence doesn't get hurt," Chuck said with a grin.

Janelle smiled back. "Fat chance." She hesitated. "Although, the way he's been looking at her..."

The sun climbed above Turret Peak, bathing the tent platform in a warm glow. The smell of frying bacon rolled up the slope from the mess tent, still enveloped in mist and shadow at the foot of the hill.

Chuck sat back in his camp chair. A mosquito buzzed at his ear, the first to find him in the Thorofare. He waved it away. Millions of the bloodthirsty insects would rise from the standing waters around camp in the weeks ahead. Fortunately, he and his family would be long gone by then.

Voices and the rustle of sleeping bags came from Sarah's tent. The zipper opened and Clarence crawled out. He stood on the wooden platform in his bare feet, his jeans low on his hips, his flannel shirt unbuttoned. He faced the morning sun with closed eyes. "Mmm," he murmured.

Chuck raised his voice. "Get any sleep?"

Sarah answered from inside the tent. "Very funny, Chuck."

He smiled, then turned to Janelle. "This should only take a couple of hours. We'll find the kill site—which everyone figures is what brought the bear and wolf together in the first place—and come right back. We'll head up to the baskets after that."

"*Bueno*," she said.

As Chuck placed his daypack beside his gear duffle, he looked up and down tent row. Clarence was busy pulling on his socks and boots. No other scientists stood outside their tents.

He unzipped his rubberized, waterproof duffle. He'd convinced himself by now that whatever he'd heard behind him in the woods last night had not been growls, and whatever he'd seen hadn't been glowing eyes. But it had taken a lot of convincing.

He dug inside his duffle until his hand closed around a chunk of cold steel—the .357 magnum he'd brought into the

Yellowstone backcountry with Janelle's grudging okay, but against all research team regulations.

Crouching, he transferred the heavy, stainless-steel pistol to the bottom of his daypack. He shouldered his pack and side-hilled down the slope to Turret Cabin.

24

After breakfast, Chuck joined the same group as the previous evening in front of the cabin. Keith reeled in Chance's leash until his dog stood at his side. Randall turned his back to Kaifong, who tightened the straps securing the drone in its frame. Toby adjusted the shoulder straps of his daypack, the tripod for his spotting scope lashed to its side. Lex tipped his head, shading his face, his straw park-service hat glowing luminously white in the morning sun.

Sarah hurried out of the mess tent to join the others, throwing her pack over her shoulder, a foil-wrapped breakfast burrito in hand. Lex set off, taking the lead, showing no signs of stiffness from the miles he'd logged the day before. He re-traced yesterday's route north and west away from camp, bypassing the blowdown. Rays of bright morning sun knifed through the trees, illuminating the last of the mist rising from the damp forest floor and banishing all hints of the shadowed disquiet to which Chuck had fallen prey last night.

Lex's raised hand brought everyone to a halt where the drone had plunged to the ground at the edge of the broad meadow. In the light of day, Chuck saw that the rolling meadow sloped downward to a thick grove of trees lining the edge of the river.

Chance pulled at the retracted leash in Keith's hand, snuffling at the grass.

"How's the scent?" Lex asked.

"Still strong," Keith said. "Lucky for us, it didn't rain last night."

"You're sure the bear and wolf were still together here?"

"One hundred percent."

"I still can't believe it." Lex whistled. "I know of only one other observed instance of grizzlies and wolves hanging around together, and that was between cubs and pups, which at least has some logic to it. That time, a sow with a pair of cubs approached the carcass of an elk killed by a wolf pack. The wolves backed off while the sow fed on the elk. The cubs yipped at the pack's pups like dogs wanting to play, and the youngsters from the two species got into a free-for-all, nipping at each other's legs and tumbling all over one another. After a few minutes, the sow woofed and the cubs ran back to her. Just like that—" Lex snapped his fingers "—the play date was over." He reached down and scratched Chance's ears. "But that was young ones not knowing any better. Quite a different story yesterday."

Kaifong spoke up. "Maybe the two of them staying together for so long is human-caused. What strikes me is that it occurred here in the park, where there's often human interaction with wolves and grizzlies—darting, placing tracking collars, ongoing observation."

Chuck waited for Lex to agree with Kaifong and mention the theory he'd shared over breakfast: that the changing behavior of other mammals in Yellowstone—including, possibly, Notch—might be the result of the park's ever increasing number of human visitors. Instead, Lex answered her with a question of his own.

"You think scientific work in the park might somehow be making bedfellows out of Yellowstone's wolves and bears?"

"I have no idea what might have driven this particular wolf and this particular grizzly to stay together over such a long distance, but I do know the extermination of a single species—the gray wolf—upended the entire park ecosystem."

"Still, what you're proposing is quite a stretch."

"I wouldn't disagree."

Lex looked around the group. "Any and all speculation aside, it's time to find out how much longer our predator buddies stayed together. Keith, will Chance really be able to tell us where they went their separate ways?"

"That's what he's trained to do." Chance panted at Keith's side. "When they split up, *if* they split up, he'll let us know."

"He's that good?"

"The Mammalian Neurological Alliance wouldn't have given me a five-year, half-million-dollar grant if he wasn't. They see Chance's tracking ability as a perfect example of what mammals can do for humans if used to their full potential."

Chuck gawked at Keith and Chance. Half a million bucks? A dog worth that kind of funding never would have missed the trail of the grizzly and wolf if the two predators had backtracked and come up behind him. No way had the noises and gleams been the two predators.

"It's taken years to get him to this point," Keith continued, his hand on Chance's head. "No canine on the planet is better at tracking non-human mammals than this fella right here."

Keith and Chance set out west, toward the river, on the trail of the wolf and grizzly. Lex and Chuck fell in line behind the others.

"Five hundred thousand dollars for a tracking-dog study," Lex said. "What are people thinking?"

"Keith must know a lot of people at that neuro alliance," Chuck responded. "That's what I'm thinking."

"Well, I don't need a half-million-dollar pooch to tell me what we're about to find. The wolf and griz are going to have split up somewhere just about there." Lex pointed ahead, where the valley floor broadened as the side ridges fell back two miles upriver from the southeast arm of the lake. "I can find it in my head to believe the wolf and grizzly happened upon one another near camp, and the scent of the piece of meat lured the two of them into the open at the same time. I'm even okay with the idea that a kill by one or the other of them brought them together in the first place." Lex shook his head. "But if the kill site is somewhere way out here, that's awfully far from camp for the two of them to have appeared there together. I'm convinced they'll have gone their separate ways up ahead, where the valley opens up and it makes sense for them to have done so."

"What if it turns out they stayed together even farther?"

"If that's what Chance determines, then either the dog doesn't know what it's doing…or Kaifong's idea may have more truth to it than I care to admit."

"'Changing behavioral patterns,' remember?" said Chuck, recalling their cafeteria discussion.

"Yes, I remember," Lex said flatly. "In fact, that's just about all I've been thinking about." He strode ahead.

Chance led everyone to the point across the meadow where the two distant, moving forms had been captured by the drone's camera before the copter's crash. The dog kept its nose to the ground and entered the grove of trees on the far side of the clearing, veering west, toward the upper Yellowstone.

Rather than stopping upon reaching the river, Chance strode straight into the current. The tracking dog halted only when the water reached his belly, his nose in the air, sniffing.

Keith called Chance back to shore. They walked up and down the riverbank, the dog nosing the ground. After working the bank of the river in both directions, they returned to where the dog first had entered the water. Chance faced the other shore, fifty feet away. Keith turned to the group lined along the bank above him. "They went into the water together, that much I'm sure of."

"Together?" Lex threw up his hands. "This whole thing is nuts."

"Chance never hesitated. No telling if they swam all the way across and continued on as a pair, though. Not from this side, anyway."

Lex studied the opposite shore, then turned to Kaifong and Randall. "Are you two up for another flight?"

"I'm not sure that would be worthwhile," Kaifong said. "It's been more than twelve hours at this point."

"Understood. But what if they're still together, just across the river?"

Chuck added, "You can fly a quick grid pattern on the far side, the same as you did over the baskets."

"The odds that we'll see anything..."

"...are not good," Chuck finished for Kaifong, nodding. "Try looking at this like an archaeologist. All we do is play long odds. The vast majority of the time, we come up with nothing. Only rarely do we find ancient baskets all lined up and waiting to be studied."

"Or a piece of bone sticking out of a wall of ice."

"Or that. In this case, at least, the trail you're following is just a few hours old rather than hundreds or thousands of years. And if you happen to get some footage of the two of them hanging around together, you'll be world famous."

"We'll all be world famous," said Sarah.

"But," Lex noted, "if you wreck your copter again, it'll be on the far side of the river."

"No worries with that, dude," Randall said. "I'll swim over there to get it if I have to."

"Brrr." Kaifong shook herself. "Not me. I know how cold the water is."

Toby pointed above the tops of the trees across the river. "Actually," he said, "it looks like something else may already have found what we're looking for."

Chuck lifted his gaze, following Toby's pointed finger. Less than half a mile to the west, a dozen turkey vultures rode the morning thermals, rotating in a tight circle, their broad wings fixed.

25

The winged scavengers, known for their keen eyesight and taste for carrion, circled high in the air, beyond the wall of trees lining the opposite bank.

"They're definitely over something," Chuck said.

"The kill," Lex said, a trill of excitement in his voice. "I couldn't have imagined it would be this far from camp."

"And might still be keeping the wolf and grizzly together," Chuck said.

Kaifong turned to the drone on Randall's back. "Let's see what we can find out."

"No," Lex said.

She stopped, her hands on the straps.

"Change in plans," Lex continued. "The vultures have done for us what you and Randall were going to do. They've given us an indication of what's going on over there. If the wolf and bear are still hanging around the carcass together, I don't want to risk scaring them off with the noise of your drone." He rubbed his palms together. "We're close. What we want, what we *need*, are verified observations without disturbing them. We'll have to cross the river." He looked at Chuck. "Remember the rigging you did for us at Navajo?"

Chuck nodded. Three years ago, Lex had asked if he would take a break from one of his Grand Canyon digs to rig a two-pitch rappel off the tip of Navajo Point on the South Rim of the canyon to access a California condor nest believed to contain an ailing chick. Researchers of the endangered species had rappelled to the nest, removed the chick, and nursed it back to health before returning it to the wild.

"This'll be simple in comparison, don't you think?" Lex asked.

Chuck studied the smooth river and the sturdy trunks of trees growing close to the shore on either bank. "Tyrolean traverse. Surface-based."

"Exactly what I was thinking. Can you do it?"

"What equipment did you bring?"

"Two rafts, PFDs, plenty of rope."

"Is the rope static?"

"The non-stretch kind? Yes."

"How about webbing?"

"Half-inch and inch. Plenty of both."

"Carabiners? Pulleys?"

"Check and check."

"Let's do it."

Chuck's thoughts turned to Janelle, waiting at camp with Carmelita and Rosie. How incredible it would be for her and the girls to see the kill site that had brought the grizzly and wolf together, or—he barely dared think it—the two predators themselves, if they were still hanging out near the site.

He drew Lex aside as the others headed back to camp to collect the necessary equipment for the river crossing. "One condition, though. My crew gets to come along."

"Clarence? Fine."

"No. My entire crew."

"Your family?" Lex gazed toward the soaring vultures, seeming to look beyond them. "I remember so many times with Jess, taking Carson and Lucy to see bugling elk, spawning salmon, migrating sandhill cranes." He turned to Chuck. "Of course they can come."

Back at camp, Chuck and Lex moved from storage keg to storage keg, collecting what they needed for the traverse, while the girls and Janelle tagged along.

"We're going in a boat?" Rosie asked, bouncing from one foot to the other.

"Just across the river," Chuck said.

"Yippee!" She leapt in the air while Carmelita stood rooted to the ground, her hands in her pockets.

"Doing all right?" Chuck asked her.

She offered a slight up and down movement of her chin and kicked at a tuft of grass.

Janelle put an arm around her. "If you decide you don't want to do it, you won't have to."

Rosie declared, "I'm going in the boat! For sure, for sure, for sure!"

"Only if Chuck says it's all right," Janelle told her.

"Just 'cause Carm's a scaredy cat," Rosie whined.

"Your sister's wise beyond her years," Chuck said. "She knows it's not always best to just do something no matter what."

Rosie crossed her arms and huffed. "I always do stuff no matter what."

"And that," Janelle said, "is your whole problem." She sighed. "And mine."

The group returned to the edge of the river after an early lunch. Clarence carried one of the tightly rolled rafts on his back while Toby hauled the other. Half a dozen PFDs and the gear to rig the crossing were distributed among Janelle and those from the morning search. Even the girls carried a pulley each in their small daypacks.

The turkey vultures continued to wheel in the western sky, dark slivers against the early afternoon clouds. The crew dropped their packs at the river's edge as a series of sharp yips sounded from beyond the river to the west.

Everyone straightened. Chuck gently squeezed the back of Rosie's neck, signaling her to remain silent. The only noise was the gurgle of the flowing river and the soft rustle of the treetops swaying in the midday breeze. Then, a single, spine-tingling howl rose from across the river. An instant later, a cacophony of howls joined the first. The chorus floated across the water, climbing to a crescendo before coming to an abrupt halt.

Toby put a hand to his chest in the sudden silence. "Oh...my...God."

"Wolves," Sarah said. "Plural."

"A pack," Toby confirmed. "But there are no packs anywhere nearby. At least, there weren't when we came out here."

"What a beautiful sound," Sarah murmured. "Every time I hear it, it brings tears to my eyes."

"We'll make a wolfie out of you yet," Toby said.

Chuck braced himself. But Sarah surprised him.

"Maybe one day," she said, holding Toby's gaze.

"Riddle me this, then," he said. "Why would any pack have traveled this far, this fast, from wherever they were two days ago?" He blew a jet of air between his lips. "There's no precedent for this. None whatsoever."

"But," Chuck said, "I thought wolves were known for covering lots of ground."

"They are," Toby replied, breaking his gaze with Sarah to look at him. "But packs generally cover set areas in set patterns. They typically make only gradual movements from their defined territories over time. And there were no packs anywhere near here when we crossed the lake."

"Which one was closest?"

Toby frowned. "Stander Pack, I guess, forty miles west of here, on the other side of Old Faithful along Little Firehole River."

"Could those wolves have made it here in just a couple of days?"

"Could they have? Sure. Wolves can cover fifty, sixty miles, easy, in a day. But would they have? I don't see why. Stander is the most public pack in the park, totally comfortable with its environs. Besides, it's denning season, when wolves stay put with their new pups. Stander Pack has been hanging out near Grand Loop Road and Old Faithful, in full view of tourists, for years. The Stander wolves have all they need there—elk herds, plenty of small game when the elk aren't around, woodlands to lay low in. They haven't moved more than ten miles in any direction from their primary denning site since I don't know when."

"What other pack might it be, then?"

Toby pressed his thick mustache into place with his thumb and forefinger as he looked across the river. "Blacktail, I guess. They'd be the next closest."

"From Lamar Valley?"

Toby nodded.

Chuck swallowed. "That's the pack your Territory Team was going in to check on when they..."

Toby nodded again, his face marble. "Joe and Rebecca."

"You knew them?"

"They were my friends, both of them. Good people. *Great* people. I still miss them, every single day."

Sarah said, "They were my friends, too. Joe made the most incredible spaghetti sauce. He called it gravy, said it was his grandmother's recipe. And Rebecca, with all her dirty jokes, she just cracked me up."

"I'm sorry," Chuck said to both of them. He asked Toby, "Do you have any idea why Blacktail or any other pack would have come this way over the last couple of days?"

Toby looked from Chuck to Lex. "I got nothing."

Lex crossed his arms over his chest. His voice was calm, assured. "Well, then, that's what we're going to find out."

26

Chuck waved for the others to join him at a place on the riverbank with everything necessary for the crossing—a pair of stout conifers opposite one another on each shore; banks devoid of brush; and smooth water between, free of protruding rocks.

Clarence gathered from everyone the gear necessary to rig the traverse—coiled ropes, loops of one-inch nylon webbing, oversized locking carabiners, aluminum pulleys, and a metal ratchet with a long-travel handle. Lex rolled out the pair of ten-foot rubber rafts and assigned Keith, Kaifong, Randall, and Sarah to inflate them with a pair of foot pumps.

While the researchers manned the pumps and Lex screwed together a pair of collapsible paddles, Toby sat nearby, tapping at a tablet computer he'd pulled from his pack.

"Anything?" Lex asked him.

"Not yet. I'm going through every article I've ever stored on this thing, searching under 'sudden pack movement,' 'pack travel distances,' any word combo I can think of." He smacked his forehead with the butt of his hand. "I can't believe I left our radio receivers in camp. The wolf that showed up at the cabin wasn't collared, so I figured we wouldn't need them out here."

"I should've brought the satellite phone from camp, too," Lex said. "I'll use it to check in with Martha as soon as we get back. It's for emergencies only, but I'd say this qualifies. She'll be able to tell us which pack has come our way."

Toby looked across the river. "If they show themselves, we'll know sooner than that. Between fur colors and collars, I'll be able to make a positive ID, no radio receivers required."

Chuck slid one of the inflated rafts into the river. He put on a PFD and turned to Carmelita and Rosie. "Don't get anywhere near the water without one of these strapped on tight. The water's cold and fast."

Janelle rested her hands on the girls' shoulders. "Got it."

"Got it!" Rosie repeated, her voice raised, prompting a "shush" from her mother.

Chuck ferried the raft across the river, paddling with J-strokes to keep the small, rubber craft aimed into the current while Clarence paid out a lightweight line attached to the stern. The ferry was easy to manage solo, but would have been dangerous with a passenger load—hence the need to set the traverse. The river carried him a hundred feet downstream during the crossing. He hopped ashore and dragged the raft upstream to the tall tree.

He used the lightweight line to draw a sheathed length of nine-millimeter rope across the river, then a stout length of static, eleven-millimeter line. He and Clarence affixed the thicker line across the river between the two trees. Clarence attached the ratchet to the rope and tightened the device, stretching the thick line until it extended across the water as taut as a bowstring, three feet above the river's surface.

Chuck looped the nine-millimeter rope through the ring on the bow of the raft and affixed the raft to the ferry line with a pair of pulleys. He tossed his PFD and paddle into the raft, and helped Clarence run it back across the river using the looped nine-mil line and pulleys.

Clarence slid the second raft into the water and secured it behind the first. Lex, Sarah, Toby, Kaifong, Randall, and Keith donned the PFDs. Randall balanced the drone, in its pack frame, on the floor of the downstream raft. Chance crouched

between Keith's knees. Lex and Sarah took places at the head of
the upstream raft, and Chuck and Clarence hauled the doubled
rafts away from shore. The loaded boats rode low in the water,
the current breaking around their bows. Upon reaching the far
bank, the scientists dropped their life jackets in the boats, shouldered their packs, and clambered ashore. Chuck and Clarence
ran the PFD-laden rafts back across the river, where Clarence
tossed life jackets up the bank to Janelle and the girls. They put
on the PFDs, Janelle double checking Carmelita's and Rosie's
straps, and boarded the rafts. Clarence knelt at the head of the
upstream raft, and Chuck pulled the rafts back through the
current.

With everyone gathered on the shore, Lex put a finger to
his lips and gestured for Keith to set out with Chance. Keith
released the leash reel and Chance surged forward, nose to the
ground, scurrying upstream along the riverbank, then down.
The dog stopped, tail in the air, several yards downstream from
the traverse line. Keith motioned the others to him.

"They were still together when they came out of the water
here," Keith reported, his voice low.

"Unbelievable," Lex murmured.

Chance headed up the bank into the forest, pulling hard at
the extended leash.

Janelle grabbed Chuck's arm. "Remind me again this is safe."

"I wouldn't be comfortable having you here if it wasn't."

"But those howls." She shuddered.

"Wolves have gotten a bad rap for centuries. The big bad
wolf in the Three Little Pigs, the wolf that ate Grandma in Little
Red Riding Hood—fear of wolves is a big part of why they were
wiped out across the West a hundred years ago, and why it took
so long to bring them back to Yellowstone. But wolves don't

attack humans." Chuck laid a hand on her arm. "This is what we came for."

Rosie tugged the hem of her mother's jacket. "They're leaving us behind." She pointed at the departing scientists. "We'll be all alone."

Janelle looked at the waiting rafts, snugged against the shore, then up the riverbank into the forest. "Okay," she said. "*Vamanos.*"

She propelled the girls ahead of her.

Chuck's pulse quickened at the thought of his family getting to see a pack of wolves here, deep in the Yellowstone backcountry.

Then, his thoughts hit a speed bump.

The pack's arrival here in the upper Yellowstone River valley was sudden, inexplicable. If Toby had no idea why the wolves had come, Chuck certainly didn't.

Concern fluttered through him. He reached back to feel the .357, solid and heavy at the bottom of his pack.

They came to a broad meadow west of the river. Everyone spread out beneath the sheltering branches of the trees at the meadow's edge. The meadow stretched half a mile to the foot of the steep, forested ridge that rose high above the valley.

Keith retracted the leash, drawing Chance to his side. Lex, Randall, and Kaifong lifted binoculars to their eyes. Toby unstrapped the tripod from the side panel of his pack, extended its telescoping legs, and attached a large, black spotting scope to its top. Next to him, Sarah pulled a tripod and scope from her pack, too. They peered through the high-powered monoscopes, studying the open field.

Chuck raised his binoculars to his eyes. He waited for his contacts to settle over his pupils, then spun the focus knob.

Hummocks of bunch grass came into sharp focus a hundred yards ahead. Fresh, green shoots sprouted through the previous year's matted, brown stalks. He scanned the meadow in bite-sized pieces, working his way across the clearing.

To his left, Sarah let out a startled gasp.

27

Chuck lowered his binoculars long enough to note that Sarah, Toby, and Lex were focused on a spot two-thirds of the way across the clearing. He aimed his binoculars but saw only the new grass blanketing the meadow. Panning the binoculars, he spotted two stripes of black sticking up from the grass in the distance.

He stilled his breathing and tweaked the focus knob, zeroing in on a pair of turkey vultures perched close to one another on a gray hump several hundred yards away. His fingertips pressed hard at the green, plastic housing of the binoculars. The vultures' heads were tiny, red specks, while the gray hump on which the birds stood was furry—a wolf, lying on its side, dead.

A vulture plucked at the carcass, coming up with a clump of meat clutched in its beak.

"Uncollared," Toby said, his eye to his mono-scope, his voice shaking. "The only thing that possibly could have killed it…"

"Not a grizzly," Sarah said. "Couldn't be. They've never been known to kill wolves."

Toby took his eye from his scope. "Wolves and grizzlies never have been known to hang out together, either." He gripped the legs of his tripod with both hands, his knuckles white. "What else could it have been?"

She took a deep breath. "I don't know."

"I hope I'm wrong." He looked her in the eye. "I liked the idea of the two of them as friends."

"I did, too," Sarah said.

"There's an entire pack here," Lex said. "Could it have been wolf vs. wolf?"

"Wolves don't kill each other very often," Toby said. "Only in the case of territory disputes, which wouldn't be happening here, far from any dens. Juveniles fight to the death sometimes, but that's when they're on their own, testing themselves. Inside the pack, wolves are family."

Lex gestured across the meadow at the dead wolf and perched vultures. The rest of the winged scavengers still circled above, silhouetted against the clouds building over the ridge to the west. "We'll go in quick," he said. "I want to get back to camp and the sat phone." His eyes rested on Janelle and the girls. "We can't all go, but I want to determine cause of death before we pull back."

Toby nodded. "That's critical."

"We'll take a four-person team," Lex said. "Big enough to be safe but small enough to move fast. Toby and Sarah, you'll come with me." His eyes flitted from Kaifong to Randall, then to Keith and Chance. "No need for a drone, and no dog."

He turned to Chuck, who glanced at Janelle and the girls and shook his head. "Sorry. I'm staying here."

"Clarence, then," Lex said.

Clarence nodded.

"The four of us will be more than enough to cause a bear to hold off—if this is, in fact, a grizzly kill," Lex said.

He left the shelter of the trees and headed across the meadow with Toby, Sarah, and Clarence behind him.

The breeze picked up, blowing hard and cold down the face of the ridge and across the meadow. The sun gleamed in the blue sky directly overhead while, to the west, the clouds gathered in bursts of white and gray. Chuck sat with his back to the trunk of a tree. He rested his elbows on his knees, steadying his binoculars as he peered through them, tracking the lead team's progress. Carmelita and Rosie knelt on either side of him.

"What do you see?" Rosie demanded. "Something's dead, isn't it? I can smell it. It's yucky."

"You can't smell anything," Carmelita chided.

"Can too," Rosie shot back.

"Can *not*."

"Can *too*."

"Carm," Janelle scolded. "Rosie. Hush."

"Can we look?" Rosie asked Chuck.

"Yeah, yeah. Can we?" said Carmelita.

"Of course." Chuck unstrapped his lightweight backpacking tripod from the side of his pack and extended it to the height of the girls' eyes. He screwed the binoculars into place atop the tripod and focused the view on the pair of perched vultures. He pinched the barrels close together for Carmelita's narrow face. She put her eyes to the lenses. He guided her hand to the focus knob, moving her finger back and forth to make the ring spin.

"See how it goes in and out of focus?" He placed her other hand on the plastic housing of the binoculars. "You can move them around all you want."

"Got it," she said.

"What do you see, Carm?" Rosie demanded. "What, what, what?"

"I just started," Carmelita replied. "Sheesh."

From behind Toby's scope, Randall said, "It's a wolf, all right. Was. You can see the wind ruffling its fur."

Chuck looked at the distant gray lump in the grass. The birds, reacting to the lead team's approach, hopped off the carcass, took a few running steps away from the team, and rose into the air with heavy wing flaps. They ascended to their fellows and circled, riding the breeze.

"Have you got them spotted?" Chuck asked Carmelita.

"I see Uncle Clarence," she reported. "He's walking."

The team was a hundred feet from the dead wolf, Lex in the lead. The other three members of the party spread out to either side of him as they neared the carcass.

Rosie pulled at Carmelita's shoulder. "My turn," she insisted. "*My turn.*"

"I'm afraid she's right," Chuck said.

Carmelita relinquished the binoculars to Rosie, who nearly knocked the tripod over when her forehead struck the lenses. Chuck grabbed the legs of the tripod to steady it.

Kaifong took a quick breath, her eye to Sarah's scope. "Oh, my God."

Chuck's heart thudded. "What do you see?"

To his unaided eyes, Lex, Sarah, Toby, and Clarence were distant stick figures. The gray hump of the dead wolf showed just above the grass.

"Bear," Kaifong said, her eye still pressed to Sarah's spotting scope. "Grizzly."

Janelle drew Carmelita and Rosie to her. "Clarence," she said, her voice pinched.

Chuck lifted the tripod and put the binoculars to his eyes. He widened the barrels and scanned the edge of the forest at the base of the west ridge. Movement—something chocolate brown, the size of a refrigerator, a bulge at its top.

Kaifong was right: grizzly.

The bear stepped from the shadows of the trees into the meadow. Its fur shimmered in the sunlight. Its broad shoulders cascaded to stocky forelegs, and a hump rose between its shoulder blades, tall and rounded and light tan.

Chuck's breath caught in his throat as the grizzly proceeded toward the dead wolf and the four members of the lead team. On all fours, the bear placed one massive paw in front of another, its pace deliberate. Halfway between the trees and the carcass, the creature halted in mid-stride, one foreleg raised. Clarence and the others faced the grizzly in a straight line, twenty feet shy of the dead wolf.

At Keith's feet, Chance whined. Keith, watching, said, "The grizzly is just asserting its rights, protecting the carcass. It won't attack; there're too many of them."

"But that would mean the griz killed the wolf," Randall responded, his eye to Toby's scope, "which doesn't make any sense." He straightened and looked across the meadow at the distant scene: the lead party, the unmoving grizzly, the carcass between.

Chuck's breathing calmed as the grizzly held its ground, its leg raised and its snout thrust out, apparently taking in the scent of the lead team. He adjusted the focus knob, bringing the view into sharp relief as the team members stepped toward the wolf carcass in unison, clearly choosing to assert their dominance and back the grizzly down rather than risk inciting it into charging at them if they were to retreat.

The bear yawned. It settled forward on its forelegs and stretched its hind legs out behind until it rested on its stomach, like an enormous dog. It watched, pink tongue lolling from its mouth, as the four team members edged toward the dead wolf.

"Aside from other wolves, no other predator in the park is capable of killing an adult wolf except a bear," said Keith. "I bet the griz got tired of the wolf's company and decided to do something about it—an agnostic killing."

"Ag-what?" Randall asked.

"That's the term for any killing by a bear, particularly a grizzly, that's not about meat or protecting cubs. From what I've read, they're fairly common."

Chuck said, "That would explain a lot—the grizzly sticking around, the howls of the dead wolf's pack mates."

The members of the lead team had reached the carcass. Toby tugged on a pair of latex gloves and probed at the body of the dead wolf. Lex, Sarah, and Clarence stood behind him, facing the lounging bear.

"Duuuuudes," Randall said, his eye to Toby's scope. "Git the frick outta there."

"They're doing what we came out here to do. They're determining cause of death," said Keith.

"But the bear's right in front of them, man," Randall replied. "A whole pack of wolves is cruising around somewhere nearby, too."

"Bears, wolves, that's what we all came here to study—except for you, sounds like."

Randall turned from the spotting scope. "This is their world, not ours, is what I'm saying. It's like we're intruding, invading even."

He bent back to the scope just as the grizzly snapped its jaws shut and rolled up on all fours.

Chuck set his binoculars head-high on the tripod, focusing on the bear.

The grizzly easily weighed five hundred pounds. Its smooth, rounded ears swiveled from side to side. It shook itself, muscles rippling, then reared back and lifted its forelegs from the grass to balance on its hind legs, rising a full seven feet above the ground. The bear batted the air with a forepaw and let out a resounding roar, its jaws stretched wide.

Chuck swallowed. The size and ferocity of the brown bear made clear to him the folly of his idea that the handgun in his daypack would somehow act as an effective deterrent against Yellowstone's massive grizzlies.

With a powerful huff, the grizzly dropped back to all fours and charged toward the lead team.

28

Chuck jerked up from the binoculars, his chest seizing. The lead team consisted of four people—four. Grizzlies didn't charge that many humans. *Ever.*

"Uncle Clarence!" Rosie screamed.

"What's happening?" Carmelita demanded. "What's going on?"

Chuck put his eyes back to the binoculars. The bear galloped across the meadow, straight at the lead team.

"It'll stop," Chuck said through clenched teeth. "It has to."

In the face of the charge, Toby rose and stepped backward toward the others. All four extended their pepper spray canisters at the bear.

The grizzly's ease of movement belied its bulk. With each leap, the bear hung above the grass like a thoroughbred for an instant, its legs outstretched.

The grizzly was thirty yards from the team.

Another leap.

Twenty.

Chuck gulped, powerless to do anything but witness through his binoculars the scene playing out before him.

The bear leapt to within yards of the gray wolf's carcass. The team stood shoulder to shoulder, ten feet from the dead wolf. A cloud of red mist appeared in front of the team as they put their canisters to use—but the steady breeze sweeping off the ridge blew the mist away from the grizzly and, instead, into their faces. They doubled over, hands to their mouths and noses.

The bear took one final leap and came to a halt next to the gray carcass humped in the grass. The grizzly rose on its hind legs, towering over the dead wolf and Lex, Toby, Sarah, and Clarence. The pepper spray melted away on the wind. Clarence gripped Sarah's arm. Again, the bear let out a ferocious roar, gnashing its teeth and shaking its head. The grizzly batted the air once, twice, its forepaw a blur of motion. Then, the bear dropped to all fours. Eyeing the team members, it lowered its head, took the wolf's body in its teeth, and lifted the carcass from the grass. The dead wolf's tail was bushy, its legs trailing.

The bear threw the carcass violently to the ground and backed away. The team backed the other direction, distancing themselves from the retreating grizzly, until Toby came to an abrupt halt. Lex reached for him, but Toby knocked Lex's hand away and returned to the carcass.

The bear stopped and watched from no more than twenty feet away as Toby grabbed one of the dead wolf's hind paws and dragged the animal backward through the grass until he reached the other members of the lead party. Toby lifted the dead wolf by its legs, threw the carcass over his shoulders, and resumed the retreat with Lex, Sarah, and Clarence. After a moment, the bear, too, recommenced its movement in the opposite direction.

When the distance between them grew to fifty feet, the grizzly turned and strode across the meadow at a stately pace until it disappeared into the trees. The team members turned and headed back across the meadow with Lex in the lead. Lex broke into a jog, the others hurrying behind, the wolf's long body bouncing on Toby's shoulders.

Chuck straightened from behind the binoculars as the lead party neared the trees. Rosie and Carmelita broke from Janelle's grasp and ran to Clarence. He bent and spoke in their ears before walking with them back to Janelle.

"*Hermana*," he said to her, his eyes alight.

"*Hermano*," she replied.

They embraced. A tear rolled down Janelle's cheek. Clarence brushed it away with his thumb.

"There, there, Sis," he said, stepping back from her. "No need for that. That's how it's supposed to go. *Exactamente.* The griz showed us who was boss, then backed off, gave us our space, without the spray doing a thing."

"Uncle Clarence told us he peed his pants." Rosie giggled.

"I did," he admitted with a tight smile, his cheeks rosy. "But only a *lee*-tle," he said, emphasizing his Latino accent.

Sarah's tone was awestruck. "It was ten feet away from us. *Ten feet.*"

Lex coughed, eyes still watering from the bear spray. "Too close. We were lucky."

Thunder rumbled from the thick bank of clouds in the west, now rolling down the ridge toward the valley floor, driven by the wind.

Lex clapped his hands. "Time to get out of here. We'll debrief at camp."

Toby lowered the carcass of the wolf to the ground. Blood streaked his daypack and the shoulders of his jacket.

The dead wolf was larger than Chance. Its torso was long and lanky, its fur the color of concrete save for the tip of its tail, which looked as if it had been dipped in tar. Its eyes were closed. Its tongue, matted with bits of dry grass, extended from the side of its mouth. A long wound slashed its side, gouged through gray fur into its ribcage.

Toby, Sarah, and Chuck set about shortening the legs of their tripods and strapping them to their packs. A chorus of wolf howls rose from the far side of the meadow. Chuck stared across the rolling grass. From the place where the grizzly had vanished into the trees, half a dozen wolves trotted out of the forest into the meadow. The six wolves—four gray, one coal black, one white as a snowshoe hare in winter—spread out as they came into the open.

Chuck's throat went dry as the wolves loped across the grass in an even line, heads high and snouts forward, as if on a hunt.

29

L et's go," Chuck said to his family, fighting to keep his voice calm. "Clarence, you first."

Clarence entered the forest, moving quickly. Janelle and the girls hastened after him. Chuck swung his pack to his shoulders and looked back before entering the trees. The wolves held their steady lope, already past the grassy indentation where the carcass of their pack mate had lain.

Chuck hustled to catch up with Janelle, who turned to him, searching his eyes.

"This isn't normal," Chuck admitted in answer to her unvoiced question.

"Will pepper spray work against them?" she asked.

"No one's ever had wolves come close enough to find out, as far as I know."

"Good." She gave a firm nod, her pony tail bouncing.

Chuck glanced back. Everyone else trailed close behind—except Toby. The lead wolf researcher stood at the edge of the trees facing the meadow, a palm-sized video camera held out before him.

Lex, following Chuck's gaze, came to a stop. "Toby," he barked. "Put that thing away and come on."

"This is incredible," Toby said. "Wolves don't do this. *They don't do this.*" He didn't move.

Lex strode to the edge of the meadow and ripped the camera from Toby's hands. "Come," Lex commanded. "*Now.*"

Toby nodded, his eyes on the wolves, the carcass of the dead wolf at his feet.

The wolves continued across the mile-wide clearing, still in hunting formation, equidistant from one another. They were close enough now for Chuck to see that two of the six wore white tracking collars around their necks.

"I don't believe it," Toby said. "Stander Pack. All the way from Little Firehole. They crossed two passes to get here, including the Continental Divide."

With obvious reluctance, he shouldered his pack. He hefted the carcass and settled it around the back of his neck. Holding the dead wolf in place by its legs, he made his way past Lex into the trees. Lex shoved Toby's camera in his jacket pocket and followed.

A second round of thunder rumbled from the approaching clouds as everyone hastened down the slope toward the riverbank. A lone wolf howl sounded from the meadow followed by answering yips. The chorus sent a shiver down Chuck's spine. Clarence increased his pace at the front of the line. Janelle and the girls hurried in silence behind him.

At the river, Janelle, Carmelita, and Rosie climbed into the downstream raft. Janelle fastened PFDs around the girls' chests.

Chuck cast a wary glance up the slope. The trees blocked much of his view. The forest filled with shadow as the clouds rolled across the sky, covering the sun. An arc of lightning pulsed through the clouds, the flash obliterating the shadows for an instant. Thunder rumbled from the clouds two seconds later—the heart of the advancing storm was two miles away. A gust of wind swept through the forest, whipping the treetops. The gale-force wind carried with it the singed odor of spent lightning and the scent of moisture from the lowering clouds.

Chuck motioned for Clarence to join Janelle and the girls in the raft. "I need you to run the traverse from the other bank."

Clarence hesitated.

"Go," Chuck said.

"Hurry, Uncle Clarence," Rosie cried.

Clarence climbed into the raft.

"Wait on the far side," Chuck told Janelle. "We'll head back together."

Keith and Chance reached the riverbank, Kaifong, Randall, and Sarah close behind them. Lex and Toby trailed, still descending through the trees.

"Keith," Chuck said. "You and Chance hop in. The rest of us will come with the second run."

Keith tugged the dog into the lead raft and settled next to Clarence as Lex arrived, out of breath, at the river's edge.

"Help me pull," Chuck told him.

They reared back on the looped nine-millimeter line, putting their combined weight into initiating the traverse. The rafts surged into the river, their bows aimed upstream, the current parting around them.

A second flash of lightning ripped through the clouds. The roll of thunder followed less than a second later. Thin tendrils of water rode the gusting wind, signaling the approach of heavy rain.

Upon reaching the far side, Clarence helped the girls and Janelle to shore and jumped to the bank with Keith and Chance. Clarence, Keith, and Janelle pulled on the looped rope, teaming with Chuck and Lex to speed the rafts back across the river.

Behind Chuck, Sarah cried, "There! Behind that tree. *Wolf.*"

Chuck didn't turn to look. The wolves meant no harm, he assured himself, trying to focus on the rafts.

"Should they be doing this?" Sarah asked Toby.

"It's been two years since the packs have seen anyone away from roads," he said. "They're just checking us out, wondering what's going on, that's all."

Chuck gave Toby's theory a mental thumbs-up. But from the corner of his eye, he saw Sarah point at the dead wolf draped over Toby's shoulders.

"That's what they want," she said. "You shouldn't have taken it."

"We have to do a necropsy," Toby said. "The grizzly must have—"

"Another one!" Sarah broke in, peering up the slope.

Chuck spotted a blur of gray darting through the trees. "Everybody," he said as the boats bumped against the shore. "Get in."

A dog-like growl came from beyond a stand of brush several yards up the hillside. The growl ended in a sharp yip.

"I don't like this," Kaifong said as she clambered aboard. "Not one bit."

Chuck clung to the rope, pinning the rafts to the riverbank, and scanned the forest and shoreline. A second flash of movement caught his eye, this one at the river's edge a hundred feet downstream. The black wolf extended its head around the trunk of a stream-side tree. The wolf stared at Chuck, its yellow eyes unblinking in its dark face, its ears standing straight up.

"Another," Chuck said. The wolf withdrew its head, disappearing from view. "They're surrounding us, pressing us against the river."

"The carcass," Sarah said to Toby. "Leave it for them."

"Sorry. Not gonna happen," Toby said.

Another growl came from up the slope.

Randall leaned the drone against the downstream raft's side and hopped in after it. Toby slung the dead wolf onto the rubber floor of the upstream raft.

The wind whistled through the trees as another crack of lightning lit the sky, this one directly overhead. An instantaneous boom of thunder accompanied the lightning, shaking the ground beneath Chuck's feet. The first drops of rain fell from the clouds, striking the brim of his cap and wetting his face.

A wolf howled from behind a low stand of willows at the edge of the river upstream. More howls answered from the surrounding forest, riding the wind.

"Hey, wolves," Sarah called out to the creatures from where she stood on the riverbank. "I've got a message for you. We don't mean you any harm. We just want to learn what happened to your pack mate."

A large wolf, its fur slate gray, emerged from a thick stand of trees fifty feet up the slope. Its mouth hung open, revealing pointed teeth. The wolf barked, a single, sharp yip.

The five other wolves of Stander Pack stepped from the trees, spaced to form a semi-circle fifty feet in diameter around the researchers. The first wolf bunched its shoulders and growled, the sound emanating from deep in its chest. A curtain of heavy rain swept through the forest to the river, large drops drumming the river bank. The wolf snarled a second time.

"Into the boats," Chuck said. Rain pelted his shoulders and head.

Rather than climb aboard one of the rafts, Sarah raised a hand to the wolves, palm out, her back to the river. "Stay where you are," she said.

The lead wolf edged toward her. The other five wolves moved forward as well, tightening the semi-circle.

"I said *stop*," Sarah said.

Beside her, Toby swung his pack to the ground, unzipped it, and groped inside. The wolves approached, moving in unison, closing the half-circle to forty feet. Their eyes, aglow in the shadowed forest, pierced the rain. Toby pulled a length of polished black plastic a foot long and a few inches wide from his pack as

Lex climbed into the upstream raft.

"Sarah," Chuck urged, gripping the haul rope to steady the boats.

She climbed into the downstream raft next to Kaifong and Randall.

Toby rooted inside his pack a second time and brought out another length of black plastic, this one with a black metal tube attached.

"Toby, come on," Chuck demanded. "Don't—"

The six wolves charged.

30

The wolves dashed toward the rafts in a powerful burst, their teeth bared. Chuck stumbled backward, fear thrumming his insides. His foot slipped off the bank and his boot plunged into the icy water between the rafts and shore. Screams from the girls reverberated from the far bank.

"Chuck!" Janelle cried out.

The wolves came to a unified stop fifteen feet from the boats, paws planted, muscles bunched beneath their smooth coats. The rank odor of the animals' wet fur drifted through the air.

Chuck hauled himself back up on shore with the traverse line, blinking through the downpour. The wolves crouched, eyeing Chuck and Toby on the riverbank.

"Toby," Lex commanded.

Toby backed to the upstream raft. He clutched the black plastic pieces he'd dug from his pack to his chest; now that he had them in his hands, he didn't seem to know what to do with them.

The wolves inched closer, growling. Lex helped Toby into the raft. Chuck stepped in after him. Instantly, the rafts moved away from shore, propelled by those on the far bank.

Chuck held out a hand to Toby, who handed over the plastic pieces from his pack as the rafts surged into the current. Still crouched, the wolves advanced to the water's edge. Chuck slid the two plastic pieces against one another as the rafts tracked along the static line. The pieces snapped together with a well-oiled click. He hefted the result of the combined parts—a short-barreled break-down rifle, popular among the hundreds of out-of-state elk hunters who flew into Durango each fall.

"Shells?" Chuck asked Toby.

Toby dove into his pack. He came up with a box of 7-mm cartridges. Chuck thumbed the bullets into the rifle's magazine. Though small in caliber compared to the 9-mm version favored by big-game hunters, the lightweight gun's size was perfect for varmint control—or defensive purposes.

The wolves paced the shoreline, their eyes on the rafts.

Chuck slotted a shell into the firing chamber, slid the bolt home, and clicked on the safety. "No scope?" he asked Toby.

"My dad thought open sights would be best."

The rafts passed the mid-point of the river. The current swept by, gurgling at the bow of the lead boat, the traverse line tight. The first wolf pawed at the water's edge and snarled at the departing rafts. At well over a hundred pounds, the wolf was the largest of the six pack members by a distinct margin. A white plastic radio collar circled its neck.

"That's right," Lex told the wolf. "Stay right where you are."

"Number 184," Toby said. "Stander Pack's alpha for the last few years. She's a beauty. And a very capable leader. I can't imagine what made her decide to bring the pack here." He rested his hand on the carcass of the wolf between his feet. "This is 217, a two-year-old male. He was really easy-going—played with the pups, got along well with the adults. We probably would've collared him this winter."

Raindrops exploded on the surface of the river. Chuck wiped water from the sides of his face. He rested the rifle across his thighs, its barrel aimed at the pacing wolves.

"You're not allowed to have that thing with you," Lex said to Toby.

"After what happened with the Territory Team, my dad insisted—not that I know what to do with it. He's a big-time hunter, goes after Kodiaks in Alaska every fall." Toby looked across the water at the wolves. "It was supposed to be for grizzlies."

"Instead, it's your wolves that have decided to go on the prowl for some reason."

"They must be reacting to our arrival out here in the backcountry."

"Reacting? From forty miles away?"

"If you have any better ideas, I'm all ears."

"What about how 217 was hanging with the grizzly?" Chuck asked.

"That I don't get at all," Toby said. He nudged the dead wolf with his boot and shook his head.

"Neither do I," Sarah admitted.

She and Toby exchanged glances. "I'm sorry about 217," she said.

He dipped his head. "Thanks."

On the riverbank, the wolves sat on their haunches, tilted their heads, and yipped and howled. Chuck thumbed the rifle's safety off and back on. Was this odd behavior the result of human interactions in the park? Or were the wolves, as Sarah believed, pursuing the carcass of their pack mate?

Stander Pack's alpha rose to all fours. Her forepaws sank into the mud at the edge of the water. She crouched, then leapt from the bank. The wolf hung in the air before landing in the river fifteen feet from shore and disappearing beneath the surface. Her head poked above the water and she swam toward the rafts, nose cutting the current like an alligator's snout, furred spine curling back and forth at the surface.

Chuck knelt in the bottom of the raft, propped his elbows on the side tube, and snugged the rifle's black plastic stock to his shoulder. Raindrops wormed their way down the back of his neck, cold and prickling on his skin. He clicked the safety off and rested the crook of his finger against the trigger as the wolf churned closer.

"No!" Sarah cried from the downstream raft.

Chuck aimed down the barrel of the gun and fired.

31

Sarah lunged at Chuck. Randall and Kaifong dove atop her, trapping her in the bottom of their raft.

Chuck raised his head from the gun's sights. As intended, the shot had passed well above the head of the alpha and ricocheted off the surface of the river and into the trees. The result was what he'd hoped. The wolf turned and swam back to the far shore, where she emerged, dripping, on the muddy riverbank. She yipped at her pack mates lining the bank, and the six wolves trotted up the slope, away from the river's edge. The rain, sheeting from the sky, blurred the wolves' departure until they disappeared into the forest.

Onshore, Chuck emptied the gun of its bullets and gave them to Toby, then broke the gun in two and handed the pieces to him as well.

"Thank your dad for me," Chuck told him.

Sarah confronted Chuck. "You could have killed her. She was just curious."

"I shot above her, to keep her from crossing to our side of the river."

Sarah pounced. "Our side? Both sides of the river are the wolves' side. The whole park is theirs." She aimed a finger at Chuck's chest. "Clarence is right. You're so old-school. First thing you do when you get a little scared is go for a gun." Her eyes burned into him. "You just had to bring your little girls along with you, didn't you? And now you're just like every other creature out here in the wild, willing to do anything to protect your young."

Chuck rocked back on his heels. Sarah's words stung—because she was right. He turned away and squinted across the river. Pinpricks of yellow glowed through the rain from the shadowed forest on the opposite slope. The wolves hadn't retreated far. He climbed the slick riverbank to Janelle. "Hanging in there?" he asked.

Her wet cheeks were crimson in the cool air, her hazel eyes bright with determination. "I know we signed up for this," she said. "But still."

The girls huddled beside her in their raincoats, water dripping from their hoods. Chuck took their hands and turned them toward camp. The rain slowed, then stopped, as they made their way through the woods.

Back at the cabin, Lex called for an all-teams meeting as soon as everyone changed into dry clothes.

Disquiet rippled through camp with the return of the group. The members of the Grizzly Initiative huddled around Sarah on one of their platforms as she filled them in. At the other end of tent row, Toby addressed the gathered wolfies. Between the two large teams, Randall and Kaifong visited on their platform with members of the geology and meteorology teams, while Keith squatted in front of his tent, checking Chance's paw pads for injury.

Chuck took in the view to the north from tent row. The clouds remained low and dark. The wind continued to slice across the valley. Thunder rumbled over the lake, a sea of shadowed gray.

Behind him, Carmelita and Rosie chattered in the tent, comparing the Stander wolves to their grandparents' Labrador retriever, as Janelle helped them out of their wet clothes. Rather than head for his own small tent, Clarence lingered beside Chuck.

He hung his head as he spoke, his voice low. "You're not paying me enough for this."

"The bear did what it was supposed to do. It stopped."

"It scared the crap out of me is what it did."

"Me, too."

"You were half a mile away." Clarence raised his head and looked into the distance. "It was so big. The smell of its breath, *Dios mio*, like something rotten. They look so sleek and clean in the pictures. But up close? Its legs were caked with mud. It had a big scar on its nose. A couple of claws were broken off its front paws. And its teeth? Like a T-Rex. When it roared, it was all I could do to keep from running."

"You sprayed your pepper spray along with everyone else. You did everything right—even if the wind screwed it up."

"Did you see the wound on the side of the dead wolf? Its ribs were snapped right in two."

"It definitely looks like the bear killed it. But the question is, why? They were hanging around together. It was like they were friends."

Clarence closed his eyes. "I'm not sure any grizzly has friends."

Lex came into sight around the corner of the mess tent. He spotted Chuck and hurried up the slope toward him, waving for him to descend.

"The satellite phone," Lex said when they met on the hillside. "Our link to the outside world."

"What about it?"

"It's gone."

32

Wat do you mean, gone?"

"It's not in the keg where it's supposed to be." The blue, plastic storage keg containing the satellite phone, emergency flares, and first aid kit sat beneath the eave at the front corner of the cabin for easy access in the event of an emergency, its list of contents facing out for all to see. "I popped the lid," Lex said. "It's not there. Just the other stuff—the med kit and extra flashlights and lanterns and all."

"Was it there when we arrived?"

"I never checked."

"Maybe Martha forgot to pack it."

"Martha? Are you kidding me?"

"Or somebody working for her forgot."

"Not the way she rides people."

"Meaning...?"

Lex hesitated, then said in a rush, "Meaning I'm sure someone took it."

"You really want me to believe—"

Lex lifted a hand. "I know, I know. Why would anyone do that? The answer is, I have no idea. But with all the strangeness going on around here..."

"At least we have our locator beacons."

"Which are of no use to us at this point. I simply want to get some information, see what people know about Stander Pack's movement, not scramble an emergency response team."

Chuck rubbed the stubble on his unshaved chin. Wind rattled the nylon walls of the tents on the platforms above him and whipped across the slope, cold and damp and biting. "Maybe somebody's got a girlfriend or boyfriend back in civilization they just had to talk to." He remembered Jorge's admission that the summer would be a long one for him.

"Everyone here knows how important the phone is to us."

"He or she may have just borrowed it, figuring to slip it back into the keg before anyone noticed."

Lex lifted his cap, enshrouded in a plastic cover, and ran his fingers through his silver hair, stringy in the aftermath of the rain. "Think I should announce it at the group meeting?"

"You don't have any choice." Chuck stamped his feet, wet and numb in his boots. The pounding sent shock waves up his legs. When he stopped, the vibrations continued.

He balanced on the soggy slope, the ground vibrating beneath the soles of his feet—another of the low-level earthquakes pulsing through the thin crust of the central plateau.

Lex crouched and pressed his hand to the ground as the vibrations subsided. "These are getting to be a pretty regular thing."

Chuck plucked a stalk of grass from the hillside. "Could the earthquakes be messing with the animals somehow?"

"I can't speak for the wolves and grizzlies," Lex said, "but the tremors sure have got *me* on edge."

Chuck forced a chuckle. "Maybe the lake's getting ready to switch oceans again, and the critters know it." He bit down on the grass stem, the taste tart and vinegary in his mouth. "Hell," he said. He moved the stem to the side of his mouth. "I mean, heck, it's only a couple of miles and fifty feet of vertical gain from the west shore of the lake to the Continental Divide. Wouldn't take much to send the whole thing sluicing out of the mountains and across northern Utah."

"All I know is, the world's getting way too complicated, even out here in what's supposed to be the middle of nowhere." Lex checked his watch. "Almost three o'clock. How about you go one way along the tents and gather everybody while I go the other?"

Ten minutes later, Lex climbed atop the weathered picnic table in front of the cabin. The scientists, grouped in front of him, quieted. Lex filled them in on the missing satellite phone.

"I don't care who did it," he said. "I just need it returned." His eyes roamed the crowd. "Anyone?"

No one responded—including Jorge, Chuck noted.

"I'd like for every one of you to go back to your tents and check your things. If one of you happens to 'stumble across' the phone—" Lex made air quotes with his fingers "—you can bring it to me with no questions asked, or leave it out in the open where it'll be found."

Upon their dismissal, the researchers angled up the slope to their platforms. Most climbed into their tents, out of the cold. Chuck worked with Clarence, tying additional guy lines to their two tents to stabilize them against the gusting wind. When he finished, he headed back down the hill to the mess tent, where Janelle and the girls were holed up. Lex and Keith approached him before he entered the tent. Lex was empty-handed.

"I take it the phone hasn't shown up yet," Chuck said.

"No. But Keith has an idea."

"If someone took the sat phone for their personal use," Keith said, "they'd have gotten away from camp to use it where no one would hear them. I'm betting they left it behind in the trees somewhere. Probably planned to return it after dark, when no one would see them."

Chuck pursed his lips and nodded. "That would make sense. They couldn't have known Lex would want the phone this afternoon."

"They figured they had plenty of time—and if I'm right, they'll have left a scent trail."

"Keith thinks Chance can find the trail for us," Lex said.

"The rain won't have helped," Keith added, "but I figure it's worth a shot. It'll take an hour, tops, to loop around camp."

"I like it," Chuck said.

Lex said to him, "I want you to tag along."

"Lex doesn't trust me," Keith said with a smile.

"I don't trust anyone right now," the ranger pointed out. "But the fact is, two heads are always better than one. And in your case, Chuck, you're probably as good at finding things on your own as Keith is with Chance."

"I'm not so sure about that," Chuck said. He turned to Keith. "Give me a couple of minutes."

His family sat at one of the tables in the front half of the mess tent. The aroma of sautéed onions and red chili filled the tent. The girls sipped hot chocolate between bites from enormous oatmeal cookies.

Janelle conversed in rapid-fire Spanish with Jorge, who stood at the far end of the table. She turned to Chuck. "Jorge thinks Lex is right: somebody took the phone. He's sure they'll give it back."

Jorge turned to stir huge pots bubbling on the stove. Chuck studied the man's back. Why was the cook so sure Lex's theory was correct?

Chuck explained Keith's idea of the perimeter search and Lex's request that Chuck go along. As he talked, her lips drew tighter together.

"I'm coming, too," she said. There was no give in her eyes. "Bears attack ones or twos, not threes."

"We'll be right at the edge of camp, and I'll have the .357 with me." He gave the bottom of his daypack a tap.

"So much the better for me to join you, then. The girls will be fine here with Clarence. You said it'll only take an hour."

"How about if Clarence comes along instead?"

"I want to come for my own sake as much as anything else. We only have a few days out here. I want to see everything I can."

"We'll be back in the trees. It'll be wet and muddy. There won't be much to see."

"Everything out here is new to me—the moss on the tree trunks, the ferns, the mushrooms poking out of the ground."

Chuck smiled. This was the Janelle he'd fallen for two years ago. He reached out and touched her shoulder. "It'll be great to have you along, *cariña*."

They left the girls with Clarence and met Keith and Chance where the trail climbed past the east end of tent row. A thick grove of lodgepole pines rose beyond the trail.

"The trees are closest to camp here," Keith said. "I figure this is where anyone who took the phone would've headed."

Chance, tail wagging, led them into the forest. A hundred feet into the trees, Keith turned so they moved through the woods parallel to the path.

"Logic says whoever took the phone hiked up the trail away from camp, then veered into the trees once they were over the hill and out of sight," Keith said as Chance tugged him forward. "If we'd have headed up the path first, Chance couldn't have teased out the scent at the departure point from among all the other trail users. But by working our way alongside the path back here in the trees, we'll cut the scent of anyone who came this way."

A patch of low sky, gun-metal gray, showed through a break in the forest canopy. A blast of wind whipped the tops of the trees, sending heavy drops of water, clinging to the branches since the rainstorm, cascading to the forest floor. Chuck hunched his shoulders against the cold as he walked, but Janelle looked as if she were out for a stroll along the paved river trail back home in Durango, her shoulders back and arms loose, the hood of her rain jacket down, her black hair glistening with fallen drops.

Chance pivoted ninety degrees and leaned hard into the leash. Keith clicked a button on the retractable lead, allowing Chance to shoot twenty feet ahead, the nylon cord unspooling with a high-pitched zing from the reel.

"Got something." Keith retracted the lead in arm's lengths until he again stood just behind Chance.

"Human?" Chuck asked.

"Can't say for sure. Something big, though. Chance's excitement level tells me that much."

Keith locked the shortened leash with a click. Chance strained forward, collar taut.

"Cripes," Keith said as Chance pressed ahead, deeper into the forest. "It's almost like he's on a blood scent."

33

Chuck followed Janelle and Keith through the trees as Chance pressed ahead. The dog's paws tore into the duff on the forest floor, sending pine needles flying. The smell of must and decay rose from the ground into the damp air.

Peering ahead, Chuck spotted something glinting in the weak afternoon light.

"Ka-ching," Keith declared.

Chance came upon the rectangular storage case for the satellite phone. The black plastic case, lined with gray foam rubber, lay open on the ground, empty. White plastic shards littered the forest floor beyond the case. A fist-sized rock rested among the plastic pieces.

"The phone," Keith said, disbelief in his voice. "Somebody smashed it to bits."

Chance sniffed at the case and phone shards, then looked deeper into the forest. The dog stood in place, trembling. It lowered its head and keened, the mournful sound almost human.

The trunks of trees and the needle-carpeted forest floor stretched as far ahead as Chuck could see.

Keith used the shortened lead to urge Chance forward, but the dog cowered, refusing to move.

"What do you smell, boy?" Keith asked. "What is it?"

He took hold of Chance by the scruff of the dog's neck and tugged the animal past the phone shards. Chance straightened at Keith's side.

"Are you ready now, boy?" Keith asked.

Chance answered with a short, sharp bark.

Keith cursed. "It's a blood trail, all right."

Chuck studied the floor of the forest. "I don't see anything."

"It's an air scent. That's what Chance's bark means. Straight ahead."

Keith moved beyond the smashed phone, his steps deliberate. Chance advanced with him, pressed to his leg.

Chuck considered digging the .357 from his pack, but there was nothing yet to see—or aim at.

Keith and Chance made their way through the trees, Janelle and Chuck trailing behind. No one spoke. Chance panted, no longer sniffing.

"There!" Keith exclaimed, his voice shaking.

Fifty feet away, a human body lay crumpled at the base of a lodgepole pine. The body, twisted and unmoving, wore brown work jeans and an insulated jacket in a camouflage print.

Sarah.

Part Three

"Where we are, there are no wolves;
where the wolf lives, there is wilderness."

— Ecological biologist Daniel Botkin

34

Chuck ran toward the body. He stumbled over the knuckle of a root protruding from the ground, caught himself, and kept running, dodging trees, his breaths coming in harsh gasps, until he fell to his knees beside Sarah's still form.

She lay on her back in the shadowed forest, her torso wrapped around the trunk of the tree, her arms and legs askew. Blotches of blood, the color of dark cherry in the shadowed forest, soaked through her jacket. Numerous cuts slashed the jacket's camo-print exterior, revealing a puffy white layer of insulation, stained with blood in several places. Sarah's bare head was flung back, her eyes open but unseeing.

Chuck knew in an instant Sarah was dead—her face was ashen, her eyes collapsed into their sockets, her lips drained of color—but he threw himself into action nonetheless, anything, anything to keep from acknowledging the horrible truth before him. He unzipped Sarah's jacket. A number of knife wounds—more than a dozen at first glance—had gone through her jacket and torso-hugging T-shirt. Some of the wounds slashed diagonally across Sarah's body, flaying open her ribcage. Others were stab wounds straight into her chest cavity. It was obvious from the severity of the stabs and slashes that Sarah had not suffered long after sustaining her injuries.

Janelle fell to her knees beside Sarah. Chuck cupped the back of Sarah's neck and lifted, clearing her air passage. Already, however, her neck was stiff with death. A whiff escaped Sarah's lips, the result of the opening of her throat, but that was all.

Chuck looked across Sarah's motionless body at Janelle. "She's gone. There's nothing we can do for her."

His stomach lurched. He put the back of his hand to his mouth, fighting the urge to vomit. Little more than an hour ago, Sarah had stood with everyone in camp, listening as Lex spoke in front of the cabin.

The skin at the back of his neck tingled. He spun on his knees, scanning the surrounding forest. Was Sarah's murderer watching?

He looked up at Keith, who stood at Sarah's feet, staring. Chance quivered at his side.

"Can Chance follow the trail of whoever did this?" Chuck asked.

Keith lowered his hand to the dog's head. His face crumpled. "No," he managed, his voice hoarse. "The blood will have overwhelmed Chance's olfactory system. Besides, whoever did this is sure to have gone back the way they came."

"You mean, to camp?"

Keith nodded. "They wouldn't have gone deeper into the forest."

"You don't think an outsider could have done this?" Chuck asked, even though he knew the answer.

"Some crazy person who happened to be waiting in the woods, miles from anywhere, just when Sarah wandered out here with the phone?"

Chuck sank back on his heels and closed his eyes. Tears pressed at his eyelids. "I know. You're right." He blinked, freeing the tears, and gazed at Sarah's pale face.

He forced himself to accept the truth. Someone from camp had killed Sarah, and her killing must have had something to do with the satellite phone.

Janelle's eyes went to the woods around them. "We should go."

Chuck worked his arms beneath Sarah and straightened, lifting her to his chest. Crime scene be damned; he wasn't about to leave her body alone here in the woods. He held her tight and turned a slow circle, taking in the site of Sarah's murder without any idea what he was looking for. No bloody knife lay on the forest floor. Nothing.

They paused on their way back through the trees long enough for Janelle to pile pieces of the satellite phone into the plastic case and snap it shut. She trudged on through the woods, case in hand. Chuck followed, Sarah's body heavy in his arms. Keith and Chance brought up the rear.

When they approached the edge of the grove, Janelle turned and headed down the slope past tent row while remaining well back in the trees and out of sight of camp.

"Best not to set off a panic," she said over her shoulder to Chuck and Keith.

"For as long as we can, anyway," Chuck agreed.

They left the forest at the bottom of the slope, below the latrines, and made a beeline for the cabin. A misty fog swept low across the valley floor, obscuring their movements from those on the tent platforms above. No one stepped out of the mess tent as they hurried past. Janelle opened the cabin door without knocking and stepped aside, ushering Chuck past her. He edged sideways through the doorway, holding Sarah's body.

A long, wooden table surrounded by chairs took up the center of the cabin's single room. Built-in benches topped with foam pads lined the log walls, providing couch-like seating by day and dorm-style sleeping at night. At the sight of Chuck with Sarah in his arms, Lex and Toby shot to their feet from where they were seated at the center table, their ladder-back chairs scraping the scarred, plank floor.

Lex swept notepads, crumb-speckled plates, coffee mugs, Toby's laptop computer, and a squat LED table lantern to the far end of the table. The light of the lantern and the feeble illumination through the room's sole window in the cabin's west wall created a subdued glow. A fire, burned down to coals, cast heat into the room from a stone fireplace set in the back wall. Wooden pegs lined the chinked logs above the benches, serving as hanging storage for an assortment of fleece coats, rain jackets, and daypacks. The combined odor of wet nylon, sweat, and woodsmoke was strong in the confined space.

Chuck laid Sarah's body on the table as Keith entered the cabin with Chance. Janelle closed the door behind them.

Lex put a hand to his mouth. "Dear God."

Chuck eased Sarah's eyes closed with his thumb and forefinger. He straightened her arms at her sides, his movements gentle.

Lex reached to touch Sarah's hand. "She's...she's...?"

"Yes," Chuck said. The sound of his voice surprised him. "She was in the forest. Chance found her...Keith...the phone..."

Toby clasped his hands together. Tears built in his eyes and rolled down his cheeks into his mustache. "Sarah!" he cried, his voice breaking, his gaze fixed on Sarah's face.

The tip of her tongue showed between slightly parted lips. Her mohawk fell to one side and her earrings glinted dully in the dim light.

Lex grasped the personal locator beacon hanging from a zipper tab at the back of Chuck's daypack and pressed and held the button at the beacon's base.

"Oh," Chuck said. "Right." The thought of the beacons hadn't even occurred to him.

During the seconds required for the light next to the button to activate, Lex gulped repeatedly, battling for each breath.

The instant the beacon lit, he spun to the wall of the cabin and pressed and held the buttons, in turn, of the emergency beacons attached to his and Toby's daypacks, hanging on the wooden pegs above the benches, until their tiny LED lights glowed red, too.

"What?" Lex demanded. "How?"

Chuck explained in fits and starts—their passage through the woods, the discovery of the phone in pieces, Sarah's body at the base of the tree. He described their return to the cabin under the cover of the mist and gathering darkness.

"Whoever did this had to have seen you. They'd have been watching for you," Lex said, his voice grim. "Help will be here soon. We'll evacuate the camp. Everyone will be questioned."

"I'm not sure how soon help will be able to get here," Chuck said. He looked out the window at the wind-whipped fog racing across the meadow. "Helicopters won't be able to fly in this, and the wind and darkness are likely to keep boats off the lake, too, maybe until morning. They'll come as soon as they can—at daylight, for sure—but they won't risk the lives of responders in bad weather for what, as far as they know, may be nothing more than a sprained ankle."

"I activated three beacons. We could activate more."

"They'll be freaking out all right. But I still think we have to plan on no one making it here before dawn."

Lex looked at Sarah's body. "She was so much like my Lucy, our Lucy." He shook his head, his cheeks wobbling. "When Joe and Rebecca were killed, it tore Jessie up. She kept seeing Carson and Lucy in those two. She couldn't get it out of her mind, even when the kids were home for Christmas. Everything should have been fine—we were all healthy, happy—but it wasn't. It was like there was a shadow over us. And then, a month later, the cancer came."

He drew a halting breath and pressed a finger to the base of his nose. A single tear dangled at the corner of one eye.

"She said she'd felt it for months, that she should have done something. But the doctors said there was no way she could have known. And of course, at that point, what could they do? Poison her with chemo. Burn her up with radiation. All for just another year. But she took it. She took it all. Those last weeks with Carson and Lucy, she made them count. She never once let them see how much she hurt."

He squeezed his eyes shut. The tear rolled down his cheek and fell to the floor, making a dark spot on the wood. He opened his eyes, taking in Sarah on the table before him. "This attack may have been personal." He looked across the room at Janelle. "Your brother, wasn't he...?"

Janelle's eyes flashed. "Yes, he was. But he was in camp with Chuck between the time you spoke with everyone and when we found—" She stopped, licked her lips, began again. "Chuck and I left him with the girls when we—" A yelp escaped her. "The girls," she said, fear rising in her eyes. She whirled for the door.

"Wait," Lex said. "Please."

She turned to him, her fingers on the handle. "I'm going to bring them here," she said, her voice firm. "I want them inside. They will be inside, with me, until help comes."

"All right," Lex said. "Understood. But we shouldn't scare them. I don't want to scare anyone." His eyes went back to Sarah. "Most of all, I don't want to scare whoever did this to her." He looked around the room. "Everyone got that? We'll be like Jessie. We'll be strong. Together."

Toby clung to the edge of the table, bent over Sarah's body. Chuck caught Lex's eye, then directed his gaze at the folding knife belted to the waist of Sarah's ex.

Toby glanced up, catching Chuck's look. "I've been here, in

the cabin, the whole time since the meeting." He looked at Lex. "Haven't I?"

Lex nodded.

Chuck stared at Sarah. To his surprise, he found that the killing itself didn't shock him as much as he'd have expected, coming as it did on the heels of everything else—the appearance at camp of the grizzly and wolf, the arrival of the wolf pack in the valley, the destruction of the satellite phone—almost as if Sarah's murder was part of a pattern he couldn't quite recognize.

"We have to play for time," Lex said. "We don't want anyone else to get hurt."

"We can't take people's knives away from them," Chuck said. "That would set everyone off. But we do need to gather everyone together. Sarah was alone; we don't want anyone else to end up in the same situation."

Lex squeezed his hands together, his fingers intertwined. "Sarah," he murmured.

"We'll put her in a sleeping bag," Chuck told him. "We'll tell the girls she's asleep, that she's not feeling well."

"We'll have to tell Clarence," Janelle said. "He'll ask. He'll demand to know."

She waited until Lex met her gaze.

"Okay," he said, his mouth sagging, his voice weary.

She left the cabin, pulling the door tight behind her.

"Keith," Chuck said. "I want you at the door. No one else is to come in."

While Keith manned the doorway, Chuck pulled a sleeping bag from beneath one of the benches and slid it from its stuff sack. Toby, choking back sobs, helped Chuck slip the nylon bag up Sarah's body.

As Chuck zipped the sleeping bag to Sarah's chin and lifted her body in his arms, he remembered the story about a member of a friend's team of rafters, floating the Colorado River through the Grand Canyon, who had drowned in notorious Crystal Rapid.

"It was awful," Chuck's friend told him. "We were in shock, all of us. We'd just lost one of our best buddies. He'd died right before our eyes. But it was amazing how we kept right on functioning—calling in the rescue helicopter, clearing a landing site, preparing his body for retrieval. The worst thing in the world had just happened, but life kept right on going—we kept right on going—because, really, what other choice was there?"

Chuck held Sarah to him. He bit his lower lip until he tasted blood. The other choice, in this case, was to find out who had murdered Sarah so as to assure her attacker did not kill again, and to assure Sarah the justice she deserved.

He settled Sarah's body on the padded bench against the shadowed east wall of the room, away from the window. He tucked the hood of the sleeping bag around her head and turned her face to the wall. Blood no longer seeped from her wounds, leaving the outside of the sleeping bag clean and unstained, and leaving Sarah looking for all the world as if she were merely asleep.

Methodically, Chuck took the phone case from where Janelle had left it on the floor of the cabin and opened it on the table. "I don't think Sarah's death was the result of a lover's quarrel."

Lex peered at the smashed phone.

"I think," Chuck said, "she stumbled across something she shouldn't have."

Lex slid his hand beneath a red bandana lying open on the tabletop amid the items he'd shoved to the table's end. "I don't think we were meant to stumble across this, either."

He held out the bandana, its corners draped over his hand.

35

A sliver of black plastic rested in the center of the cloth in Lex's palm. "Toby found it," he said. He plucked the thin, rectangular object, no larger than a communion wafer, from the folds of the bandana and held it close to the lantern. Metal lines etched the surface of the plastic. "It was in the dead wolf. It's some kind of computer chip."

Chuck's brow furrowed. "A chip?"

"I'm as confused as you are. We all are."

"It was in 217's neck," Toby said, his voice scratchy and weak. "Under the skin, above where a tracking collar would have been."

"But 217 didn't have a collar," Chuck said.

"Or any signs of ever having been fitted with one—no rub marks, no callouses." Tears continued to well in Toby's eyes, but they no longer coursed down his cheeks. "I felt a lump when I ran my hand down 217's body. The chip was encased in scar tissue."

"Which means it had been there a while."

"At least a year, I'd guess. Maybe longer."

"Could it have been there its whole life?" Chuck turned to Lex. "Was this wolf raised in captivity?"

"No," Lex said. "Every wolf in the park was born in the wild."

"What about a past research project involving chip implantation?"

"There's never been any such study that I'm aware of."

"But lots of the wolves have collars."

"Sure. That's a big part of the Wolf Initiative—dart individuals in each pack, affix the collars, and track where they go. But not computer chips."

"Someone could have stuck it in the wolf while it was darted and asleep."

"That's possible, I suppose. But why would someone do that? Besides, there's a whole bunch of people on hand when wolves are collared. The idea of someone sticking a chip into a wolf without anyone else noticing? Impossible. Anyway, like Toby said, there's no sign the wolf was ever darted and collared in the first place."

"What are you thinking at this point?"

Lex took a deep breath. "I'm thinking the chip doesn't really matter. Not anymore. The phone doesn't matter, either. None of it matters, not with what's just happened." He exhaled, his cheeks sunken. "I just want to get out of here. All of us. Get everyone back to civilization and let the investigators do their work."

"That's what we all want," Chuck said. "But we're not there. Not yet. There's a killer, a murderer, right here in camp. Are they planning to try to bluff their way through the investigation team's questioning? Who knows. I'm convinced Sarah's death had something to do with the smashed phone. Whatever that something is hasn't gone anywhere—which means we have to stay on guard."

Lex looked as if he'd aged ten years in the past few minutes, but he straightened and looked Chuck in the eye. "Okay," he said. "I'm with you."

The door to the cabin burst open. Clarence rushed inside. He scanned the room until he saw Sarah. He went to her and draped himself over her body, his head pressed to hers.

"*Dios mio*," he wailed, his cry muffled by the sleeping bag. "Sarah! *Jesucristo.*"

He lifted her upper body from the bench and rocked her in his arms. After a minute, spent and sniffling, he lowered her to the bench.

"Janelle said..." he began. He stared at Sarah's wan face, encircled by the collar of the sleeping bag. "Janelle said..." He drew a tortured breath and ran a forearm across his face.

A quiet knock sounded on the door. Clarence jerked. He turned Sarah's face to the wall and stepped back just as Janelle entered the room with Carmelita and Rosie.

Chuck expelled a sharp breath. He hadn't realized how nervous he'd been since Janelle had departed from the cabin on her own to retrieve the girls.

Taking Carmelita and Rosie by the hand, Clarence ushered them to the bench at the back of the room next to the small fireplace. Janelle pointed to Sarah and put a finger to her lips. "You know to be quiet, right?" she told the girls.

They nodded as they climbed onto the bench and sat with their backs to the log wall, their booted feet hanging off the edge of the foam pad.

Rosie eyed Chance. "Can we pet the doggie?" she asked in a loud whisper.

"Of course," Keith told her, his voice hollow.

He reached for the clip that attached the leash to Chance's collar. Before he detached it, a chorus of wolf howls echoed through the cabin.

36

"Good," Chuck said. "They've crossed the river."

Lex gawked at him. "What do you mean, 'good'?"

"That's what we need."

"I don't see—"

"We're holding out until the response team gets here." When the girls leaned forward, listening, Chuck chose his words with care. "In the meantime, we want everyone together so no one can do anything bad to each other. The wolves are our excuse."

Lex looked out the cabin's rain-spattered window. Chuck followed Lex's gaze. The patch of western sky framed in the window was growing darker with each passing minute.

More howls sounded, their proximity indicating the wolves were in the woods below the cabin.

"*Lex*," Chuck urged.

Lex turned to Clarence and Toby. "Would you two head up to tent row? I want everyone down here at the cabin and mess tent. We'll do a head count, make sure we're all together before nightfall."

Chuck followed Clarence and Toby outside. "Don't make any waves," he said. "Keep everyone calm. Sarah's killer could be any one of us. We've all got knives." He tapped his own all-purpose blade, sheathed and belted at his waist beside his canister of bear spray. "Whoever it is will be laying low. We want to keep it that way until we can get everyone out of here."

Toby headed up the hill to tent row with Clarence. Chuck still wasn't certain of the wolf researcher's innocence, but he was sure of Clarence's ability to look after himself in the public setting of the camp.

Lex joined Chuck outside.

"I think," Chuck told him, "you should keep everyone together at the cabin and mess tent until help gets here."

"Agreed." Lex's face was a hard mask. "Keep your friends close, and your enemies closer."

Chuck looked across the meadow. The grass sloped gently away to the north and west. The pines at the foot of the clearing stood tall. "I never should have brought Janelle and the girls out here."

"Don't say that," Lex said. "You're conflating, as Jessie would have said. This is murder. We're dealing with it. We *will* deal with it. But it has nothing to do with your bringing your family out here—on my okay." His voice was strong, assured. "If I've learned anything from losing Jessie, it's that life happens so fast you can't even believe it, like a meteor. It flares, it's terrific, it's gone." He looked Chuck in the eye. "You were right to want to bring them here, and you were right to bring them."

He gripped Chuck's elbow. "I've been watching you. You're a good dad. You're going to make a great father. Your wife and girls are indoors. They're safe." He let go of Chuck's arm. "We just have to keep everyone else safe until the emergency team gets here."

Chuck nodded. "We can post people on all four sides, set up all the extra lights we have around the cabin and mess tent."

"There's no way the wolves will attack."

"It's not about that. It's about keeping everyone occupied and safe, in one place."

"We just have to make it till morning."

The two men watched Toby and Clarence work their way along tent row. The researchers left their tents and gathered on their platforms, zipping rain jackets and shouldering packs.

A single wolf howl rose from the forest below the cabin.

Chuck turned with Lex, scanning the wall of trees at the bottom of the meadow. The wolves were back there in the forest somewhere, out of sight. But why were they here at all?

The howl hung in the air like the high note of a stringed instrument before dissolving into a series of high-pitched yips. Chuck tensed when a deep growl reverberated across the clearing like a bass drum.

"That's a grizzly," he said. "It's with the wolves."

Lex faced the forest, his back stiff. "What the hell is going on out there?"

Chuck studied the sky, dense with clouds. He checked his watch. An hour until full dark.

More than enough time to see about answering Lex's question.

37

The drone," Chuck said to Lex.

"No. It's too much. We just need to make it through the night."

"It'll help keep everyone engaged, focused."

Lex studied the darkening sky. "Okay," he said. "Think there's enough daylight?"

"If we hurry."

Lex turned to the closed cabin door. The bags of wrinkled flesh beneath his eyes were dark half-moons. "I'm sorry," he said, and Chuck realized he was addressing Sarah's body, inside the cabin. "I never thought...I couldn't have imagined..."

Chuck put a hand on Lex's shoulder, wanting to give him strength, to return the favor Lex had paid him a moment ago. "The superintendent will put the park's investigative team on this. They'll work with the FBI and whoever else to find her killer. That's their job."

He turned Lex away from the cabin, back to the mist-shrouded meadow. "Keep it simple when everyone gets here. No details. I'll go find Kaifong and Randall."

Chuck passed the mess tent and angled up the slope. He studied the scientists making their way down the hill in the gathering gloom but failed to spot either of the Drone Team members. On its platform in the middle of tent row, the Drone Team's large, red tent glowed with light from within.

"Randall?" Chuck called as he approached. "Kaifong?" Nothing. He climbed onto the platform and batted the nylon wall of the tent with the flat of his hand.

Randall unzipped the front entrance. He removed ear buds strung to a music player in his palm as he stepped out. He looked past Chuck at the researchers gathering in front of the cabin and his eyes grew wide.

"You don't know what's going on?" Chuck asked.

"Sorry." Randall lifted the music player. "Violent Femmes. Sickest retro on the planet."

"You didn't hear the wolves?"

He shook his head. "No, man."

"They've crossed the river. They're approaching camp. Sounds like they might have a bear with them."

Randall took a quick breath. "A grizzly?"

"Lex and I are thinking you and Kaifong might be able to answer that question for us. We're wondering if you could do a flyover, see if you can make out anything."

Randall faced the strong breeze coursing across the hillside from the west. "Windspeed's cranking, but manageable." He turned to Chuck. "You got it. I'll load up."

"Where's Kaifong?"

Randall pointed at the three dozen scientists forming a half-circle around Lex in front of the cabin. "Down there, I guess. She was hanging with the wolfies the last I saw of her." He turned to the tent. "I'll be just a sec."

"Need any help?"

"Nah," he said as he ducked inside. "I can get it all, no prob."

Lex finished addressing the group as Chuck returned to the bottom of the hill. The researchers headed for the storage kegs lined between the cabin and mess tent, their faces set.

"I told them Sarah's sick," Lex said to Chuck as Randall approached with the drone in its frame on his pack. "I said we were caring for her in the cabin, that help wouldn't get here until morning, and that no one was to bother her in the meantime."

"All ready to rock and roll," Randall announced.

"Still no sign of Kaifong?" Chuck asked.

"She's not down here?"

Chuck aimed a questioning look at Lex, who shook his head.

Around them, the scientists hung LED lanterns, taken from the storage kegs, on hiking poles driven into the muddy ground.

"Do me a favor?" Chuck called to Clarence, who worked with Toby to fasten one of the lanterns to a pole in front of the mess tent.

"*Sí, jefe.*" Clarence's voice was subdued, but his gaze was resolute.

"We're not sure where Kaifong's gone off to. Would you and Toby track her down?" Chuck clenched his jaw. Surely, Sarah's killer hadn't struck again, not this quickly, and not in such a crowd.

"We'll find her," Clarence said.

He and Toby set off while Randall went ahead of Chuck and Lex to the west side of the cabin.

Chuck peered at the fog filtering through the trees at the foot of the meadow. No more howls or growls came from the woods. Had the grizzly and Stander Pack really teamed up? The fact that the grizzly and the single wolf, Number 217, had traveled across the valley away from camp together was unlikely enough. The idea that the entire pack of wolves had forged some sort of alliance with the same grizzly, particularly after 217's death, was unfathomable. But so was Sarah's murder.

Chuck shuddered at the realization that Sarah's killer still lurked among the researchers. Lex had assured him Janelle and the girls were safe in the cabin, where they were alone with Keith.

It was Keith who'd led the search that resulted in finding Sarah's body. That meant he couldn't be the killer—could he?

215

Chuck put the side of his hand to the cabin's window and looked inside. Keith stood with his back to the closed door. The girls squatted on the floor in front of the fireplace with Chance resting between them. Janelle sat on the rear bench above the girls, speaking with Keith.

Chuck exhaled. Janelle and the girls were fine. But where was Kaifong?

He turned to Lex. "She wasn't there when you spoke with everyone?"

"Kaifong?" Lex shook his head. "When we counted off, only she and Randall were missing. But I saw the light in their tent, up on their platform. I figured they were on their way."

"She *was* at our tent, up until just a bit ago," Randall said. "She's around. Clarence and Toby will find her." He glanced at the dusky sky. "If we're going to do this, though, we'd better get airborne, like, right now."

He handed the drone to Chuck and retrieved the tablet computer from his backpack. He held the tablet out to Lex. "I'll need you to hold that up for me until Kaifong gets here."

Lex took the computer. Randall freed the control console from the holster at his waist and pressed a switch. The four rotors kicked in. He nudged the console's left toggle forward. The rotors spun faster. The craft trembled in place before lifting from Chuck's hands and rising into the cloud-covered sky with a loud whine.

Randall looked from the hovering drone to the view of the cabin and meadow streaming on the tablet screen. He thumbed the right toggle forward and watched the drone zoom across the open field, the whine of the rotors dying away.

When the drone was a black speck against the clouds, Randall eyed the computer screen, where the view of the meadow disappeared, replaced by treetops.

Chuck pointed at the video feed. The tops of the trees passing beneath the drone looked as if they were only inches from the hanging camera. "Make sure you stay—"

"We're golden," Randall said before Chuck could finish. "The wide-angle lens makes the trees look way closer than they are." The drone slowed as Randall worked the controls. "Okay," he said to Lex, "what is it you want me to do?"

Lex looked from the tablet propped in his hands to Chuck, who said, "We should check nearby meadows, see if we can catch sight of anything. You said animals will come into the open sometimes when they hear the drone, out of curiosity."

Lex said, "Maybe the wolves will—"

"Wait," Randall broke in, his eyes locked on the computer screen. "Did you see that?"

Chuck stared at the tablet. "See what?"

"Movement, I think."

The tablet showed a tight clearing in the forest. Randall nudged the console's toggles with his thumbs. The drone descended into the shadowy opening. The scene on the tablet grew grainy in the reduced light below the treetops. The drone came to a halt, hovering a few feet off the ground. A phalanx of tree trunks and pine branches surrounded the clearing.

Something moved at the base of a tree.

The camera continued to focus on the gray trunks of the trees and the green of the tree branches spreading above.

Seconds passed. Had he imagined it? The drone hovered. The camera streamed the unchanging scene. A burst of light gray entered the video feed, moving fast, straight toward the camera.

Randall nudged the controls. The drone climbed. On the computer screen, a wolf flung itself at the rising copter. Its mouth snapped shut as it disappeared from view beneath the dangling camera.

"That was close," Randall said.

The drone circled as it climbed, the camera capturing a panning scene of tree trunks and branches and something else, barely visible at the edge of the shadowed clearing, dark on top, lighter below.

Randall leaned toward the tablet as he worked the controls on the console. The copter and camera plunged back toward the ground.

Chuck's heart leapt into his throat. On the tablet screen, the object grew in size and grainy focus until it became a person dressed in a navy jacket and khaki slacks, bound to a tree trunk by loops of rope, mouth gagged, head slumped forward.

38

The tablet shook in Lex's hands. "That's...that's..."

"Kaifong!" Randall cried, staring at the screen.

Chuck pointed across the meadow to the west, where the drone had disappeared above the treetops. "She's there." He grabbed Lex by the arm, tugging him toward the meadow. "Let's go."

"I'm coming, too," Randall declared.

"No," Chuck said.

"It's Kaifong!" Randall pleaded.

"Chuck's right," Lex told him. "We need you to stay here and fly the drone to keep tabs on her. You can use it to fend off any wolves. Its noise will help guide us when we get close."

Clarence and Toby appeared around the corner of the cabin.

"We couldn't find—" Clarence began.

Chuck cut him off. "We need your help."

Clarence and Toby stared at the scene on the tablet, their mouths falling open.

"Lex and I are going after her," Chuck said. "She's not alone. A wolf almost took down the drone."

Toby pressed forward. "A wolf? I'm coming with you."

"Good," Lex said. "That'll make three of us."

He handed the tablet to Clarence, who raised it in front of Randall with shaking hands. An orange light flashed in the screen's lower corner.

"That means we only have ten minutes of battery power left," Randall said. He looked at the leaden sky. "About the same amount of flying time before full dark."

Chuck hurried across the meadow behind Toby and Lex. Toby's knife bounced against his hip. At the edge of the forest, Chuck slowed and swung his pack around to his chest. He dug inside until his fingers wrapped around the .357. While Toby and Lex strode into the woods, he unlocked the trigger guard with the small key stored in his wallet, then racked a round into the chamber from the gun's magazine. He checked the safety and shoved the pistol into his waistband at the small of his back before setting off once more, catching up as Lex picked a path around downed trees and pools of water ahead of Toby.

"Faster," Toby insisted.

"We're almost there," Lex replied between heavy breaths. "We can't run; I don't want to trigger any attack responses, even with the three of us."

The tall trees allowed little of the waning evening light to reach the ground. Chuck struggled to see what lay ahead. He sensed something behind him and spun, yanking the .357 from his belt and brandishing it at the shadowed forest behind him.

Silence. No signs of movement.

He replaced the gun at his back, chiding himself.

Brighter light showed between the trunks of trees—the clearing. He hurried forward, nearly tripping on Toby's heels. The drone whined out of sight ahead. The forest grew lighter, the whine of the copter blades louder.

Lex broke from the trees in front of Toby and Chuck and crossed the small opening, passing beneath the hovering drone to Kaifong. Unsheathing his knife, he slashed at the ropes binding her to the base of the tree. Toby went to her and freed the length of rope gagging her mouth and knotted at the back of her neck. Chuck turned a slow pirouette in the center of the clearing. The fetid smell of wet fur blew past him from somewhere in the trees; the wolves—and, perhaps, the grizzly—were nearby.

Chuck gave a thumbs up to the drone hovering overhead, the camera facing his direction. The copter rose into the air with a noisy whine and sped east above the treetops toward camp.

Toby held Kaifong in his arms, her head resting on his shoulder. The loops of rope, which Chuck recognized as multi-purpose line from the camp's store of supplies, fell away from her body as Lex worked at the back of the tree. She collapsed forward against Toby with a half-cry, half-sob. Lex cut the last of the cord at her ankles, freeing her from the tree. Toby clutched her to his chest. Her head fell back. Her eyes remained closed.

A canine-like snarl sounded behind them, from the section of forest through which they'd just passed. A second snarl followed, this one from the forest in the opposite direction, beyond the tree to which Kaifong had been tied.

Toby propped Kaifong in his arms. Lex entered the clearing, his eyes darting. Chuck pulled the .357 from his waistband. He held the pistol in both hands, barrel pointed at the ground. A pair of glowing yellow eyes shone from the trees beyond Toby and Kaifong. As Chuck watched, a second pair of eyes appeared, unblinking, alongside the first.

Chuck stepped past Toby and Lex and aimed the .357 at the wolves. The creatures were more than thirty yards away, too distant for an accurate shot with the handgun. He considered assembling the far more accurate rifle from Toby's pack, but rejected the idea as too time consuming.

The wolves held their distance. Chuck turned toward camp, pointing with the barrel of the .357. "Let's go."

"There was a growl that way, too," Toby said.

"It'll fall back," Chuck replied, summoning assurance he didn't feel. "If it doesn't..." He lifted the pistol.

Knife in hand, Lex took long strides through the opening and back into the forest. Toby draped Kaifong over his shoulder and crossed the clearing behind Lex.

Chuck looked back. A third pair of eyes glowed alongside the first two. He edged across the clearing, gun raised, and entered the trees behind Lex and Toby.

The forest stretched at least three hundred yards from the clearing to the foot of the meadow below the cabin. Chuck covered Lex, Toby, and Kaifong from the rear with the pistol as they headed for camp. Twenty yards into the woods, he turned to see three forms, just visible between intervening trees, trotting across the clearing toward them. He hurried on. Lex and Toby, with Kaifong over his shoulder, moved steadily through the forest. In the gathering darkness, Chuck stumbled on the uneven ground, righted himself, and made his way around a pool of water behind them.

Where was the meadow? It had to be near by now.

A flash of gray rocketed from the shadows. A mid-sized wolf leapt at Toby and Kaifong, slamming into them with gnashing teeth before Chuck could so much as lift the .357.

"No!" Toby cried. He fell beneath the onslaught while clutching Kaifong. He turned his back to the animal and hunkered over Kaifong's limp form on the ground.

The wolf clamped its jaws around Toby's shoulder and tore at the researcher's backpack and jacket. Chuck aimed the .357 but didn't dare pull the trigger; in the commotion and deepening shadows, he was as likely to shoot Toby or Kaifong as he was the wolf. He stepped forward and grabbed the creature by the scruff of its neck. He yanked, and the wolf spun with a snarl and went for his forearm, jaws snapping.

"Look out!" Lex yelled.

Chuck let go and stumbled away. Lex leapt forward and buried his knife in the wolf's spine. The animal yowled and ripped into Lex, who cried out as he fell to his back next to Toby and Kaifong.

The wolf planted its forepaws on Lex's chest. Lex gashed the creature's snout with his knife. The wolf snatched Lex's wrist in its mouth and slung its head back and forth. Droplets of blood flew from Lex's arm. He transferred his knife to his free hand and again slashed the animal across its face, cutting into one of its eyes.

The wolf sprang away and crouched. It snarled, blood streaming from its wounds. The animal jumped at Lex, its legs spring-coiled, returning to the attack. Chuck swung his arm, tracking the wolf as it sailed through the air. He fired, aiming for the chest cavity behind the foreleg, where the wolf's heart was suspended between its lungs.

The gun blast ripped the night air, the flash of the shot bright in the gathering shadows. The wolf collapsed atop Lex. Its legs twitched, then went still.

Lex slid the animal to the ground and climbed to his feet. "Are you all right?" he asked Toby.

"I'm glad I was wearing my jacket." Toby rose and again lifted Kaifong to his shoulder despite the fresh blood soaking through his coat where the wolf's teeth had ripped into him.

Chuck toed the downed wolf. It didn't move. Death did not diminish its beauty, its lean physique that of a distance runner, its fur sleek and unruffled, its paws nearly as long and wide as his hand. What had led it to attack Toby and Kaifong? And—more important—where were its pack mates?

He scanned the surrounding trees. "Let's get out of here."

"Almost there," Lex said. He set out for camp once more, his bleeding arm pressed to his chest. Toby followed with Kaifong. Chuck came last. He looked back after a few steps to see the three trailing wolves—one black, one white, and one the big, slate-gray alpha—emerge from the forest and trot silently toward him.

Chuck backed away, the .357 outstretched. The wolves stopped to nose the carcass of their pack mate. They lifted their heads and growled, their eyes golden yellow in the gloom.

Before their snarls died in their throats, the three wolves leapt over their downed comrade and came at Chuck.

39

The wolves approached too fast for Chuck to draw a bead on them. Instead, he raised the .357 and pulled the trigger, firing past the animals into the woods.

At the percussive crack of the shot and the bright flare from the mouth of the pistol, the wolves slid to a halt. They crouched ten feet from Chuck, who held his ground. He glanced behind him to find Lex and Toby stopped and looking his way.

"Go!" he yelled.

Lex set off through the trees. Toby followed, Kaifong's limp body over his shoulder, her arms slung down his back. Chuck hustled after them, glancing back every few steps. The wolves stayed crouched until he lost sight of them among the trees.

Lex tripped over a downed branch and plunged face-first to the ground. Toby stepped past him and kept moving with Kaifong. Chuck hauled Lex to his feet and they hurried together through the forest after Toby.

Chuck looked back while keeping a firm grip on Lex's arm. No sign of the wolves. But where in God's name was camp?

Lex inhaled mouthfuls of air as he stumbled through the trees at Chuck's side. Lights lanced into the forest from the edge of the meadow ahead. They emerged from the woods into the open to find several scientists, including Clarence, waiting for them. Clarence and three others lifted Kaifong from Toby's shoulder and carried her across the grass. Chuck shoved the .357 into his pack. He and Toby propped Lex between them and headed for the cabin.

Janelle stood aside to allow Kaifong inside, then guided Lex through the doorway. In the lantern light in front of the cabin and mess tent, Chuck held out a hand to Toby, who handed over his pack.

"The longer barrel will be better in the open," Chuck told him.

And the rifle no longer would be in Toby's possession.

Working fast, Chuck dug out and assembled the gun and loaded it to capacity, five rounds in the magazine and one in the chamber. He hefted the compact rifle. It rested comfortably in his hands. Its open sights didn't trouble him; he'd developed his initial marksman skills as a kid hunting squirrels and rabbits around Durango with an old, open-sight .22.

Toby entered the cabin clutching his bleeding shoulder. Chuck squeezed past Clarence and the researchers who'd carried Kaifong as they left the cabin, setting the rifle and his pack on the floor next to the door inside.

Kaifong lay on her back on the plank table, arms at her sides, eyes closed, a fleece jacket bunched beneath her head. Randall stood over her, his face drawn. Janelle held two fingers to Kaifong's neck below her jawline.

Lex sat catching his breath on the bench beneath the cabin's west window, his glasses fogged. Keith squatted in front of him, wrapping gauze around the ranger's mangled wrist. Perched at the edge of a wooden chair pushed back from the table, Toby peeled his mauled jacket off his shoulder and down his arm. The girls sat next to Chance on the floor at the back of the cabin, their fingers trailing through the dog's fur, their eyes saucered as they took in the scene before them. Against the far wall of the cabin, Sarah's body lay enveloped in the sleeping bag.

Randall turned to Chuck. "They're saying you shot a wolf to save Kai. Thank you, man."

Chuck flushed as he pictured the wolf, majestic even in death. "I'm just glad we managed to get her back here." He went to Kaifong's side. "Well?" he asked Janelle.

"Pulse is strong and steady. She's breathing evenly. No signs of trauma."

Kaifong moaned. She pitched from side to side, her arms and legs jerking. Janelle leaned over Kaifong, holding her in place until her movements subsided and she again lay still and quiet atop the table.

Janelle lifted each of Kaifong's closed eyelids. "Her pupils are normal, but she's showing no signs of awareness. It's like she's been drugged or something."

"You'll stay with her?" Randall asked.

"Of course."

"I'll get back to work next door, then. Let me know if she comes around, would you?" He shot a quick look at Sarah's body and left the cabin, pulling the door closed behind him.

"I told him about Sarah and the phone," Keith said. "I had to."

Chuck glanced at the girls.

"He pushed his way in," Keith explained, "while you were on your way back with Kaifong."

Rosie nodded emphatically. "They had a whisper talk."

Carmelita petted Chance. "Rosie tried to sneak up on them," she said, "so they moved away from her."

"But first they made bad faces at me, didn't they, *Mamá*?"

"Yes, they did," Janelle confirmed.

Chuck studied the closed door, then scanned the room, his gaze moving from Lex, who wiped his glasses on his jacket with one hand while Keith tended to his injured wrist, to Kaifong, motionless on the table, to Toby, who gingerly probed his shoulder with his fingers.

A blast of wind rattled down the chimney. The coals in the fireplace glowed bright red, then broke into low flames, casting broken light around the cabin. In front of the fireplace,

Carmelita scratched Chance's neck while Rosie leaned forward and rested her head on the dog's back.

"What's this?" Carmelita asked, her fingers digging into Chance's fur.

Rosie sat up. She pushed her sister's hand away and pressed her own fingers to the side of Chance's neck, just below the dog's skull. "Yeah," she said. "What's this, huh?"

Keith left the roll of gauze dangling from Lex's arm and went to Chance. He buried his fingers into the dog's fur alongside Rosie's. His face went white.

"There's a cut." He looked up. "And a lump. Something hard."

40

"The lump is right up under the edge of the skull, against the bone," Keith said. His fingers continued to probe. "The cut's still fresh."

He pressed at Chance's neck. The dog whined.

"There, boy," Keith soothed. Then, to the room: "Got it."

He held up a beige-colored object a quarter-inch thick and an inch square, glistening in the light of the fire.

Chuck studied the object from across the room. Its color triggered something in his brain. He unzipped the outside pocket of his pack and took out the clear plastic bag containing the sliver of bone he'd collected from the wall of ice at the base of Trident Peak. He crossed the room and dangled the baggie beside the object Keith had removed from beneath Chance's skin. In the firelight, the sliver and object shone with the same off-white color.

Keith handed the object to Chuck. Like the bone sliver from the glacier, it was moist and slippery in his fingers. He tucked the baggie containing the bone sliver beneath his arm and applied pressure to the object, bending it back and forth with both hands. A tiny, black, rectangular piece of plastic popped from its center.

"Ah ha," he said. "The chip was inside." He held it out for Toby's inspection.

"Identical to the one from Number 217," Toby said. He looked toward Sarah's body. "What did you know that you shouldn't have?" he asked her. "What was it you found out?"

"Whatever it was, we need to find out, too," Chuck said. Anxious to learn what Randall was up to in the mess tent, he handed the chip to Toby. He returned the sliver of bone to his pack and picked up the rifle from beside the door. "I'll do a quick reconnoiter," he said to Janelle from the doorway. "You're doing great in here."

She rested her hand on Kaifong's arm. "I just wish there was more I could do for her."

He stepped outside. The air had chilled with the onset of night. Scientists in clusters of three and four stood watch along the front of the cabin and mess tent. LED lanterns swung on hiking poles in the wind, casting an eerie glow into the meadow. Inky blackness pressed toward the cabin and tent from beyond the thirty-foot perimeter of muted lantern light. Mist and clouds blotted out the stars.

He found Randall seated at a table inside the mess tent. Jorge sat opposite him. A lantern swayed from the ridge pole, lighting the interior of the tent. Randall's pack rested beside him, the drone strapped in its fiberglass frame.

Shattered bits of the satellite phone lay on the tabletop in front of Randall. He turned one of the pieces over in his hand. Its smooth plastic surface reflected the combined light of his headlamp and the lantern overhead. "I thought I might be able to put it back together."

Chuck eased his grip on the rifle. So this was what Randall was up to. "Any luck?"

"It's pretty much hopeless, man."

"Keep trying," Chuck said. "It'd be great to get through to somebody."

He ducked outside and studied the researchers to his right and left, their folding knives belted to their waists. Someone had murdered Sarah and drugged Kaifong. But who?

He wormed his way through the crowd to the cabin's west side, where half a dozen flashlight-wielding scientists stood with their backs to the log wall, facing the meadow. Three lanterns illuminated wet grass at the side of the cabin, while the concentrated beams of the flashlights reached to the edge of the forest two hundred feet away. The scientists acknowledged Chuck's presence with glances and curt nods before returning their attention to the black wall of trees rising at the bottom of the clearing.

Chuck continued on around to the back of the cabin and mess tent. There, a handful of researchers aimed flashlights up the hill at the tent platforms. Chuck studied the slope alongside them—no sign of movement.

Clarence's full-throated cry came from the east side of the mess tent. "Hey!" he yelled. "Back off!"

A deep roar ripped the night air.

Chuck sprinted around the corner of the mess tent, rifle raised. Clarence stood alone, his back to the canvas wall of the tent, his flashlight piercing the darkness beyond the dim half-circle of light cast by a pair of lanterns set on poles against the tent wall.

"It's gone," he said.

"A grizzly?" Chuck asked, his chest heaving.

Clarence nodded.

"You're on your own over here?"

"They took off around front when the bear showed up." He pointed at the corner of the tent. "Probably the smart thing to do."

"Are you okay?"

"I barely saw it. As soon as I yelled, it disappeared back out of sight, roaring as it went."

"It must be the one from the west side of the valley. It crossed the river, too." Chuck shook his head, flummoxed. Common sense said the grizzly should not have followed after the wolves. He stopped himself. Why was he thinking in terms of common sense? Nothing about the last few hours—Sarah's murder, Kaifong's entrapment, the wolf's attack in the woods—was, by any measure, common.

Clarence swung his flashlight, revealing the empty trail climbing south away from the cabin. "*Nada*," he said.

Another roar sounded, this time from north of camp. A handful of scientists surged back around to the east side of the mess tent.

"Stay here, would you?" Chuck asked Clarence.

"*Por supuesto.*"

Chuck slipped through the researchers to the north-facing side of the tent.

"Look!" Justin cried out from the front of the cabin.

Flashlights swung north. The combined wattage illuminated the wall of forest at the bottom of the meadow. Something big and brown appeared among the trunks of trees at the edge of the forest before disappearing deeper into the woods, moving from east to west.

Seconds later, someone shouted from the west side of the cabin, "There it is, see? It's running!"

A chorus of wolf howls rose from the forest to the west.

Chuck pushed his way through the knots of scientists gathered in front of the cabin. He met Lex as the ranger stepped outside.

Lex's bandaged wrist hung at his waist. Fire burned in his eyes. "What's going on out here?"

Chuck filled him in.

"So they're circling," Lex said.

"The grizzly, at least."

"It's a standoff, then."

"We just have to keep it that way."

Clarence's cry came a second time from the east side of the mess tent: "Bear!"

Chuck frowned as he and Lex sprinted back toward Clarence. Mere seconds ago, the grizzly had shown itself two hundred yards away, on the opposite side of camp. It couldn't be in two places at once.

Half a dozen researchers stood in a clump at the northeast corner of the mess tent. Chuck muscled through them, then came to an abrupt halt.

Captured in the beam of Clarence's flashlight, a massive grizzly charged from the trees, its jaws wide open.

"Stop!" Clarence pulled the canister of pepper spray from his belt.

The bear did not slow as it neared the semi-circle of lantern light. Clarence released his spray. A cloud of red mist formed in front of him. Lex slipped past Chuck to Clarence's side, yanked his canister from its holster, and sprayed it alongside Clarence. Chuck leaned his shoulder against the tent's corner post and sighted down the barrel of the rifle.

Tongue trailing from its mouth, the charging grizzly reached the edge of the lantern light, thirty feet from Clarence and Lex. Another leap. Twenty feet.

Chuck thumbed off the rifle's safety, peered down the barrel, and aimed at the bear's head.

A deep, ragged V gouged the grizzly's right ear.

41

The grizzly—Notch—entered the cloud of pepper spray. A shiver passed the length of its immense body. Its snout turned down and it closed its eyes. Despite the spray, however, it gathered itself and took another enormous leap.

The grizzly landed scant feet from Clarence and Lex. Before Chuck could draw a bead on it, the bear swung an enormous forepaw, batting Clarence across the chest. Clarence flew backward. He struck the canvas wall of the tent and collapsed to the ground. Chuck sighted down the barrel of the rifle as the grizzly hunkered over Clarence and turned to face Lex. Chuck set the bead at the front of the gun's barrel on the bear's sloped forehead. He raised the rear V of the gunsight to the base of the bead, lining up the barrel. He took a breath, held it, and squeezed the trigger.

The report of the rifle shot was jarring, the flash from the barrel's mouth bright in the dim glow of the lanterns.

Chuck blinked to reestablish his eyesight as the bear fell. His ears rang. The tang of gunpowder filled the air, mixing with the sharp bite of the dissipating pepper spray and the rotten odor of the bear's breath.

He levered another shell into the chamber and sighted down the barrel at the grizzly, lying in a heap on the ground. Chuck held his position, shaking, and eyed the bear over the top of the gun. A dime-sized hole in the bear's forehead led to the blown-out back of its skull. Bits of brain matter speckled the creature's shoulders. The grizzly's eyes were open and unblinking, its chest still.

Notch, the bear that two years ago had attacked and killed Joe and Rebecca of the Wolf Initiative's Territory Team, was dead.

Chuck lowered the rifle. In the space of hours, he'd killed one each of Yellowstone's magnificent, top-of-the-food-chain predators. He exhaled sharply. In both instances, he assured himself, he'd exercised the only option available to him.

Clarence lay against the canvas wall of the tent. Blood spread through the front of his jacket where the bear's paw had struck him, but he managed a pained smile. "Lured it in for you, didn't I, *jefe*?"

At Lex's direction, the scientists who were gathered at the front corner of the mess tent lifted Clarence and carried him to the cabin. When Lex followed them, Chuck found himself alone with the bear.

He squatted beside Notch, his heartbeat slowing. The grizzly was enormous, easily seven hundred pounds. Chuck stroked its thick fur. Even in death, the creature was awe-inspiring.

Bile built in his throat. He'd acted in defense of Clarence and Lex, but at enormous cost.

Randall approached with the drone in his hands. The lantern light caught the sadness that filled his eyes the instant he saw the grizzly. "It charged?"

"Right through the spray."

Randall nodded, stiff-necked. He aimed his chin at the drone. "I gave up on the phone and got to jonesing on this instead."

He lifted the copter to reveal a headlamp taped to the side of the hanging video camera. "I've never flown at night, but I thought we could give it a try with the light." The headlamp's beam was aimed the same direction as the camera's lens. "I was thinking the noise combined with the glare might help keep the animals at bay." He looked at Notch.

"The wolves are still out there," Chuck said. "And the other grizzly."

Randall nodded. "Let's do it, then. Grab the tablet from inside, would you?" he asked before disappearing back around the corner of the tent with the drone held out before him.

Chuck stroked the bear's shoulder once more before following Randall. Two dozen of the camp's researchers milled in front of the mess tent and cabin. Chuck sent the nearest four to keep watch where Notch's body lay. He studied the scientists' faces as they passed him, wondering if he was looking into the eyes of Sarah's killer.

He grabbed the tablet computer from the mess tent and exited in time to see Randall round the far side of the cabin. Before joining him, Chuck pushed open the cabin's front door. Kaifong still lay on the table, unconscious, while Toby leaned far back in his chair, his eyes closed, and Keith crouched in front of the fireplace, dabbing antiseptic into the cut on Chance's neck.

Clarence sat in a chair between the fireplace and table, his shirt unbuttoned to his waist. Blood ran from four parallel gouges centered on his bare chest, the trickles gathering on his bulbous belly. Purple bruises outlined the ragged edges of the cuts. Lex, Carmelita, and Rosie hovered at Clarence's side. He winced as Janelle pressed a wad of gauze to his wound.

"How're you doing?" Chuck asked him.

"I'm alive." He shifted in his seat to look across the room at Sarah's still form.

Chuck ducked outside and caught up with Randall, who stood among the scientists on sentry duty along the west side of the cabin. Chuck rested the rifle against the cabin's log wall and took the drone from Randall in exchange for the tablet computer.

Randall focused on the tablet, gripped in his left hand, while he fingered the toggles on the face of the control console, slung at his waist, with his right.

The drone's rotors kicked in and gained speed, whining, until the copter lifted from Chuck's palms into the night sky. Randall handed the tablet to Chuck, then freed the console from its holster and balanced it in both hands, his thumbs on the toggles.

Chuck held up the tablet for Randall. Its screen displayed only grainy grays and blacks.

Randall's eyes roved between the departing drone and the fuzzy screen. "I'm not sure this is going to work," he admitted. "I'll have to fly just above the trees to be able to see anything."

The drone ascended as it traveled west across the meadow, the glowing light of the headlamp receding until it appeared as one more among the handful of stars now visible between openings in the clouds.

The drone disappeared beyond the treetops to the west. The video feed remained grainy, but its hue was now green instead of gray, and the treetops passing close beneath the drone were easy to make out on the screen.

"This might actually work," Randall said.

"What are you thinking to do?" Chuck asked.

"I want to find the wolves. Maybe the other griz. I'm hoping the noise plus the light will push them away from camp."

He brought the drone to a halt. The tablet provided a stationary view of the forest canopy. Another round of wolf howls rose from the forest to the west.

"Come on," Randall said. "Show yourselves."

He nudged the toggles. The drone and camera described a slow circle. Here and there, small sections of forest floor appeared as patches of dark gray amid the green treetops. A flicker of movement appeared in one of the dark gray patches. The flicker stopped, becoming a spot of dusty gray centered in the small opening.

"There," Randall breathed. "Gotcha."

The drone flew lower. On the tablet screen, the spot of lighter color became an oval, an oblong form—then a wolf, head up, watching the copter as it approached.

"Careful," Chuck said, remembering the wolf that earlier had flung itself at the drone.

Randall extended the console in front of him, working the toggles as the copter descended. In the camera frame, the wolf backed off. Its eyes were white, refracting the light of the headlamp. The drone hovered a few feet above the ground. The wolf stood directly in front of it.

"Shouldn't you be higher?" Chuck asked.

"Not if we're gonna get it to do what we want, man." Randall advanced the drone toward the wolf. "Scat!" he shouted. "Git!"

The wolf took a tentative step toward the drone, then another. The creature crouched, its eyes fixed on the craft hovering before it.

"Don't do it," Randall said.

He shifted the controls. The drone lifted just as the wolf leapt. The animal opened its jaws, aiming for the dangling camera and headlamp. The tablet screen went dark.

Randall cut loose with a long string of curses as he frantically thumbed the console's toggles. The screen remained black.

"We're down," he said. "I can't believe it!" He shoved the console into its holster and sprinted toward his downed craft, his headlamp lighting the way.

"Randall!" Chuck yelled. "Stop! Don't be stupid!"

He dropped the tablet, grabbed the rifle, and took off in

pursuit, pulling his headlamp from his jacket pocket and centering it on his forehead as he ran.

Randall disappeared into the woods, the forest swallowing the light of his headlamp. Chuck entered the trees behind him, Toby's rifle swinging at his side, his free hand clenched in anger. Randall was risking his life by going after the drone, and risking Chuck's life as well.

"Randall! Come back!" Chuck called ahead. The woods absorbed his cry. He looked around him as he ran, his headlamp beam flashing past bushes and tree trunks. His foot caught on something. He tripped and sprawled forward, extending his hands to break his fall, the rifle flying free of his grasp.

As he struck the ground, he tucked his shoulder and rolled. Springing to his feet, he swept the beam of his headlamp across the forest floor in front of him.

Grass. Twigs. Rocks. Mud.

But no rifle.

42

"Whoops," Randall said, turning on his headlamp. "Did you trip over my foot? Sorry about that, dude." He stood ten feet away, holding Toby's rifle at his waist. The rifle's barrel was aimed at Chuck. "I figured you'd follow me."

Randall released the rifle's safety, a metallic click in the quiet forest. Only the bottom half of his face showed in the downward glow of his headlamp.

Chuck raised his hands. He pictured Sarah's body in the cabin. She, too, had faced Randall. And she had lost.

"What's going on? What are you doing?" Chuck asked, his goal to keep Randall talking long enough to...well, to do what, he didn't yet know. What he did know now was that, wide grins and bro-speak aside, Randall was a murderer, and he had Toby's rifle in his hands.

Chuck expected a reply thick with menace. Instead, Randall's tone was light, almost playful. "I'm doing what I should have done two years ago, Chuckie."

"The Territory Team?"

"I thought they'd get the message."

"What message?"

"To stay the hell out!" He jerked the gun for emphasis before re-aiming it toward Chuck's torso. "They shouldn't have been there."

Chuck lowered his hands, the movement gradual, careful. "They?" he asked. "You mean," he continued, stalling, "the animals?"

"No!" Randall said. "Not the animals. You don't belong

here. I don't belong here. Scientists don't belong out here in the wilderness."

"Is that why you killed Sarah?"

Randall froze. "She..."

"You murdered her, Randall."

"You...you know what she's like," Randall said. He rubbed the side of his head with his hand.

"She's *dead*." Chuck bit off the word.

"I'm not a killer." Randall exhaled, the air whistling out his nose. "I'm working for the predators. Don't you see, man? These lands were preserved, set aside. They were to be left to nature, to the animals, forever."

"Of course they were," Chuck snapped. "Every bit of land in every direction for miles and miles around us is set aside."

He recalled with a start that Randall had emphasized Yellowstone's having been preserved by Congress "for the animals," and had called Yellowstone National Park the grizzlies' "pad," likening park visitors to invaders.

Randall's hands tightened around the rifle. "You know Yellowstone's history—the animals wiped out by poachers. You think this place is preserved? Wrong. The way humans are allowed to swarm all over the place, the wolves and grizzlies and everything else might as well be specimens in a freakin' zoo."

Chuck's eyes strayed toward the cabin. No lights approached through the trees. He was on his own. "They got a handle on the poachers decades ago," he said. He had no choice but to ride the conversation, search for a way out. "The animals came back, even the wolves."

"Sure, they brought the wolves back—to a place that had been totally developed while they were gone. Millions and millions of visitors every year and no end in sight. It's just as bad outside the park, too, bulldozing new roads, drilling wells, pumping chemicals into the ground. You've felt the earthquakes, we all have. It's a full-on assault. I saw it my first summer here. I tried to talk to the others about it, but no one would listen, no one wanted to hear."

"So you took matters into your own hands."

Randall's headlamp moved up and down. "Nonviolent confrontation, that's what I settled on."

"You didn't achieve it."

"I tried. I really did."

Chuck fought his nerves, seeking focus. The tiny, plastic computer chips, the ones implanted in the wolf and Chance, they matched up perfectly with Randall's high-tech skills. "The chips. Those are yours, aren't they?"

"Bing-*go*," Randall said. "I use a crossbow and a projectile point made of beef cartilage. The cartilage dissolves and the projectile shaft falls out, leaving the chip in place."

"I don't see..."

"Of course you don't. You're an archaeologist, stuck in the past. This is about the future. About making things right in Yellowstone after all these years."

"Making things right for who?"

"For the wolves, the grizzlies."

"By scaring people out of the backcountry?"

"The concept is simple, really. Tiny electrical pulses applied where the spinal cord meets the brain. I can make the animals do what I want. My chips are based on the neurological biosensor chips developed for humans by Effiteon Technologies. The developers at Effiteon don't understand the true potential of their work. My improvements are straightforward—circuitry upgrades, a transistor boost, paint-on battery power. My enhanced chips create what's called cortextual suggestion in my animals, setting them on certain paths based on the strength and directional intensity of the pulses I deliver." Randall lifted the control console in its holster at his waist. "At their base operational level, the pulses free the animals to follow their natural instincts, minus their fear of humans. From there, I can use the pulses to encourage the animals to do more. Much more."

"But how...?"

"Standalone computer chip design and manufacture is simple these days. You don't need a factory anymore. You can lay circuitry on individual chips now. And you don't need a big lab to test chips prior to implantation, either."

"But why Chance? Why the dog?"

Randall dropped the console back to his side and again gripped the gun with both hands. "I chipped it the first night, outside on its sleeping pad, while Keith was in his tent. It didn't make a sound. Not even a yelp." Randall's teeth flashed white below his headlamp. "Did you see the way that thing took off across the thermal basin? Like a shot. Talk about natural inclination."

"But Chance isn't one of your predators."

"No. But the dog's tracking ability was going to be a problem."

"So you tried to kill it."

"I gave it its freedom, that's all—though, I admit, I did wait until we reached the basin to do so." He laughed.

"But you launched the drone to herd the dog back to safety."

"That was Kai's doing, not mine. I had to go along with her."

Chuck worked backward in time. "The Territory Team—Kaifong wasn't there to stop you, was she?"

"I chipped the grizzly when it was on a kill in Lamar Valley, right next to the road. The wolves were just as simple, and more grizzlies, too. It's a sin, really, how comfortable all of them are around humans. It's so easy to get close to them. Each chip is GPS-enabled. I know the location at all times of every single one of my test subjects."

"So you knew the grizzly had taken over the wolves' carcass."

"I knew its locational coordinates, sure."

"You gave Notch a pulse when the Territory Team was scheduled to arrive, didn't you?"

Randall shrugged. "They're the ones who chose to hike into the heart of grizzly country. They gave me the chance to test the chip in real-world conditions."

"You killed two wolf researchers, two people, Rebecca and Joe."

"I didn't kill anyone. I simply freed the bear to do what its natural tendencies told it to do—defend its food source."

"You're insane."

"On the contrary, I may be the only sane researcher in all of Yellowstone National Park. I was a kid when my parents first brought me here. The wolf reintroduction program was only a decade or two old at that point, but the good the wolves were doing for the park already was obvious. Even so, the wolves were under assault. Anytime one of them wandered outside the park boundaries, it was gunned down."

"Everything was going well inside the boundaries, though—the elk population declining, beavers rebounding, the rivers coming back."

"But they couldn't leave well enough alone, could they? They couldn't just look around and realize things were on the mend. No way, man. They had to do all their darting and collaring. They had to treat the park like one, big, human-run science project." Randall took a deep breath. "Yellowstone's predators are not zoo creatures. They're *not*."

"I'm not sure I—"

"It's not what nature intended!" Randall said. "I watched it play out when I was in college. I visited the park, chatted up everybody, went on to grad school. I got the posting here with the Yale program three years ago. Finally, I was where I needed to be. I could set up my own protocol with my own subjects."

"You decided to play God."

"Wrong. All the other scientists were playing God. The goal of my study was, is, to restore equilibrium, to turn the grizzlies and wolves back into the free, kick-ass predators they were before the white man showed up here."

"The white man?"

"Back in the day, the Indians who left the baskets you came here to study knew who was in charge. They came up to the central plateau a few weeks each summer, picked nuts and berries, harvested a little meat, and headed for lower ground."

Despite the gun aimed at him, Chuck thought of the loamy contents of the Trident One baskets—contents that might well have been meat. "The ancient Indians who came up here may have done a lot more hunting—and killing—of your animals than you want to admit."

"What are you saying?" Randall demanded.

"Your precious predators may not have been so kick-ass compared to the Indians, back in the day, as you'd like to think."

"Doesn't matter." Randall jutted his jaw. "The bears and wolves did just fine until the Europeans showed up. They were the ones who screwed everything up. Instead of allowing nature to take care of itself, the white dudes destroyed the Greater Yellowstone ecosystem. We knew it was time to fix things. So we set to work."

"We?"

"Of course, we. I couldn't do it alone. But it took me a while. Everyone at Yale, Harvard, Brown was too citified. They didn't understand the first thing about the natural, animal world, and they didn't care, either. They just wanted to do their science. They had no appreciation for what was really happening in Yellowstone. Finally, I met Kai at a conference. She was from Stanford, out here in the West. She'd seen the crowds at Yosemite and Sequoia; she knew what was at stake. We decided to team up. She understood—for a while."

Chuck's eyes widened. "When you slapped her on the shoulder and she fell into the lake," he said, "that was no accident, was it?"

"I—" Randall's voice caught in his throat. "I had the idea in mind, but I don't think I knew if I would go through with it. It was so easy, though. I barely touched her shoulder." He released the gun with one hand long enough to squeeze the bridge of his nose between his thumb and forefinger. "She thought we were only studying wolves. She was convinced they wouldn't attack humans. She believed grizzlies were too dangerous, too unpredictable."

"She was right."

"I'd say the data is still inconclusive."

"You've been documenting all of this, haven't you?"

"Of course. It's a study. And, I must say, its design is flawless. The data we've collected over the last three years is fully suggestive that my primary theory is one hundred percent correct."

"Your theory?"

"That given the freedom they deserve, the park's top predators will assert their dominance over all other animals in the park, humans included. Once they're chipped, all I have to do is give them the tiniest of jolts to set them off. Sometimes, not even the pepper spray stops them. It helps that firearms are outlawed on the research teams, of course. Or, it helped—until you came along with Toby's gun." Randall's voice sharpened. "You killed two of my study subjects, Number 6, the wolf, and Number 1, Notch, my very first chip placement. There's no excuse for what you did, Chuck. None whatsoever."

He raised the rifle, aiming at Chuck's face, his finger on the trigger.

43

Chuck looked down the barrel of the gun, its mouth a small, black hole aimed at his forehead.

The lower portion of Randall's face, visible in the light of his headlamp, was slack, his breathing steady. Chuck didn't move. Randall lowered the gun back to his waist.

Chuck said accusingly, "You sicced the wolves on us when we were trying to get Kaifong back to the cabin, didn't you?"

"Even after the lake, she didn't get the message. She kept asking questions. She claimed I'd summoned too many animals here too quickly, that I was abusing the pulses. I tranqued her water bottle. When she got groggy, I led her away from camp. I wanted you and Lex to go after her. With the three of you out of the way—plus Toby, as it turned out—I'd be able to take care of everyone else. When you reached her, I pulsed the wolves and got the drone out of there."

"But they didn't attack. At least, not right away."

"That's the difference between wolves and grizzlies. Pulse a grizzly, it goes berserk. Pulse wolves, they go on a hunt. They're very methodical about it."

"They sent one in on its own first."

"Number 6. Testing the defensive ability of the prey."

"When I fired past the others, they held off."

"It's called cortextual suggestion. There's no guaranteeing the precise effect the pulses will have on test subjects, especially in the face of gunfire."

Chuck gritted his teeth. "The first day, the wolf and bear below camp, that was you, too, wasn't it?"

"Yabba dabba doo. The griz—Number 11—and the wolf—my Number 9, the Wolf Initiative's Number 217. I used a pulse sequence that synchs the species. I thought if I could show everyone how bitchin' cool grizzlies and wolves were together, people would understand."

"When we went after them that evening, I heard growls behind me, and I saw eyes, too, in the dark."

"I'm happy to hear that. I was busy, busy, busy—pulsing the dog to keep it moving ahead while I brought the two of them around behind."

"But they didn't attack."

"I made sure they didn't. That was still for show. But I kept the two of them together too long. My mistake. I knew there was trouble when Number 9 stopped moving. I came along with everyone when the vultures revealed the carcass location. The lead group was lucky the griz only bluff-charged despite all the pulses I gave it."

"You pulsed the Stander Pack wolves after the bear backed off, didn't you?"

"I had no choice."

"But the wolves didn't attack, either."

"They would have before we reached camp, I'm sure of it. I was ready for them to attack at that point, with Number 9 dead. I was finished trying to impress people. It was time. I kept pulsing them, but your gunshot from the boat was too much."

"You were going to have them attack even though you were with us?"

"I've incorporated a paired-charge, repellant force field around the control console that interacts with the chip circuitry to keep test subjects a few feet away."

"The walls of the cabin will repel your test subjects, too. It doesn't matter what you do to me out here. Everyone will be safe inside. Your chipped animals won't be able to get to them in there, no matter how many times you pulse them."

"With my help, they will—now that I'm armed. By the time the emergency responders show up, no one will be left alive. The predators will have asserted their dominance in an overwhelming way, which will keep humans out of the Yellowstone backcountry for decades, longer maybe, the way it should be."

"But when your body isn't found with the others, they'll come looking for you."

"I'll leave a trail to the river, then wade upstream before I leave the water and head south, out of the park. They'll assume I was chased in and drowned, my body swept downstream to the bottom of the lake. "

"You've got it all figured out, haven't you?"

"As a matter of fact, I do. And it all starts with you. I appreciate how predictable you are, Chuck-a-dee, bringing me what I needed." Randall put the stock of the gun to his cheek and aimed down the barrel. This time, the lower half of his face was stiff, his lips a flat line, his breaths coming hard and fast through his nostrils.

Chuck sensed Randall's finger tightening on the trigger and ducked as the gun spit a burst of flame. The blast echoed through the trees and the bullet seared the air just above his head. He hit the ground and crawled, elbows and knees digging into the dirt.

"Nice effort, dude," Randall said from behind him. "Very commendable."

Metal slid on metal as Randall worked the bolt, reloading. Chuck spun and sprang, wrapping his arms around Randall's legs. Randall pulled the trigger as he tumbled backward. The gun blasted again, the bullet flying into the night sky.

Chuck scrambled atop Randall, who rolled to his stomach and clutched the rifle to his chest, the barrel protruding past his shoulder. Chuck tugged hard on the gun. He couldn't free it from Randall's grasp, but the rifle's chamber was empty, affording him time. He leapt to his feet and sprinted for camp. At his back, the rifle snicked as Randall chambered another round.

Chuck dug for the cabin, putting trees and distance between himself and the gun. A third shot rang out, struck a tree, and ricocheted away. He kept running.

Behind him, Randall laughed. "You can run as fast as you want, Chuck," he called, "but you can't outrun my wolves."

Growls sounded from the darkness to Chuck's left. Adrenalin surged through him as he dashed headlong through the forest. He broke out of the trees and sped up the tilted meadow toward camp.

"Chuck!" Clarence yelled from the front of the cabin.

"It's Randall," Chuck hollered. "He's—"

A wolf struck him from behind, sending him to the ground. He wrapped himself into a ball and folded his arms over his head. The wolf tore into his back, ripping at his jacket. Chuck peeked between his arms. His headlamp illuminated four wolves—one black, one white, and two gray—padding out of the trees toward him. He ducked as the wolf on his back shifted position, gnashing at his forearms.

A second wolf wrapped its jaws around his upper arm. The two wolves growled as they tore at him, their snarls vibrating through his body. Another vibration joined the growls of the wolves, this one rising from the earth beneath Chuck. The wolves paused. The tremor became audible, its sound increasing from a distant hum to a thumping beat.

The wolves released Chuck. He twisted and squinted through his crosshatched fingers at a bright floodlight, aloft in the sky, approaching up the valley from the direction of the lake. The light shone from the front of a helicopter swooping in from the north, framed by the starry night sky.

The two wolves bolted back into the forest with their pack mates. Chuck sat up. He pressed his forearms, bruised through the thick, torn fabric of his jacket, against his stomach as the helicopter skimmed the tree tops, heading for the clearing in front of the cabin.

He struggled to his feet and ran toward the descending helicopter, waving his arms to warn the aircraft's oblivious occupants. The chopper's floodlight was trained on the crowd of researchers gathered in front of the cabin. The thrum of the aircraft's rotors deepened as it slowed to a hover above the meadow.

A whirring noise sounded behind Chuck, blending with the low-pitched beat of the hovering helicopter. He turned and his headlamp beam lit Randall, standing at the edge of the forest with Toby's rifle at his feet. Randall balanced the drone at a forty-five-degree angle in his left hand while the fingers of his right hand worked the console at his waist.

The drone hadn't wrecked after all. Rather, Randall had settled it safely to the ground in the forest.

Chuck ran at Randall. But he was too late.

The whirring noise increased to a loud whine. The drone rose from Randall's hand, leveled, and shot toward the hovering helicopter. Chuck turned, tracking the trajectory of the drone as the helicopter settled toward its landing, still twenty feet off the ground.

"No!" he cried out.

A metallic ping reached his ears as the drone struck the helicopter's rotor. The whop-whop-whop of the helicopter blade became erratic and the chopper sank sideways toward the grass. The spinning rotor blade struck the ground first. The rotor snapped off and the freed drive shaft sped to an ear-splitting screech. The long, aluminum tail crumpled to the meadow with a metallic crunch. The body of the helicopter settled on its skids, its battered tail in pieces on the ground behind it.

Chuck ran toward the craft as someone inside cut its engine and the screech died away. The helicopter's side doors opened and two people tumbled out and scurried away from the downed craft. The smell of spilled fuel permeated the air. Flames licked from beneath the damaged chopper, engulfing it and climbing into the night sky.

Two men ran from the helicopter toward Chuck. He backed from the heat of the burning aircraft with them. Fit and in their thirties, the men wore blue flight suits. Framed by their white helmets, their faces were pale, their eyes panicked.

"This way," Chuck told them, pointing at the cabin. "Run."

A rifle shot rang out. One of the men screamed. He gripped his upper leg with both hands and fell to the ground.

Randall advanced across the grass toward them. He worked the rifle bolt, chambering another round. "Don't move," he said.

The uninjured man, backlit by the flames, waved his hands at Randall. "Wait," he said. "Don't. We're here to help. There was an emergency call."

"You weren't expected until dawn."

"The storm broke. We came on in. But something went wrong with the rotor. Thank God we were so close to landing."

"You came too early," Randall said.

"No," the man said. "You don't get it." He pointed at the injured man on the ground beside him. "Ted's a flight nurse. I'm the pilot. Just tell me what's going on. We can radio back—" He stopped in mid-sentence, looking at the blazing helicopter.

"Get your nursey-nurse on his feet." Randall pointed at the cabin with the rifle. "That way."

The pilot clamped his mouth shut and grasped one of Ted's arms. Chuck took hold of the other. Together, they hoisted the nurse and helped him toward the cabin.

"What's going on?" the pilot whispered to Chuck.

"Silence," Randall commanded from behind.

Chuck glanced back. Randall's fingers flew across the face of the console at his waist. The five wolves of Stander Pack reemerged from the woods, their eyes bright in the light of the burning helicopter. The rumbling growl of a grizzly came from the woods. The bear stepped out of the trees, its light brown hump aglow in the firelight. The grizzly stood apart from the wolves. It held its head high, one foreleg raised.

"Number 11," Randall said. "There you are."

44

Chuck hurried toward the cabin with the pilot and limping flight nurse. Smoke from the burning helicopter bit into his lungs.

"Run, Chuckie, run," Randall ridiculed.

"Inside," Chuck yelled ahead as they neared the cabin. "Everybody inside. Now!"

The scientists crowded through the cabin door.

"As if that'll do you any good," Randall called. "When I put a match to the place, everyone will come right back out."

Clarence and Lex met Chuck and the pilot in the arc of lantern light at the front of the cabin. They took the flight nurse between them and guided him inside, the pilot following. Chuck spun, his back to the cabin, his eyes on the rifle in Randall's hands, ten feet in front of him.

"Time to let nature do its thang," Randall said. Behind him, the bear and wolves approached camp, keeping their distance from one another. The bear lifted its snout, testing the smoky night air. The wolves spread apart, on the hunt.

"One more pulse," Randall said, his hand poised over the console, "and it'll all be over for you."

"Which will prove everything you've been working toward to be wrong," Chuck said. He pointed at the animals. "You claim you're setting them free, but nothing could be further from the truth. You've turned them into robots. Automatons. You're forcing them to serve you as their master."

"No," Randall said.

"Yes. Everything you've done is about you. You've taken control of the park ecosystem for your own sick reasons, with your computer-chipped animals as your slaves."

"You're wrong," Randall insisted, raising his voice. "I'm freeing the park's predators to do what comes naturally to them."

"What comes naturally to them is being left on their own—not being turned into test subjects controlled by some megalomaniac."

"No!" Randall cried out. He tapped furiously at the console. The wolves surged past him toward Chuck. The grizzly charged, too, trailing the wolves.

Chuck crossed his arms over his face as the wolves struck. He toppled backward, their paws digging into his chest. He rolled to his stomach, peering over his shoulder, as the grizzly entered the melee.

The bear swatted the wolves aside with its massive forepaws, sending first one wolf tumbling away, then another. The grizzly stretched its long neck and bit into the hind leg of a third wolf, the one with white fur. The white wolf yowled as the bear lifted it off the ground by its hind quarters and flung it away.

"Stop!" Randall yelled at Number 11. "Stop it!"

The last two wolves ran off. The grizzly charged after them, dragging one to the ground with an enormous paw. It bit into the downed wolf's back. The bear clenched its jaws until a crunch sounded, then released the wolf and raised its head.

The wolf lay on its side, pressed to the ground by the grizzly. It craned its neck, failing repeated attempts to rise.

"What are you doing, 11?" Randall screamed at the bear. His fingers flew across the face of the console. The four remaining wolves formed a semi-circle around the grizzly. The white wolf balanced on three legs, its injured hind leg lifted off the ground. The wolves snarled, their eyes on the bear. The grizzly slashed at them and they fell back, remaining just beyond the bear's reach.

The bear took the downed wolf's neck in its jaws and ripped powerfully upward. The grizzly lifted its head high, clutching a length of the wolf's windpipe in its teeth.

"No!" Randall screeched. "Don't!"

He raised the rifle and fired pointblank at the bear. The grizzly collapsed. A red blotch on its shoulder marked a gaping exit wound. The bear's eyes remained open, its legs trembling.

Randall worked the rifle bolt, ejecting the spent brass casing to the grass beside the fallen grizzly. He rammed the bolt home and aimed down the barrel at Chuck, who sat upright a few feet away.

"You," Randall said through tight lips, his eyes narrow with fury. "All of this is your fault."

He centered the barrel on Chuck's forehead. Chuck held still as Randall pulled the trigger. A metallic ping sounded as the firing pin struck the gun's empty chamber. Chuck exhaled. He'd counted correctly. Randall's pointblank blast into the grizzly had been the last of the rifle's six rounds.

A pistol shot rang out from the front door of the cabin. Randall dropped the rifle, clasped his upper chest, and fell to the ground.

Clarence stepped from the cabin with the .357 in his hands, his bandaged chest showing between the folds of his open shirt. "That's for Sarah," he said.

He looked down the gun's barrel at Randall as the four remaining wolves of Stander Pack charged.

45

Chuck dove to Randall's side. The wolves darted around him, skirting the control console's force field. Clarence had no time to aim and fire the .357 before the wolves lunged at him and he went down beneath their growling mass.

Chuck drove a fist into Randall's nose and clawed the console from its holster. He worked its controls madly, pushing buttons and throwing switches, but the wolves continued to rip into Clarence. Chuck tossed the console to the ground, grabbed the rifle by its barrel from where it lay in the grass next to Randall, and brought its heavy stock down on the console's housing. The console shattered and the green diode light in its upper corner blinked out.

Instantly, the wolves' growls died in their throats. They released their grips on Clarence, backed a few feet away, and stopped.

Clarence rose on an elbow and aimed the .357 at the nearest of the four wolves. The wolf, Stander Pack's alpha, did not move. Clarence did not pull the trigger. The three other wolves spun and surged around Chuck and Randall and past the downed grizzly and their dead pack mate. The alpha held its position until the three wolves were out of the lantern light. Then it turned and loped after its fellows, headed for the cover of the forest.

At Chuck's side, Randall's eyes blinked open. He drew a deep, rasping breath that turned into a choked sob. "Help...me," he gasped.

The grizzly, lying atop the wolf it had killed, struggled to its feet, a string of saliva dangling from its mouth. The grizzly huffed when its close-set eyes came to rest on Randall's prostrate form.

"No," Randall moaned. "Dear God, no."

Keeping his eyes on the bear, Chuck dragged Randall toward the cabin by the ankles.

Blood dripped from the exit wound in the grizzly's shoulder. The wound was on the same side of the bear as the rifle shot's entry; Randall's bullet had struck the creature's scapula and ricocheted out of its body, stunning the animal but causing no lethal damage.

Clarence aimed the pistol at the grizzly as Chuck drew even with him.

"Don't," Chuck said. "If your shot isn't perfect, you'll only enrage it. It'll rip us to pieces."

Clarence set the pistol on the ground and held out his hands to the bear placatingly before shoving himself backward toward the cabin alongside Chuck and Randall.

"Faster," Randall whimpered.

The grizzly pounced. It took Randall's skull in its jaws, yanked him from Chuck's grasp, and flung him from side to side. Popping noises issued from Randall's flailing body as his neck and spine snapped.

Chuck tumbled to a sitting position next to Clarence. A cry rose from the cabin. He looked back to see Kaifong squirm her way past Janelle and the researchers crowded in the doorway. She scooped the .357 from the ground and strode toward the grizzly, extending the gun before her in both hands.

"No, Kaifong!" Chuck barked. "The pistol's not enough."

The bear went still, its eyes on Kaifong, its grip vice-like around Randall's head. Kaifong aimed the pistol at the grizzly, then lifted the gun higher and pulled the trigger. The gun blasted, spitting fire, and the bullet passed harmlessly above the bear. Kaifong took another step forward and fired past the bear a second time.

The creature opened its jaws, dropping Randall. The grizzly looked at Kaifong without blinking, much as Notch had eyed the Territory Team camera after its attack two years ago. Then, the bear pivoted lightly on its paws and ambled away from the cabin.

Kaifong sank to her knees beside Randall's unmoving body, her back to Chuck and Clarence, her shoulders bowed, the .357 clasped in her lap.

Blood seeped into Randall's curly hair from a flap of scalp ripped from his skull. His open eyes stared upward, unseeing, at the smoke-smudged sky.

Chuck pushed himself from the ground and stepped toward Kaifong. She stiffened when a twig snapped beneath his foot with a subdued pop. She turned on her knees to face him and raised the pistol, centering it on his chest.

46

Whoa there," Chuck said.

Kaifong's shoulders slumped even as she kept the gun trained on him. "Randall," she murmured.

"He was a murderer," Chuck said.

She studied the ground, her lips pressed together. Then, she squared her shoulders and looked up at Chuck, her eyes shining. "I won't have you think that of him," she said. "Not Randall. Not my Randall. He did whatever I told him to do. Always. He was the perfect soldier."

Chuck gaped at her as she continued.

"We didn't want this." She waved the gun around her, taking in Randall's body, the burning helicopter, and the cabin, where Sarah's body lay. "He didn't want this. Any of this. He only thought about the animals—the wolves, the bears. That's why I brought him in."

"Wait," Chuck said, astonished. "What? You brought him in?"

"He was everything I needed, everything I'd been searching for. He had the technical skills, the physical abilities, and, most of all, the desire."

"He told me he met you at a conference, that he convinced you to join him."

She inclined her head in the affirmative. "That's exactly what I wanted him to think. I studied up on him. He was an open book—his beliefs were in everything he wrote, everything he posted online. When I saw he was coming to the conference, I arranged to bump into him."

"He said you only knew about the wolves. He made it sound like he was running things."

"That's what I let him believe. The power of suggestion is an amazing thing. I barely had to mention an idea to him and he was on it, thinking it was his brainchild the whole time. It was even better than that, actually. He thought he was protecting me, when, in fact, it was me constantly protecting him—putting out the piece of meat to be sure the bear and wolf came in close to camp when he pulsed them, herding the dog back across the basin when he got carried away and tried to kill it. I protected him every time, always."

"But he tried to kill you," Chuck insisted, "on the lake."

"I know. I deserved it."

"What do you mean, you deserved it?"

"He knew what I was capable of. He knew I...I..."

Chuck recalled what Randall had told him just minutes ago in the forest: "I'm not a killer." His animals, yes. But Randall, himself? No. He'd even admitted he hadn't fully committed himself to pushing Kaifong at the back of the boat, that he'd barely touched her shoulder.

Chuck gaped at Kaifong. Her grip on the pistol was firm, her hands steady. Her small body was muscle-packed after her summers of work in the park, her shoulders sturdy, her biceps pronounced. She was more than capable of using the folding knife sheathed at her waist as a murder weapon.

"Sarah," Chuck breathed. He looked into Kaifong's dark brown eyes. "You."

"Yes," she said. "Me."

"But why?"

"What I've been doing with Randall is critically important. But you'll never understand that. You're not a biologist; you don't work with living creatures. It's different than with your old, rotting baskets. You can't possibly comprehend the deep understanding those of us who work with animals come to have of their needs, the awareness we develop for how debased they've become in our modern world. Here in Yellowstone, people are nothing but a blip on the evolutionary timeline of the wolves and grizzlies. But humans are threatening to destroy the foundation of their existence nonetheless, a foundation they've developed over thousands and thousands of years."

Kaifong's voice grew cold, steely. "We needed more time. I needed more time. I took the phone. I thought no one saw, but she came up behind me, demanded to know what I was doing. She ran, but I caught her. I just...I just..."

"You killed Sarah," Chuck finished for Kaifong, his words hard. "You stabbed her to death."

"I did what I had to do," Kaifong said, "for the wolves, the bears. My wolves, my bears." She looked behind her, taking in Randall's broken body. "Our wolves," she said, her voice softening. "Our bears."

While Kaifong's head was turned, Janelle passed Chuck with purposeful strides. She lashed out with her booted foot, kicking the pistol from Kaifong's hands. The gun spun away into the darkness. Kaifong swung her head toward Janelle, who centered her foot on Kaifong's chest and drove her backward to the ground next to Randall.

"Like Clarence said. That's for Sarah," Janelle said. She leaned forward, pressing Kaifong into the wet grass.

Chuck whipped off his belt and knelt beside Kaifong. Janelle lifted her foot, and he rolled Kaifong to her stomach and strapped her wrists together at the small of her back.

She grunted as he yanked the belt tight. "That's for Joe and Rebecca," he said.

He hoisted Kaifong to her feet and turned with her toward the cabin as the researchers spilled out the front door. Carmelita and Rosie ran to Janelle and buried their faces in her torso.

Lex approached Chuck and Kaifong. "I'll take her from here," he said. He pulled the knife from the sheath at Kaifong's waist and stuck it in his pocket, then pushed her ahead of him across the patch of muddy ground to the cabin. She twisted in the doorway, craning to look at Randall before Lex thrust her forward and they disappeared inside.

Justin, the rookie grizzly researcher, edged past Chuck and Clarence. He extended his cell phone, aiming it at Randall's body.

Chuck stepped in front of Justin's phone camera. "What do you think you're doing?"

"Yeah, dude," Clarence said in a decent imitation of Randall's voice. "What are you up to, man?"

Justin lowered his phone. "Nothing. I'm not doing anything." He slipped the phone into his pocket.

Chuck went to Janelle. Carmelita and Rosie put their arms around him, including him in their embrace. Janelle turned her face to his.

"That's some kick you've got," he told her.

"Let it be a warning to you," she said. Her face shone in the flickering light of the burning helicopter.

Chuck smiled as he looked at her. Beautiful.

He drew her to him, along with the girls, and looked up at the stars. Somewhere in the distance, a wolf howled, its cry at once mournful and triumphant, and wild and free.

About Scott Graham

Scott Graham is the author of *Canyon Sacrifice* and *Mountain Rampage*, books one and two in the National Park Mystery Series from Torrey House Press, and *Extreme Kids*, winner of the National Outdoor Book Award. Graham is an avid outdoorsman and amateur archaeologist who enjoys mountaineering, skiing, hunting, rock climbing, and whitewater rafting with his wife, who is an emergency physician, and their two sons. He lives in Durango, Colorado.

ACKNOWLEDGEMENTS

First and foremost, my thanks go to my earliest reader, my wife Sue, my additional early readers, Mary Engel, Anne Markward, Chuck Greaves, Kevin Graham, and Pat Downs, and Torrey House Press editors Kirsten Johanna Allen and Anne Terashima. Their selfless work made *Yellowstone Standoff* far better than if it had been the product solely of my own efforts.

With each additional book in the National Park Mystery Series, I respect all the more the crucial role independent book-sellers play in helping new writers of fiction like me find a place in the American literary scene. To indie booksellers across the country, and to my hometown team at Maria's Bookshop in Durango, Colorado, thank you all.

My appreciation goes to the countless scientists dedicated to studying the West's incomparable wild lands and creatures with the aim of their protection and preservation. In particular, former Yellowstone wolf researcher Molly McDevitt provided me great insight into her work in the field, which I used—and abused—liberally in *Yellowstone Standoff*.

In conjuring the fictionalized version of Yellowstone's remote Thorofare region featured in *Yellowstone Standoff*, I am indebted to Gary Ferguson and Tim Cahill for the precise, dead-true descriptions of the region in their respective nonfiction books, *Hawks Rest* (republished by Torrey House Press in 2015) and *Lost in My Own Backyard*. In addition, Fort Lewis College professor of history Andrew Gulliford was forthcoming with his vast store of knowledge of Yellowstone National Park and the Greater Yellowstone ecosystem.

Last, my tremendous thanks go to the rangers and staffers devoting their lives to preserving and protecting Yellowstone National Park and America's other national park gems.

ABOUT THE COVER

Famed nineteenth-century landscape artist Albert Bierstadt painted "Geysers in Yellowstone," a portion of which is featured on the cover of *Yellowstone Standoff.*

Bierstadt's paintings of geysers, waterfalls, and other magnificent topography in the Yellowstone area, based on a trip there in 1871, played a significant role in Congress' decision a year later to preserve the region as America's first national park. Mount Bierstadt, a 14,065-foot peak south of Rocky Mountain National Park in Colorado, is named in Bierstadt's honor.

"Geysers in Yellowstone" is used by permission of the Whitney Western Art Museum, Cody, Wyoming.

Also by Scott Graham

Mountain Rampage: A National Park Mystery

The anticipated second installment in the highly praised National Park Mystery Series, *Mountain Rampage* brings the rugged Rocky Mountain landscape, Colorado's violent gold-mining past, and animal-poaching present vividly to life. *Rampage* provides readers an inside perspective into Rocky Mountain National Park and the fascinating world of professional archaeology with the return of archaeologist Chuck Bender.

"Filled with murder and mayhem, jealousy and good detective work—an exciting, nonstop read." —**ANNE HILLERMAN**, *New York Times* bestselling author of *Rock with Wings*

"Graham's clever tale is tailor-made for those who prefer their mysteries under blue skies…" —*KIRKUS REVIEWS*

Canyon Sacrifice: A National Park Mystery

In Tony Hillerman fashion, this page-turner brings the rugged western landscape, the mysterious past of the ancient Anasazi Indians, and the Southwest's ongoing cultural fissures vividly to life. A deadly struggle against murderous kidnappers in Grand Canyon National Park forces archaeologist Chuck Bender to face up to his past as he realizes every parents' worst nightmare: a missing child.

"A terrific debut novel..." —**C.J. BOX**, *New York Times* bestselling author of *Stone Cold*

"Graham has created a beautifully balanced book, incorporating intense action scenes, depth of characterization, realistic landscapes, and historical perspective." —*REVIEWING THE EVIDENCE*

YOSEMITE FALL

A National Park Mystery
by Scott Graham

Forthcoming June 2017 from Torrey House Press

TORREY HOUSE PRESS

SALT LAKE CITY • TORREY

"Fingers of steel, zero body fat, and lots of testosterone."

— Famed female rock climber Lynn Hill, describing the historic, male-dominated Yosemite Valley climbing scene in the documentary film *Valley Uprising*

1

Twelve-year-old Carmelita was fifteen feet off the ground and climbing higher, her yellow T-shirt bright in the morning sun, before Chuck, caught off guard by her speedy ascent, reacted.

He took up the growing slack in the climbing rope, sliding the line past his brake hand and through the belay device attached to the harness at his waist. The rope's braided sheath warmed his skin as it slipped through his cupped palm.

Skinny as a whiffle bat, her navy tights hanging in loose folds from her tiny thighs and calves, Carmelita balanced the rubber soles of her climbing shoes on the resin holds bolted below her on the climbing tower and grasped additional holds above her head with chalked fingers, hoisting herself skyward.

"Take it easy," Chuck called up to her, pride edging his voice, as he took up the last of the slack in the rope. "Give me a chance to keep up, would you?"

She hesitated for only a heartbeat before climbing higher, her helmeted head back, her moves fluid and natural as she moved from hold to hold up the vertical tower.

Chuck shot a quick grin at Janelle, standing beside him in a form-fitting fleece top and black yoga pants. "You sure she hasn't snuck off and done this before without our knowing it?"

His grin widened as he looked back up at Carmelita. A sweet spot, that's where he found himself, three years into parenthood, on a working vacation with his family in the heart of his beloved Yosemite Valley in the middle of Yosemite National Park on this warm and sunny mid-August morning, hired to explore the fascinating particulars surrounding a pair of hundred-and-fifty-year-old murders in the valley.

Everything on this day was right in his world. Perfect.

A loner turned sudden husband to Janelle and stepdad to Carmelita and Rosie thirty-six months ago, he was well settled in to his new life now, squeezing in his runs with Janelle before the girls awoke, working in his small study in the back of the house during their school hours, and helping Janelle with household chores and the girls with their homework in the evenings. He'd learned to bid for work close to Durango these days, too, assuring he could make it home on the weekends while he conducted the fieldwork portion of his contracts.

His morning runs with Janelle kept him fit at forty-five, fifteen years Janelle's senior, even as gray emanated from his sideburns through the rest of his scalp and new wrinkles pleated the edges of his lips, matching the crow's feet that for years had creased the sun-scorched corners of his eyes.

He took in another arm's length of rope as Carmelita continued her ascent. Her bravura climb, so out of character for her, took him aback. She shouldn't be doing this. Such brash, public displays were the province of her openly exuberant ten-year-old sister, Rosie.

His sidelong glance had caught a smile on Janelle's face that matched his as she watched her older daughter's confident moves up the portable, forty-foot tower set at the edge of the Camp 4 parking lot.

Janelle's smile reinforced what she'd told Chuck in the truck last night, after the girls had fallen asleep in the rear seat of the crew cab as they'd driven deep into the night on the way here from Colorado. She'd spoken softly, so as not to awaken the girls, of her pride at having passed the last of her Emergency Medical Technician certification courses, her EMT application now pending with Durango Fire and Rescue.

"She must have gotten this from you," Janelle said at Chuck's side, her heart-shaped face turned skyward. Her dark hair, long and silky, hung free down her back, and a purple gemstone glittered in the side of her small, pointed nose.

"Not me," Chuck said. He took up more slack, maintaining slight tension on the line to assure it would catch Carmelita the instant she fell—if she fell. "I'm a grunter. I climb by force of will. But look at her. She's defying gravity, and she's doing it with pure grace."

Carmelita passed the tower's halfway point, still moving higher despite the decreasing size and number of holds on the top half of the structure. She grasped the small resin grips with the tips of her fingers, her weight on her toes. The climbing rope extended from her harness to a pulley at the top of the wall and back down to Chuck in the parking lot below. Her chestnut hair, gathered in a ponytail, gleamed in the sunlight. She showed no hint of fear as she passed thirty feet off the ground, nearing the top of the tower.

"You go, girl!" Janelle's brother and Chuck's assistant, Clarence, called up to Carmelita from where he stood back from the tower's base with a knot of onlookers, several waiting their turn to climb.

"Yeah! You go, girl!" ten-year-old Rosie echoed her uncle from where she watched at his side.

Rosie's stocky frame contrasted sharply with that of her slight sister, but she could have been her uncle's twin, he with his squat physique and pot belly, if not for the difference in their ages.

"No way am I going up that thing," Rosie declared as she eyed her sister, her thumbs slung through the belt loops of her jeans. "No frickin' way."

"Rosie!" Janelle admonished. Her reprimand was half-hearted, however, focused as she was on Carmelita three stories above. Janelle put her hand to her forehead, shielding the sun. "Isn't that high enough?" she asked Chuck.

"She might send the thing," Chuck said. "She might actually top out."

Carmelita clambered upward, the widely spaced holds at the top of the tower presenting her no apparent difficulty until, suddenly, she was forty feet off the ground and there was no more climbing to be done. She gave the top of the fiberglass tower a tap. As Chuck had instructed, she leaned back in her harness and planted her feet flat on the wall. She shook out her hands at her sides while he held her in place, his brake hand gripping the rope.

"How's the view from up there, sweetness?" he called up to her.

She looked at the granite cliffs lining the valley thousands of feet above her. "I've still got a ways to go."

Janelle shuddered. "Don't get any big ideas, *niña*," she warned.

Chuck relaxed his grip and lowered Carmelita, the rope running through his palm. "I'm glad I belayed her," he said to Janelle as Carmelita descended, walking backward down the wall. "As light as she is, I wouldn't have wanted to trust the auto-belay to kick in and catch her."

When Carmelita reached the ground, the tower attendant, thickly bearded and in his early twenties, approached from where he'd been talking with a female climber his age waiting her turn on the tower beyond the line of large boulders dividing the parking lot from the campground.

The attendant's broad, tanned shoulders extended outward straight as a crossbeam from his tank top, and his powerful quads filled the leg holes of his shorts. The climber wore shiny black climbing tights cut low across her hips and a magenta bikini top. Her bare stomach was smooth and bronzed and flat, and a gold ring sparkled where it hooked through the skin above her belly button.

The attendant untied the rope from Carmelita's waist. "Good going," he told her, offering his palm for a high-five.

Carmelita slapped his hand and pranced over to Janelle and Chuck, a grin plastered on her face. "That was a blast."

"You made it look easy," Janelle said.

"It *was* easy."

Chuck lifted an eyebrow at Carmelita. "Not for mere mortals."

He freed the rope from his harness, and the attendant set about reattaching it to the cylindrical auto-belay mechanism at the tower's base.

Carmelita's white teeth flashed. "When can I do it again?"

Chuck indicated the climbers grouped and waiting behind the boulders. Jimmy Anderson stood at the front of the group, in animated conversation with Bernard Montilio, the two of them clearly enjoying the opportunity to catch up with one another after so many years.

"The line got pretty long behind Jimmy while you were up there," Chuck said. "I'm glad we came over here first thing this morning." He hesitated, avoiding Janelle's gaze, the idea coming to him even as the words formed in his mouth. "The only way you're going to get to climb any more this weekend is if you enter the Slam."

"The what?" Carmelita asked.

Janelle stiffened at his side as he continued. "The Yosemite Slam. It's Camp 4's big climbing competition. It starts tomorrow, runs for three days, through Sunday. That's why the tower's here.

Jimmy timed the reunion for this weekend to coincide with it. He started it a few years ago to raise money for Camp 4, and it's gotten bigger every year since. Once the Slam begins, entrants will be the only ones allowed on the tower."

Carmelita begged Janelle. "Can I, *Mamá*?"

Janelle turned to Chuck, no longer smiling. "A climbing competition? Those are only for adults, right?"

"The best sport climbers in the world these days are teenagers. Their strength-to-weight ratios are off the charts thanks to the fact that—" he reached out and encircled Carmelita's upper arm with a finger and thumb "—they're so skinny."

"But that's teenagers you're talking about."

"I'll be thirteen in December," Carmelita reminded her mother.

"I don't want to think about that."

Chuck said, "She was a natural up there just now."

"Do they actually have a kids' division?"

"Maybe. Even if they do, though, I'd say she should enter the Open division." He tipped his head to one side. "The way she climbed that thing, you never know."

Carmelita's face glowed pink beneath her olive complexion, but Janelle's brows drew together. "You mean, where she'd be going up against anybody and everybody?"

"All the female climbers, anyway."

"But that was the first time she's ever climbed anything in her whole life. You just got her those climbing shoes last week, before we came out here."

Chuck eyed the top of the tower. "I don't imagine she'd win," he said to Janelle. "But sport climbing isn't as much about experience and repetitive practice as other sports. It's a matter of strength and balance—both of which, clearly, Carm's got by the bucketful. From what I just saw, I don't think she'd have anything to be ashamed of."

Carmelita beamed at him. "Really?"

Chuck cupped the back of her head in his hand and looked into her luminous almond eyes. "Really."

"Cool," Rosie declared. She jigged at her sister's side, her arms swinging. "You should do it for sure, Carm."

Janelle rested her hand over Chuck's at the back of Carmelita's head. "You really think you want to try it?"

Carmelita nodded, bouncing up and down on her toes.

"You won't be sad when you lose?"

"*If* she loses," Chuck said.

"No," Carmelita told her mother. "I won't. I promise."

Rosie chimed in, "But I'll be sad for her. Would that be okay, *Mamá*?"

The corners of Janelle's mouth ticked upward. "Okay," she said. "You two win."

Jimmy threaded the climbing rope into his harness. Still talking to Bernard, his back to the tower, he tied the rewoven figure-eight with knowing fingers and gave the rope a tug, assuring it ran from his waist, up through the pulley at the top of the tower, and back down to the auto-belay mechanism.

Faded tattoos purpled Jimmy's sinewy forearms below the short sleeves of his shirt. A long, braided, salt-and-pepper beard curved outward from his jaw like a scorpion's tail. Stringy brown hair streaked with gray fell from the back of his battered straw cowboy hat to his shoulders. His faded blue jeans hung loose at his waist, and the top buttons of his plaid cotton shirt were undone, revealing a gold necklace with a bear tooth pendant nestled in a patch of silvery hair on his chest.

"Show us what you can do, Jimmy," Chuck said.

"You're the man," Bernard said. "Let's see how much gas you've got left in the old tank."

Bernard had driven to the valley early this morning from his home in Sacramento. His pasty face and jowly cheeks spoke of his current life as an office-bound attorney, as did his horn-rimmed, turquoise-framed glasses, which could have come straight from a fashion magazine. His waistline pressed at the top of his pleated khaki slacks and the lower buttons of his crisply ironed dress shirt. His brown hair, closely cropped, showed no hint of gray.

Jimmy turned to the climbing tower and settled his hands on two large holds above his head. "You guys are next," he said over his shoulder to Chuck and Bernard.

"Not me," Chuck said. "No way."

"I'm ground-based these days," said Bernard.

"You're scared you can't do it anymore," Jimmy said.

"You got that right," they replied in unison.

Jimmy tightened his grip on the two holds and lifted himself off the ground. He ascended the large, easy-to-grasp holds on the lower portion of the tower with no apparent strain, the auto-belay mechanism taking up the slack in the rope as he climbed. Each of his moves was precise, his fingers set, his feet poised on holds beneath him. He angled left and right, scaling the wall with the effortlessness of a gecko, as if he hadn't aged a day over the last two decades.

He passed the halfway point on the tower and reached above his head for a small hold thirty feet off the ground. Only two of his fingertips fit atop the tiny protrusion, which sloped outward, providing little purchase.

He grunted, his first sign of exertion, as he transferred his weight to the hold. He clung to the tower, his knuckles turning white. Then his fingertips lost their purchase on the hold and he fell.

The ratchet in the auto-belay mechanism should have kicked in, catching him when he dropped no more than a few inches. Instead, he cartwheeled away from the wall and plummeted toward the ground unimpeded, his arms and legs flailing, while the climbing rope zipped freely through the auto-belay device bolted to the base of the tower.

TORREY HOUSE PRESS

The economy is a wholly owned subsidiary of the environment, not the other way around.
—Senator Gaylord Nelson, founder of Earth Day

Love of the land inspires Torrey House Press and the books we publish. From literature and the environment and Western Lit to topical nonfiction about land related issues and ideas, we strive to increase appreciation for the importance of natural landscape through the power of pen and story. Through our *2% to the West* program, Torrey House Press donates two percent of sales to not-for-profit environmental organizations and funds a scholarship for up-and-coming writers at colleges throughout the West.

Visit **www.torreyhouse.com** for reading group discussion guides, author interviews, and more.

CPSIA information can be obtained
at www.ICGtesting.com
Printed in the USA
JSHW022325081121
20270JS00001B/94